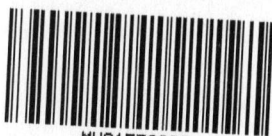

ALL BOYS TOGETHER

ALL BOYS TOGETHER

EDITED BY ROBIN YEO

First published 2000 by Millivres Ltd,
part of the Millivres Prowler Group,
Worldwide House, 116-134 Bayham St, London NW1 0BA

Introduction World Copyright Robin Yeo © 2000
Individual stories World Copyright the authors © 2000

A CIP catalogue record for this book is available
from the British Library

ISBN 1 902852 11 7

Distributed in Europe by Central Books,
99 Wallis Rd, London E9 5LN

Distributed in North America by InBook/LPC Group,
1436 West Randolph, Chicago, IL 60607

Distributed in Australia by Bulldog Books,
P O Box 300, Beaconsfield, NSW 2014

Printed and bound in the EU by WS Bookwell, Finland 2000

Preface

There are many gay men, I'm aware, who hate boys and everything to do with them. If they happen to pass a school gate in mid-afternoon, with a horde of boys rushing out untidy and probably unwashed, they're immediately reminded of the horrors of their own younger days. I have some friends – don't we all? – who practically deny that they ever were boys themselves, even if technically they must at one time or another have been ten, twelve or fourteen. But in no way were they were ever 'one of the boys', and even at a tender age their minds were set on higher things. They will tell you how they seduced the lodger, or carried on a passionate affair with an uncle. I'm afraid that this book will not be their cup of tea.

The authors of the stories collected here are more likely to have been at the other end of the scale. They were boyish enough to take part in the timeless games of boyhood, including those sexual games that boys naturally gravitate into around puberty. Perhaps they experienced this sex play rather differently from most boys, as involving stronger feelings; we can never be sure. But it would seem that they drew a great deal of pleasure from this phase, while it lasted.

The typical reader of this book, however, will probably have gone through puberty rather like me. Desperately desirous of the bodies and organs burgeoning around him, but generally too shy to have joined in much of the action. Which is why, whatever kind of sex we prefer as adults, we still like to read about what might have been.

Over the last twenty years, some of my favourite books from Gay Men's Press have been those that recaptured, in fiction or as memoir, the special feeling of early adolescence. And as several of these are no longer readily available, I had the idea of bringing together some of the most interesting passages into a collection. Once the idea took shape, it provided an outlet for a number of original pieces that would not otherwise have made

it to publication, as well as extracts from some new books still in preparation. The result is a book that is definitely about sex, and appeals to the reader on this basis, yet I believe is quite distinct from pornography. What's the difference?

Pornography, or what nowadays appears on bookshop shelves as 'erotica', is written with the sole aim of arousing the reader, which it does by its physical description of sexual organs and acts. The kind of writing about sex that we have here, however, which would have been called 'erotic' before the term was hijacked, aims above all to convey the subjective feeling of its characters, in the complex mix of sensual and emotional sensations that sex always involves. A good example would be Andrew O'Hare's story 'Padraig'; it is admittedly about lust, it does not claim to be great literature, and it focuses close up on precisely what two boys do with each other's dicks. But 'Padraig' is very different from what you might find, for example, on a typical Internet porn site; it takes the reader inside the world of its characters, indeed inside their minds. You might still get a sexual buzz from it, but you'll also get something more lasting.

We made a definite decision in this book to combine fiction and memoirs. On the one hand, fiction on this subject generally draws heavily on personal experience. On the other, there is no way of checking whether what is billed as memoir actually happened. The test in both cases is authenticity, that a story faithfully captures real-world experience. The greater part of these stories are set in England, though there are also one each from Scotland and Northern Ireland, three from the USA and one from India. But they span a considerable interval of time: from the 1930s (though recorded half a century later), through the postwar decades, to the more recent period. Compiling the collection confirmed my impression of a certain trend – and not a very positive one. Until the 1960s, it seemed to me, it was tacitly accepted that if boys had sex in their early teens (never mind earlier), it was going to be homosex. Psychologists even spoke of a 'homosexual phase'. But to the extent that gay people acquired a higher profile in society, this homosexual phase lost its legitimacy. Today, children are pressed into charades of boyfriend and girlfriend even before they reach puberty, and the sex play among boys that was once innocent and normal now acquires a dangerous 'gay' connotation. The place we have

won as gay adults has in a way been at the expense of the sexual freedom of boys.

In the stories in this book set before World War Two, when Peter de Rome and Jack Robinson were young, there's no question mark over boys having it off; they just get down to it. In the postwar time, evoked for example by Martin Foreman and James Beresford, the question whether it's ok for boys to have sex together lurks in the background, and this also was the experience I drew on in my own piece. Of the more recent settings, however, Chris Anderson's 'Twelve and Thirteen' hinges most sharply on the conflict between desire and taboo, and Nick Ellwood's 'The Private Life of Sheds' describes how the heterosexual dictatorship puts an end to boyish slaggishness at an early age.

This at least is the impression given by the memoirs and fictions in this book. But some recent evidence suggests a new and more positive trend. Shere Hite, in her *Hite Report on the Family* (1994), claims:

> In the 1940s, Kinsey reported that 48 per cent of the men in his sample either masturbated or had sex with other boys as adolescents or in their early teens. In my own work for *The Hite Report on Men and Male Sexuality*, I found that 43 percent of the sample were doing this. Now, in the 1990s the figure in my sample has increased to almost 60 per cent... Equally intriguing is the kind of sex boys are now having together. In the 1970s, the contact was mostly mutual masturbation, often without touching each other. Now, it seems much more common for boys to touch each other, masturbate the other boy, while 36 per cent of boys also perform fellatio together. Around 20 per cent have experienced anal penetration.

Hopefully this trend is a reality, but it is still suppressed, both in Britain and America, by a macho homophobic culture that is all too apparent. Perhaps a new aim for the gay movement should be to give boys back the freedom to follow their desires without the fear of stigma. A year or two back, I read an interview that a gay journalist did with his fourteen-year-old nephew. Two

phrases from it echoed around in my mind: "You don't have to be gay to do gay stuff," and "It takes a boy to know what a boy really likes." Right on, nephew! – those would make good slogans for the new century. And if books can make a modest contribution, then we might hope to see this book in school libraries, where it could be browsed by the pubescent boys of tomorrow. It shouldn't be too far above their reading age!

Robin Yeo

PART ONE: MEMOIRS

Martin Foreman

When..

Thirteen years old, gawky, buck-toothed, black-suited and ill-suited to the next four years of my life, I waited with my mother at the entrance to School. If architecture is frozen music, my new home was a clash of chords on half the instruments of the orchestra. A mass of grey stone rose out of colonnades and curves to be crowned in green-roofed flourishes of turrets and towers. On a summer's day School overlooked Edinburgh with the serenity of a castle on the Loire; on a winter evening it lurked behind trees like Dracula's home. That grey autumn afternoon, it loomed over me, dark, cavernous, unknown.

Beside me, a curly-haired, large-nosed boy my own age, as embarrassed as I was, tolerated my mother's questions and her repetition to me of his name and provenance. Thus my first acquaintance was Anthony Turnbull (I rechristen him with all the others) from Aberdeen. To call him Anthony was impossible. He was Turnbull, of course, as I was Foreman; first names were never used, even by friends, in public schools in the mid-1960s. Turnbull was pleasant enough, although a little too self-confident and unaware of his own presence for me to be comfortable with him. Like most of the boys I was about to encounter, he was long-accustomed to boarding, while I was a scholarship pupil, a refugee from a direct-grant school and middle-class poverty. With only my mother's introduction in common, Turnbull and I seldom spoke to each other, except for stilted conversations on the long Sunday afternoons when, with nothing else to do, he accompanied me to my home in the south of the city where he, my single parent and I sat and politely drank tea.

My mother left; Turnbull and I helped each other carry our trunks, neatly packed with the grey, green and black clothes that comprised our formal and informal uniform, over the threshold. In the dimly-lit entrance dusty glass cases preserved

photographs, medals and record books of years long past. A wide stone staircase curved up an extravagant height to the first floor and an unlit corridor where door after door suggested a Wonderland of unexplored rooms. Another flight led to my House and the illusory welcome of bustle and light as we dragged our burdens past half-open doors to the junior dormitory at the end of the hall.

Fifteen low beds with a squat clothes cupboard at the foot of each lined the walls of a high-ceilinged room. Half a dozen or more boys facing their first term were already unpacking. By default I chose a bed near the door and next to the prefect. It was, I soon realised, a haven. A bed in the far corner or by the window offered no protection or means of escape from hostile neighbours. Violence was rare, but there were other forms of aggression: the apple-pie bed, which I dreaded, unable to imagine what it was or how it could be undone, or the pillow stolen and passed from boy to boy, as each called out the body fluid with which he was smearing it. The pillow never came to me and for years I was convinced that it returned to its owner as stinking and sodden as it had been described. Even these activities were uncommon, but each night after lights out insults and mockery roamed the dorm as I lay silent and relieved that the target was almost always in the centre of the group, leaving me forgotten at the edge.

Sixty boys between thirteen and eighteen shared the two floors of my House and twenty-five my own age sat beside me in class. In eight years of day school I had learned to live peacefully with my contemporaries but I had almost no contact with those who were older or younger. Here, uncertain of my status, my duties and my rights, by the time I understood this hothouse society it was too late for such understanding to bring me respect. Marked as an outsider by my accent and my ignorance, deprived of a home to retreat to, I was at the mercy of fifteen-year-olds with bulky bodies, deep voices and fierce expressions, who nonchalantly changed my name to Foreskin, broke into my tuck-box with impunity and laughed as I cringed at their slightest gesture. My own age group was less fearsome, but their self-confidence still cowed me. Prefects I held in the same deference as masters. Only those boys of seventeen and eighteen who had achieved age without authority were outwith my orbit.

Winter approached. Mornings were spent at graffiti-carved desks, my willingness to learn inhibited by ageing, ill-tempered and eccentric masters. Lunch was forty minutes of relief, a long table of banter with one of the younger masters. The pain of rugby followed, an hour each damp grey afternoon squashed in scrums and trampled in tackles, only returning to the grim changing room as the early darkness fell. In the concrete communal bath up to ten of us, from the hairless pre-pubescent to the hirsute young adult, would cram at any one time as the initially hot and soapy water turned lukewarm and brown with mud. Ten minutes of soaking, the surface dirt dissolved, we dressed to face an hour's freedom or late afternoon class.

There was humour and occasional name-calling, but neither in the changing-room nor anywhere else in School, neither between boys and masters nor between boys was there any suggestion of sexual activity: no friendly arm around a housemate's shoulder, no light-hearted grope at another's genitals. Sex was nonetheless constant in our speech, especially at night when darkness hid what words described. I lay in bed and tried to relate such terms as spunk and wank and root-on to the dry explanation of human intercourse that, with sepia diagrams of wombs and testes, had been my introduction to the subject at day school. Finally I deduced that if I rubbed my penis when it was stiff, semen would come out. Once or twice, therefore, in solitary silence before the early morning bell, I briefly stroked my erection. Nothing happened. Convinced I had misunderstood, I gave up the experiment, disappointed and still curious.

The hesitancy that governed all my actions was seen by my housemaster as responsibility. In my second term I found myself in a three-bed dormitory without the supervision of a prefect. Fourteen years old, in the upper stream, Markham, Menton and I were at the age where the intellect develops faster than the body and demands even greater exercise. Night after night, staring up at the dark ceiling, we argued every subject from the existence of God to the possibility of non-carbon life forms, our debates only occasionally interrupted by a master or prefect flinging open the door to insist that we keep quiet. Unperturbed, we stayed silent for a few minutes until the intruder had passed on, then resumed our enquiries at the precise

point of information at which we had been forced to stop.

That spring and summer term my senses, awoken by adolescence, threw School, and therefore Life, into a new dimension. The stone corridors and wooden desks, the notice boards detailing cricketing teams or shooting colours, the sward we had to walk round and the tuck shop where we bought ice-cream, were all suddenly more real and intense than any aspect of my previous existence. The boys I talked to or avoided and the begowned teachers who ruled each classroom became predictable, solid personalities whom I could, to a certain extent, understand and with whom I could, in one way or another, negotiate. Dimly, I became aware of potential strengths within me. Yet marvellous as all this new perception was, I was sure that it was only a first stage, that behind what I saw and now understood there must lie layer upon layer of further secrets and mysteries.

My second winter term, a year older and another dorm. This one had waist-high partitions which allowed a modicum of privacy should a prefect or master open the door; those who were standing could be seen while those in bed were hidden. Bolder now, protected by these wooden walls, I chose a bed by the window at the far end of the room. I had a friend opposite: Fraser, a fat, round-faced boy with a sense of humour close to my own.

My status rising as younger boys entered school, I was more confident and relaxed. Classes were enjoyable. In my free time I had my own study cubicle, where I pinned to the wall pictures of rockets, starving children and ponderous quotations. There and in the privacy of the dorm I could listen illicitly to the world through the earplug of my transistor radio, wakening one morning to the opening broadcast of Radio One and retiring each night to the late night comedy of Radio Four.

Sex was ever more present, yet still beyond my understanding. My morning erection was a daily occurrence and I woke more frequently from powerful, formless dreams to find my pyjamas and sheets wet and stained. I noticed more and more those of my contemporaries who were slimmer, more athletic and bore fine or handsome features. Such growing awareness did not strike me as queer, for I maintained a healthy distance from the hostility directed towards the few boys who appeared

effeminate or too interested in other boys' affairs.

My second spring term. Monday to Saturday, first light to bedtime, our days were filled with classes and games. On Sunday, however, we rose late, lingered over breakfast and waited for lunch; Sunday afternoons stretched before us like a featureless desert made more depressing by the prospect of the long church service that closed the day. We could go into Edinburgh but few did so; shops were closed, the streets were empty and wind-blown, enlivened only by the rare passage of a red and white bus. Too old now to go home for tea, I loitered in the House, wanting to do something and not knowing what to do.

* * *

And so one Sunday after lunch Thompson, Grant and myself mooched restless in the dorm. Fifteen years old, we were of similar height and build, although our personalities were very different. Thompson's high-pitched voice reflected immaturity and naiveté, while Grant's deep tones, sullen expression and sharp features gave the impression of easy violence. I was neither one nor the other, physically and mentally more mature than Thompson, while less assured, although of fuller body, than Grant.

Energy within us sought release. We piled onto Thompson's bed, each trying to subjugate the others, our bodies heavy and close. When tired, we lay back, and in that pause Thompson accused Grant. "You've got a root-on!" "So what," Grant replied calmly, "so do you." So, I admitted silently, did I. We sat up slowly and straightened clothes. "I'm not playing this game any more," said Thompson truculently. Grant shrugged, looked at me. "Well, we are," he said. And because Grant said so, because no-one ever bullied him, that both absolved me of guilt and included me in whatever he wanted to do.

Tension hung between us. Thompson stood up, said he was leaving, which forced Grant and me to leave his cubicle too. My throat was dry. I feared to speak, to shatter what I had suddenly found. I followed Grant out of the dorm, in unspoken agreement to find a place where we could continue what we had started. One of us suggested the ground floor urinals where porcelain and stone walls, partly unroofed, allowed in rain and

snow. It was here you came to smoke, if you dared. We stood side by side, unzipping the flies of our regulation black suits. My heart seemed to have stopped; my breathing was still. We stood holding out our erections. I stared at Grant's. Although I had showered with him and a dozen other boys every day, it was the first time I had seen another penis hard. The thin tube of flesh looked strange. "Touch it," Grant ordered. I put out my hand and held it. It was warm, welcoming. I felt his hand on mine. What might come next I did not know and did not care; this permission to touch each other's sex was more than I had ever imagined, more than I could ever desire.

Grant had more presence of mind. "Not here," he warned, manoeuvring the hard flesh back into his trousers. Reluctantly, I did the same. I wanted more, without knowing what more was, but even in this remote place we were in danger of discovery. Just holding each other as we had done would surely have had us expelled, as two boys in another House had been made to leave the year before. The thought made me nervous, but much less nervous than eager to continue whatever we had started. "Where can we go?" I asked. He shook his head. "Nowhere," he said, then added, "Tomorrow. Wake me early." I asked no more, unquestioningly trusting his judgement.

We left the toilet, separated without a word, whatever intimacy we had shared immediately dying. Tea and the evening service came and went. I slept as usual and, with a talent long since lost, woke half an hour before the morning bell. Apprehensive, but with no hesitation, I rose, pulled on my dressing-gown and tiptoed into Grant's cubicle. He woke at my hand on his shoulder. Wordless, we left the dorm, walked to our study and closed the door. There was just room in my cubicle for us to stand side by side, dressing-gowns and pyjamas open, erections thrusting into view.

I watched in silence as he put his hand on my penis, felt for a moment nothing more than if he had brushed against my shoulder, then realised he was rubbing up and down for longer and much faster than I had ever thought to do. Powerful tremors of pleasure flooded through my body. The shock was so great that my legs almost gave way, until I relaxed and gave in to the sensation.

Startling though it was, what I was feeling was not new.

Since nine or ten I had willingly climbed ropes in the gym for the unworldly tingle between my legs that would make me almost lose my grip. With the onset of puberty, each time my penis hardened unbidden, the feeling was stronger, although less acute. It was there in the indescribable emotion that slipped from my grasp as I woke from a wet dream. But all that I had felt had been no more than muted premonition of what was now occurring. It was as if for years I had been hearing a Mozart symphony in another room and the thick doors which separated us had suddenly burst open to reveal its incomparable beauty.

I had no sense of time, nor expectation of what was to come. Grant's hand was implacable, his expression complicit and triumphant. My body was vibrant, my mind hypnotised. When it seemed I could not tolerate the sensation any more, there was an explosion within me and I saw my semen shoot into the air. I trembled, uncertain of what had happened, of whether it was still happening. Something incredible had occurred, something I wanted to repeat again and again.

I was still overawed when I became aware that Grant was waiting for me to perform the same action on him. I did so willingly, eager to give him the same overpowering pleasure that he had given me. Reaching out for his thin, solid penis, I rubbed it as he had rubbed mine. His eyes closed, he began to groan, his body rocked slowly, rhythmically pushing his erection in time with my hand. I wanted this to go on and on, just to watch him, to see him transformed, to know that it was I who was giving him this ecstasy. Soon, however, he trembled, shuddered as I had done and semen spat out of the flesh in my hand. To see it, to have caused it, was as awe-inspiring as my own orgasm had been; the world, it seemed, had been reduced to this exultation of our bodies and at that moment that was all I ever wanted the world to be.

No orgasm since has achieved the perfection of that first time. Never has my body, my mind, my soul, been so completely absorbed. It is the orgasm that all my life, consciously or not, I have sought to repeat. In my twenties I matched it in intensity and in my thirties I more than matched it in affection and love; in my forties it has become gross and mechanical, its soul slowly dying. Now, over thirty years later, I finally recognise that such a incredible product of youth and energy and ignorance can never

return.

Pyjamas buttoned, dressing-gowns closed, we left the room. The intimacy gone, we were no closer to each other than before. Nothing was said that suggested what we had done was of great moment. Perhaps we did not speak to each other again that day, perhaps not for another week. In the same House but in different classes and with different friends, there was little to bring us together. So we passed in corridors, stood together at roll-call, slept a few feet apart and not a gesture, not a word, not a smile acknowledged the secret we had shared.

Over the next few days the euphoria that had gripped me faded, to be replaced by the fear that what we had done was wrong. I countered feelings of guilt with the rationale that our actions were excusable in a single-sex school. We were merely adolescents going through a homosexual phase. It was something I would grow out of, although for the sake of conscience and fear of discovery it might be better if I were not to do it again.

* * *

But I was fifteen years old, with a growing desire for sexual release that I could not control. At least I could now substitute my own hand for Grant's, at last initiated into the knowledge that had tantalised me for five terms. And so my occasional wet dreams gave way to a much more frequent and intense pleasure. Yet it was not enough without Grant, without his hand on my penis, without his erection in my hand.

And Grant, it seemed, wanted me. The circumspect manner in which we spoke, walking back from the dining-hall after lunch one day, masked a shared urgency to be alone and in greater privacy. Time could be found – at the weekend, in the early evening or an afternoon when we had no class – but the place was more difficult. Somehow we obtained the key to the storeroom at the top of the school tower, where boys' trunks gathered dust from the beginning of term to the onset of the holidays.

We wound our way up three flights of narrow stairs to the dark octagonal room with its low windows overlooking School grounds in every direction. With dry mouth and hollow stomach I undid my trousers and watched Grant open his. It was there

again, this hard, erect, desirable flesh for which the only words I had – cock, penis – were inadequate or obscene. It jutted before him, expectantly. Now that I knew what it represented, what it could give me, I was both more eager and more patient than before. We experimented, stroking each other at the same time, more slowly or with different rhythms, until first he then I was overtaken by the orgasm which came with the same intensity as before.

The door locked, the key replaced, regret returned. But again I persuaded myself that I was just acting my age, that I was not queer and I would not repeat the experience. And again my resolve was weak and I found myself wondering when Grant and I could be alone again. My desire was purely sexual. I did not imagine myself in love; I was obsessed only by performing the act with another male, not by Grant himself. Indeed, I continued to be wary of his mockery and anger. But I wanted him because he was the only boy I knew whose penis I could hold and who would willingly hold mine.

Time melts and intermingles in my memory. The third time we met may have been several days, weeks, even a term later. By then I had become secretary and key-holder of the model railway club, although my interest in trains was little more than a hangover from younger days. The club was moribund, the butt of school jokes, with only a few of the youngest boys as members. The only other person with a key was the master nominally in charge, a married man who lived outside School and only attended the weekly meetings.

The club met one flight beneath the storeroom. The room was tall, bright and cluttered with the trestles on which the half-built layout ran. Grant was impressed by the convenience of a meeting-place that was ours alone. This time, despite the cold, we stripped completely, an act that to me was a sign of maturity. We took turns to lie back on the dusty wooden floor, the other on top, erections pressing hard into each other's stomachs. Not quite sure what to do, our actions were tentative. We almost kissed, but drew back; awkwardly, we hugged. In turns we placed our penises between the other's thighs, but the position was uncomfortable. I wanted to experiment further, but was restrained by his reticence and the fear of seeming queer, of wanting more than adolescents going through a phase were

permitted to do.

The privacy of the club allowed us to become different, almost adult. We spoke quietly, murmuring impersonal compliments. Here I was Grant's equal, perhaps more than equal as he admired my bigger penis. Finally, when words threatened to lead us into greater intimacy, we brought each other to orgasm, and once again I found that for me his was as overwhelming and ineffable as my own. Despite myself, I felt the first inklings of affection, of desire for Grant himself.

And perhaps because this emotional response had appeared, the guilt and unhappiness that followed were much stronger than before. Within an hour I had plunged from ecstasy into despair. One encounter or two could be excused as ignorance or adolescence; a third could only be confirmation of my perversion. Not knowing what to do, I found myself in a music room, hammering out a hymn on the piano against a cacophony of instruments being practised around me. I had no musical talent at the best of times and now I pounded the keys as if they were a drum, convinced against all hope that I was queer, queer, queer.

Yet even this black mood lasted little more than a day. Guilt gave way once more to the reassurance that I was a victim of my age and circumstances, that as soon as I left School my inclination would turn to Girls. And so, although doubts sometimes returned, each time Grant and I returned to the model railway club, the pleasure he offered me was much greater than any disapproval I offered myself.

We were not frequent lovers. Weeks might pass between encounters. I was held back by the thought that to be eager was to be queer; Grant perhaps had the same doubts. Perhaps, despite the security, it was fear of discovery. Not that anyone suspected us. In public we behaved no differently, Grant occasionally insulting me as he would insult others; it was his role and mine and I felt no resentment. Yet every so often we would find ourselves alone and the suggestion from one or other to visit the club premises was never refused. There we held each other briefly, as we had done before, but we never extended the limits that had already been defined. The orgasm was our goal and once each had been achieved, we would dress and depart.

* * *

I recognise now that what drew me was not just Grant's penis, but all his body, from the dark, slightly curly hair, past the prominent nose and high cheekbones, down the narrow chest and stomach to the athlete's thighs and calves. His back too, and to a certain extent his buttocks, although I had not yet learnt that men could penetrate each other, far less that they could enjoy it. In short, without realising it, I began to want much more than his sex; I wanted to explore and share all his masculinity.

I do not know Grant's motives. While my actions tentatively tried to go further, his focused no further than our penises. Although I sometimes resented it, he always wanted me to come first, so that I was already returning to normality as he ended on a high, his semen splattering across his chest, as high, sometimes, as his shoulder. His selfishness went no further for he was as willing to hold my penis and make me come as I was to hold his. And the orgasm he gave me was always more intense than any I could give myself. Yet apart from commenting on each other's hardness or the last time we had masturbated, or how high the semen rose, we never discussed what we were doing. Nor did we wonder aloud whether others did the same or whether either of us was attracted to other boys. I wonder now whether we should have done so, whether the silence we maintained allowed us to conceal our misgivings and so to meet again and again, or whether words would have helped us understand more and given our sexuality greater depth.

For almost two years we met. Two years in which I turned from an adolescent into a young man. Two years in which I briefly fulfilled the expectations of my scholarship, proving to myself and my teachers that I had an intellect and a talent for learning that were worth cultivating. Two years in which I learnt to avoid the rituals of rugby and cadet force in favour of the easier options of athletics and community service. Two years in which I learnt to drink and get drunk. Two years in which I began to escape once a week to cinemas where X-rated films promised an adulthood of far greater meaning than the claustrophobic world in which I lived.

I changed dorms a third and a fourth time. With two friends I shared a study and a reputation that verged on the effete. A-

23

levels approached – French and German, which I enjoyed, and English, which bored and baffled me with its incomprehensible and inconsequential analysis of long-dead literature. I grew both physically and mentally, yet School remained a Gormenghast that dominated my psyche as it dominated the grounds in which it sat, a century of history and ritual that I could never quite fathom. It was the end of the 1960s, when the world outside woke to Sergeant Pepper, hippies and flower power, while I was held hostage by the ghosts of Dickens and Kipling.

My trysts with Grant ended in irony. No master would confirm or deny details, but it transpired that a boy in the year below us had been caught in the model railway club with a boy a year his junior. Their relationship, it was claimed, was more perverse than simple queerdom. Tales of torture circulated, stories that the older had tied the younger's penis to the rails and switched on the current. Neither would speak; to our surprise, Matheson, the older boy, was not expelled, although he left at the end of the term. Williams, the younger, stayed, to little sympathy; he was not generally liked and we all wondered why, if he had not enjoyed the experience, he had allowed it to be repeated again and again.

A quiet sentence with Grant confirmed that we should stop using the model railway club for a time. We never returned and had nowhere else to go. In partial compensation, my interest in other boys was growing. I had learnt to fantasise as I masturbated and two or three boys were recurring themes. In particular, there was Bartholomew who studied German with me, a sixteen-year-old from another house with dark hair and strong yet delicate face. Once, and only once, we had been in the swimming-pool together, playing some game that not only allowed me to see but briefly grasp his body. To my inexperienced eye, his slender form, hairless yet mature, punctuated by tight dark trunks, appeared perfect. Night after night, hand on erection, trying not to make the bed shake, I had him stand by me as I had seen him in the pool, held him tightly, kissed him and felt his erection hard against mine. The frequency with which he and other boys recurred sometimes worried me and I would occasionally force myself to orgasm over a naked woman, but she was a vague, distant figure that could not compensate for Bartholomew's taut muscles or some junior's smile.

Other incidents marked my emerging sexuality. Six of us broke into the pool one midnight to swim in the nude. The flouting of laws excited my mind, while the potential of naked bodies around me excited my body; I lingered in the water, aware there was enough light to prevent me climbing out of the water lest others saw my erection. On another occasion I was intrigued by the rumour, never substantiated, that all but three of the boys in another house had been involved in nightly orgies. What made the story more piquant was the fact that the unwitting housemaster under whose nose these events were allegedly occurring was the school chaplain. I wondered then whether the whole school had been involved for years in a series of private couplings and dorm-wide debaucheries that continued to pass me by; even then, however, I did not have the courage to see if others might respond to the secret that Grant and I had shared.

*   *   *

He and I met one more time. I returned after summer holidays to my last winter term. I had been in Switzerland, where for the first time strangers had treated me as an adult. Back at School, to my surprise and some reluctance, I had become a prefect. Grant, meanwhile, had no such authority and joined contemporaries in treating all prefects with amused disdain. The barrier between us appeared insurmountable.

Yet early that term we found ourselves alone in his study, with others at games and the House deserted. It needed few words before I lay back on cushions in an alcove while he brought me to orgasm again. This time, however, the deep pleasure was somehow overlain with responsibility. "I think I'm getting too old for this," I said, words spoken to Grant but meant for myself. He shrugged. For the first time, I did not reach out to satisfy him, but tucked my shirt in, pulled up my zip, stood and left the room.

A year of frustration and growing hostility to all that School represented ended the following July. In that year Grant and I never spoke to each other. I do not remember the last time I saw him; no doubt it was the morning of the last day as we passed on the stairs and in the corridors, saying goodbye to our friends and loading trunks into separate taxis.

Turnbull, Fraser, Grant: I soon lost touch with all the boys I had known. For the next two years I assumed I was not queer, yet the day after I lost my virginity with a woman I rushed to a gay friend to admit I might be bisexual. Six months later, even that last shred of self-deceit had gone.

Fifteen years later, in my mid-thirties, I saw in the Old Boys Newsletter that Grant had become engaged. I scanned the lines several times for more information than the simple announcement could give. Then I sat back and wondered if he too read the Newsletter each time it appeared, looking for my name, seeking clues that would never appear.

* * * * *

Martin Foreman's most recent fiction is *The Butterfly's Wing* (Gay Men's Press, 1996) and his non-fiction *AIDS and Men* (Panos/Zed, 1999). Excerpts from his work can be seen on www.martinforeman.com.

Nick Ellwood

The Private Life of Sheds

Boys are slags! The younger they are, often the more voracious their appetites. Shortly out of nappies, you can be sure they've lost their innocence and it's only adults, who, for all sorts of reasons, delude themselves otherwise.

Every boy likes to have his nipples touched or a warm hand furrowing busily inside his shorts and conversely, he likes to stroke the warm flesh and hidden regions of peers. The baring of flesh, of touching and being touched by soft hands that aren't ancient, callused and threatening, is thrilling. They love doing it in groups and the more hands and bodies available, the better.

They're slags, too, because they don't particularly mind who they do it with and some *even* do it with girls though this is loathsome and frowned upon. Girls are always second-best simply because adults threaten boys with the female gender and sex if they don't correctly conform to boyish behaviour. Just as boys don't like to play with Barbie, neither do they like being touched by girls unless as a very last resort.

Boys prefer to play with boys, that is their nature at least until the onset of puberty when social pressures are concentrating for the final assault to drive them towards the boredom of monochrome heterosexuality. Adults have always been an unhealthy influence on the natural development of children.

As a boy, looking at boys and sensing strange unidentifiable urges that churned my stomach and fluttered my chest was one of the first feelings I remember. It's that time of morning when people go to work or school and, stood on the lawn, under bright blue skies, alone, I look up at the world of houses, roads and trees that rise up and dwarf me. The boys wear white shirts as they cycle past; white shirts that billow out in the fresh morning air. I was captivated by their pink flesh, the outline of their torsos highlighted through thin, flimsy material. I lacked the ability to

identify my interest, to name it by language but it evoked the sensation of beauty, admiration and I know it now, lust.

I looked at others boys right through childhood and I wasn't alone. The art of fiddling with other lads was learnt from older boys and was part of some unspoken heritage. With excited, grinning faces, they educated us younger boys in the ways of laddish sluttery.

Boys have special places they like to go and these include the shed, garage and secluded places exclusive to them. All over the world boys share and discover physical pleasure in shadowy locations from which the adult world is excluded.

Rats were under my shed; big, fat brown rats with leathery tails that twisted and tweaked like skinny snakes. It was only a small shed but large enough to house the mower, garden tools and a tool box and to a child, a fantasy playground. The summer sun lit the cracks between the wood slats and in its beams hung a suspended shower of dust. In the heat, the shed perspired and the still air was stained with the rich smell of creosote oozing from gnarled, woody knots.

In slatted light which striped our torsos we stroked flesh, teased nipples and looked in each other's pants while his Mummy, the next-door neighbour, mowed her back lawn. We knew what we were doing was to be hidden from adults and the whirling of the mower gave us a sense of security. He was a skinny lad of four or five with a rib cage like pale, corrugated iron. Like many of the boys I played with, I don't recall his face and only have a vague recollection that he was blond-haired. Their penises, however, I remember with vividness, sadly, often before I recall their names. With a thumb tugging down the front of his tight, white underpants, his little dick poked out looking like a flimsy strand of bacon rind. It wobbled amusingly when touched. There was an immense thrill in being touched by foreign hands in unexplored areas and we soon had stiffies which we pressed together and held. In such musty surroundings, I experienced my first intimate sexual experience. We did little other than look and touch as our bodies and inclinations demanded little more. In the invigorating heat of summer boys are often driven to intimacy.

Acts which adults deem 'sinful', bizarre and perverted are practised by a significant number of the boy population. There

were several circumcised boys in my road and to have a foreskin or not was a major source of identity. Being circumcised wasn't cool and deriding those who'd fallen under the scalpel was common. Neil, a skinless boy, used to invite me to watch him shit. I was never very interested but knew that after he'd evacuated himself we'd start playing with each other. Defecating didn't come easy to him. With his little bald-headed acorn poking from between his marbled, bony legs, he turned red in the face and began to will a turd into the toilet bowel.

"I can feel it coming," he wheezed. "It's a big one, I can feel it." The effort twisted his face and knotted his eyebrows. I quickly learnt to tell when a turd was on the move as his little dick gradually began to stiffen. "It's coming. Any moment now," he gasped. After a moan or a lengthy, exhausted sigh, his face relaxed and his eyes quivered as a turd plopped heavily into the pan. You couldn't just watch him shit, that was never enough. After wiping his arse you had to look at his crap in the toilet. In silence we peered into the bowel and nodded in appreciation of something which eluded me. Water rapidly soaked into the thirsty paper and slowly, it floated around the turd like delicate layers of translucent filo pastry. I was always more interested in his erection than the contents of his bowel and eager to start fiddling. Though he tried to encourage me to shit in front of him, I always declined, knowing once he'd washed his hands he'd take out my dick and play with my balls. I think most boys in my road, and even some of the girls at one time or another, watched Neil crap.

* * *

In the fields and woods behind our houses, we played free from policing parents. In secret we built camps in thickets or bushes and decorated them with bits of old junk. Entry to the gangs involved having to drop your underpants for some reason usually of mere pretence. Sometimes your dick was teased with a stick or fingers or you had to bend over and show your arse. While vigorous protesting was obligatory, it was always insincere. Once humiliated, an unwritten code demanded the older and bigger boys bare their own privates and a primitive contract was sealed. It was an intriguing experience to glimpse their

assorted shapes, sizes and stages of development. The girls, relegated beyond the perimeter of the camp, occupied themselves with inane tasks such as collecting sticks or blackberries. That this behaviour was born out of natural curiosity or harmless, male bonding is true; but it was also sexual, as the variety, regularity and intensity of such acts suggest. Mild sado-masochistic games were common. Another boy, Warren, enjoyed being tied up and having stinging nettles stroked over his dick. It was a thrill to watch him struggle and strain as the tiny needles stung his excited erection.

We entertained ourselves with games such as *conkers, toad in the hole* or *stretchy sacks*. All involved mutual, graduated squeezing, poking or stretching of various parts of the genitals until one party surrendered. Humiliating gang reprisals consisted of smearing dog shit on captured boys' cocks with the aid of a stick. I once administered this punishment to a bad boy in my gang and in guilt paid him ten pence not to tell his parents.

Throughout childhood and into puberty the variations of cock fun and exploration masqueraded as games, competitions, dares or punishments. Simply asking a playmate to stroke your cock was taboo and so the pursuit of sexual pleasure was elaborated into rituals and formalities. Slags aren't motivated by curiosity and most boys know exactly what they want.

When cock fun was exhausted and we were bored, we roamed the woods, built and repaired camps and raided other gangs with sticks and missiles. At other times we picnicked by the river and feasted on lemonade and jam dodgers or fished tampons out of a nearby sewer opening with the end of bamboo canes. Swinging the cane upwards, we flipped the sodden towel at whoever was within range. It was a disgusting game but we had no idea what tampons were or where they'd been.

What discretion boys may apply in terms of partner is undermined by the intensity of their inclinations. Not until puberty will preference become of importance and even then this may be lacking. In the pursuit of pleasure they are quite willing to endure partners with piss-stained underpants, spotty faces and smelly dicks. To have a cock is the only prerequisite, and character, personality or appearance are of little consequence. Any sacrifice in terms of dirty, cold or damp surroundings is negated by the physical experience and in this sense boys are

undignified.

When the winter winds blew away the leaves and exposed our camps, when the cold draughts and damp soiled our sheds, we invented games to play at school. Restricted, we still managed to feel each other up under desks or play with each other in toilets. In the playground we chased one another in a game of tag we called *catch the bender*. When cornered, you had to put your hands in the bender's pants. One boy I loved to both catch or be caught by was a tall lad a year older than me whose voice was already beginning to break. He lived on the council estate and his clothes and body exuded a stale biscuit smell for which we ridiculed him. Some boys deliberately avoided catching him but I quickly discovered that he had more to offer in his underpants than the rest of us.

"Don't push so hard," he giggled as I eased back his foreskin and swirled my fingers over his greasy head. My hand always lingered as I explored a long, skinny dick that was almost always hard. "You've had long enough now," he ordered without pushing me away and I knew I still had time for a quick squeeze of his hefty balls before being chivvied to take my turn catching someone else. His cock was always smelly and his cheesy juices scented my fingers for hours afterwards. In class, I sniffed them and transferred the clingy smell onto pencils, rubbers and my nostrils.

* * *

At secondary school our dicks sprouted wiry hairs and our bags began to sag. Underpants once baggy and empty began to fill and voices slipped towards contralto or cracked into tenor. For a short while, before the guilt of adults was brutally imposed upon us, it was so much fun.

That same year a neighbour introduced me both to the pleasures of electrical appliances and masturbation. Neither having seen a boy come, or having wanked one off, I was fascinated. I'd been busy tingling his dick with two small metal terminals leading from an electric train transformer. While he stretched back his foreskin, I tapped the terminals on his dick end and adjusted the voltage. We took it in turns to administer small shocks to each other but it was an odd sensation which in

itself wasn't particularly thrilling. He quickly grew restless and asked if I wanted to wank him off. Agreeing, he instructed me how to hold it, rub it and how fast to pump. His dick felt different to all others and unlike the cold, pale wobbly dicks of little boys, was to the touch hot, clammy and full of life. It was fat and defined with a head so swollen it felt like the skin of a taut balloon. Engorged veins ran throughout his shaft in an anarchical, crazy-paving fashion.

"Rub faster! And harder!" he gasped as legs squirmed and flailed.

"When's it going to happen? My arm's starting to ache."

"Soon. Soon," he hissed. "Just keep pumping."

"Will much come out? Will it make much mess?" I inquired, watching his balls jingle up and down like chestnuts in a silk sack. He wasn't listening and sighed deeply through his nose. I persisted.

"What does it look like?"

"Christ, just keep rubbing. You're slowing up and I'm gonna lose it."

"Sorry," I replied as I tightened my forefinger and thumb around his girth and willed my arm to shunt up and down at greater intensity.

He couldn't get any more excited without having a heart attack and suddenly his dick swelled in my hand. A sticky, clear liquid oozed from his eye and made it possible to slip and slide my grip all over his head. His narrow stomach sucked in and out a few times and with a little kick in his prick, a thick porridge streamed out.

"Wow!" I gasped as it slopped over my fingers. Sinking into the mattress, his body relaxed and his slippy dick began to soften.

I scrutinised the blob that had slid onto my hand. "There aren't any tadpoles in it," I commented, "and it doesn't move."

"They're too small. You'd need a microscope to see them."

"Oh, they must be small, then," I replied staring at his emission in wonder. He eased himself onto his elbows while I amassed the spunk still remaining on his dick in one clump on my fingers until it resembled an opaque, misshapen jellyfish.

"What happens if you keep it keep it warm, like you do chicken eggs? Will anything happen to it?"

"I should imagine it would go all smelly and rotten. Go and chuck it down the bog." He didn't seem to like it but it quite fascinated me and in the toilet I secretly sniffed it. I flicked the best part of it into the toilet bowl where it clung to the sides like thick paste then wiped the remaining blobs onto my handkerchief. Back in his bedroom I unzipped my jeans and pulled out my erection.

"Do it to me," I asked.

"I can't. There isn't time," he sighed pulling up his shorts.

"Go on," I begged. "I'll buy you some sweets."

"Later! My mum and dad will be back soon but we'll do it together next weekend – for a bag of Toffoes. A big bag," he added.

"A deal," I replied as I tucked myself away. Before the following weekend I'd already discovered the pleasures of ejaculation in the solitude of my own bedroom.

Bored of the train transformer, we developed a relationship with the Hoover, titillating various anatomical locations as foreplay before tossing each other off. The sucking nozzle was best before our dicks got really hard as in a pliable state it stretched and flapped them around in its forceful stream. A boner just blocked the flow and started the Hoover whining in effort. We sucked everywhere; balls, bags, bums and nipples were all frottaged with the dusty nozzle. Nipples were always a major centre of arousal. Most boys like to have their nipples touched but to admit they are sensitive is to admit being a girl. They have to hide the fact they may touch them for pleasure and to divulge they are petted during solitary masturbation is completely taboo.

* * *

Not only are boys by nature slags but they are also voyeurs. Boys are fascinated by the bodies of other boys partly because they are taught to perceive a little girl's slit as aesthetically barren, amusing and threatening. When boys are unable to look at other boys for fear of ridicule, they access their goals by play making or ribaldry. In changing rooms they covertly compare and contrast their tackle sometimes to the point of arousal, compiling a catalogue of comprehensive wank material.

Unless continually cleaned, boys' toilets have a stench that can only be compared with the worst urinals in Morocco. It's the stink of unflushed toilets and urine-soaked floors which has some pungent quality absent from adult piss. Boys piss everywhere partly through choice and partly because plenty of them have tight milk-bottle foreskins that fizzle pee all over the place including down themselves. Amidst the ammoniac stench and spraying piss, they ogle other boys' penises, compete at pissing and hold them out for all to see.

* * *

As a teenager, my interests developed. In changing rooms I was excited by hairy legs, by the flash of a white vest through shirt buttons or by the bounce of a dick in underpants. I began to position myself close to boys I found attractive so I could watch them undress in the hope they might shower.

A new boy arrived, he was fourteen and already marked by puberty. He interested me with more intensity than I'd experienced previously. Of course I couldn't admit it, but with a close friend I spent hours discussing David's attributes. We both wanted to see him in the showers yet never discussed why. We predicted what he'd look like right down to the probability he'd have hairs on his balls. Hairy bags was our benchmark of physical maturity. We knew he must have a big dick as his voice had broken and an Adam's apple bobbled in his throat. Inside his trousers something big bashed when he walked and lay squashed to one side when he sat. He is the youngest boy whose face I recall with detail and this is indicative of some change in my youthful perceptions. His eyes were the darkest of brown, almost black and his hair sandy gold. It was fine, silky hair that slipped onto his forehead and often fell over one eye. His gentle smile was enlivened by bright white teeth.

Being in a different class I never got to see him changing but on a series of lunchtime cross-country competitions I eventually had opportunities. It was a vivid, memorable event when, stood by his clothes peg, he unbuttoned his white shirt to reveal a sinewy torso with broad, pale nipples all succulent and tender. In the depths of my stomach a new sensation churned like a relentless engine. Daring thoughts entered my mind and I

wanted to lick his skin and snort and suffocate in musky, scented crevices. His hand moved towards the belt of his trousers, his fingers flicked, my heart jumped and his trousers fell to his ankles. He wore a pair of grey striped underpants which wrapped his genitals like cling-film and through which the undulations of balls and penis were discernible. I sat down to tie my trainers and provide myself with the best possible position for an eyeful of his wares. When his pants were peeled down, his dick dropped out and quivered as he moved. It was a funny shaped dick that curled to one side. It was so close that had he turned quickly it would have slapped me in the face. Suddenly, a boy amongst us commented.

"What a fucking mess," he complained, blatantly looking down between David's legs. It was a legitimate excuse to stare at him.

"What is?" asked David, turning slightly so that his dick was inches from my eyes. The head was a beautiful, soft, bluey pink.

"Down there," the boy replied nodding towards David's swaying dick. "Between your legs." In my face his dick swung and wibbled in a clumsy, disjointed manner. "Looks like you've had a fight with a cheese grater," added the boy. It was true, David's dick looked like it had been savaged by a mincing machine, it had been trimmed so tight it was scarred. It was a beefy, fat dick full of shape, movement and texture. Much to my annoyance, he quickly pulled on his shorts and ended my feast.

David obsessed me for weeks and in my wank fantasies I prized pokers into orifices and tore his flesh with pincers. In screams that wrenched his mouth wide, I sucked on hot breath and kissed pained, tender lips.

* * *

While I lusted after David, others began developing an unhealthy interest in girls who, as though only just invented, were suddenly becoming the centre of conversation. This interest spawned itself shortly after a biology class on sex education where we were taught how babies were made with the aid of ridiculous cross-section diagrams that bore little resemblance to our dicks

and reduced female organs to hideous alien aberrations at which we giggled.

"What's a clit?" asked one boy and "where's the vulvex?" asked another. The teacher, bearded and red-faced, pointed to the squiggles defining the organs while outlining their various functions. He pointed with a stick, arm fully extended, as if trying to distance himself from the blackboard. As he spouted about love, fidelity and happy families the pointer hovered and he identified what did what and what went where.

"What's a homo?" asked a boy.

"A *homosexual*," announced the teacher in a loud voice through which he diverted his gaze to the ceiling, "is a man who is sexually attracted to other men." He paused a moment, still staring upwards. "*Homosexuals* find other men's bodies enjoyable and they do things together." He spoke in a dry, emotionless drone that suggested disapproval. We were riveted and silent.

"What sort of *things*, Sir?" someone asked in a squeaky, timid voice while we sat transfixed and agitated by the nature of such inquiry. Still afraid to hold our gaze, the teacher's voice boomed.

"*Things!*" He paused. "*Things* such as masturbating each other, kissing, touching privates and sometimes anal sex." Suddenly, in uproar, we feigned horror. Cries of *disgusting, revolting* and *sick* were spat unanimously. In conformity, I joined them. We glimpsed nervously around the room avoiding the eyes of lads we'd wanked, fiddled or played with. And how quickly they fell in terror of their past, now inclinations and experiences lay exposed, named and accounted.

Other boys must have gone home that afternoon to lie in quiet bedrooms. How many suddenly prostrated themselves before the dogma of conformity, drove homoerotic thoughts from their minds and buried snippets of pleasurable history? Suddenly we started talking pin-up models, tits and getting laid. I'd been admiring boys for years and wasn't as physically developed as many, yet even the lads with the tiniest tinkles were avidly talking about girls. A tacit war against homosexuality, engineered by adults and targeted at the weak, was being waged. And won. We aided and abetted by inculcating heterosexuality both amongst and within ourselves. At fourteen I was left feeling alienated and alone.

* * *

Childhood's end, for me at fifteen, and in some twist of circumstance I end up walking towards home with David. We'd left the Christmas party early, both slightly drunk. He was tottering and I had to support him. Under my fingers and through layers of warm clothing, I felt the rhythm of stringy muscles. He'd grown taller, broader and in the appropriate angle of street light a small, dark fuzz of hair was noticeable on his upper lip. We didn't talk much, mostly because we didn't really know each other, but being liberated by alcohol, it felt comfortable. There was a tingle on my skin, a persistent thump in my chest and a voice in my head willing me to make something happen and not let him slip off into the darkness. Against my chest, his head nudged and his fingers seemed to linger over my shoulder. It was only a short distance to my house and I panicked that I'd run out of time; that'd we'd part and never be so close to something happening again.

"I'm nearly home," I stated with displeasure. Hanging onto my shoulder, his thumb rested inside my collar and gently rubbed against my neck. I pulled him tighter in my grip, pressing his head against my chest while letting my hand fall onto his chest.

"I'm feeling *really* strange," he muttered.

"So am I. It's the alcohol," I replied as my finger-tips prised between jacket buttons and trailed gently over his sternum. We weren't as tipsy as we pretended and hid our intent behind faltering steps and slurred voices.

Though I hadn't played in the shed for years its creosote and musky odours welcomed us. Stood in a beam of silvery moonlight, he was beautiful. It was too cold to fuck around playing games and I braced myself to confront the both of us.

"Have you ever done it with boys?" A nervous chatter seized my jaw.

"*No*, of course I haven't. Why, have you?"

"No! Never," I lied. Leaning forward I kissed him on the cheek. It was a soft, solitary kiss that had been unplanned. He stood his ground and said nothing.

"Would you rather go home?" I asked.

"No, not yet at least." Clearing a space on the small floor,

37

we lay down on the wooden boards through which a freezing draught penetrated. Pulling up his jumper he exposed his stomach and unzipping his jeans, pulled out his dick.

He lay like a corpse on a morgue table as I jerked his curved dick up and down. On the floor, hidden in darkness, I couldn't even see it and worse, I lost my hard-on. Straining my neck, I managed to fix my lips on his dick-end. He liked that and almost imperceptibly, I heard him gasp. He let me suck for a few moments before pushing my head away.

"Don't do that. It's too homoey. Just rub it," he whispered. Any venture towards his balls met with a similar response. I didn't want him to come so I slowed down in anticipation that things might improve. In response he grabbed my hand and dictated the speed.

It was sad kneeling next to a sexy boy and just rubbing him off. Had I stopped playing he would probably have finished himself off, and who or what I was, was irrelevant. Slags are governed by the pleasure principle and his only concern was what could wank him off better than his own hand without suggesting or implying he was queer.

My body trembled and my dick leaked slimy lubricants. In my emotions grew something additional and new; an immense need to communicate, to feel his embrace and hear his tender words. Such feelings ventured beyond bodily gratification and I realised we were playing different games. As I pulled on his dick, preoccupied with my emotions, a lump swelled in my throat and a feeling of pity flowed through my body. Boys rarely sense regret when rejected – but I did.

I blinked, pressing tears from my eyes. Soft moonbeams had shifted and now illuminated his stomach. In the cold light his skinny belly shimmered.

"I've come,' he announced. I hadn't noticed. It was only after looking that I saw a glistening trail up his abdomen. I wanted to touch it and rub it into his skin but knew that spent, he wouldn't want me to. Finding an oily rag on a nearby shelf, he wiped clean his dick and pulled up his jeans.

* * *

We boys had a shit sex education from parents and adults. Denied, distorted and shamed, it was hardly surprising we viewed grown-up, parental sexual practices as disgusting.

"Do your parents fuck?"

"Christ! What a gross thought," we joked. The very idea was repugnant.

In ignorance, silence and solitude, we were left alone to navigate the confusing complexity of our own bodies. No one taught us that we could love and while it was okay for girls, men and women to be intimate and gentle, we were supposed to avoid each other and be tough. No one taught us we could be tender or passionate; that such possibilities existed was censored from all but derogatory representation. Boyhood is an experience destitute of positive images of male relationships unless premised on aggression or competition. Once perverted and converted, we transferred our guilt on outgoing girls with accusations and slurs of promiscuity, and in process bonded. Slags have neither allegiance nor loyalty and neither do boys.

After a brief, boyish, farewell, as if we'd just played tiddlywinks or marbles, David left my shed. Watching him disappear into the darkness, I was aware that part of me had changed for ever and that emotions of guilt, longing and disappointment had vanquished childhood. With a sigh, I closed the shed door behind me. David and I never spoke again and in school corridors hung our heads when passing. He still lives in my village and now has two sons. Behind their facade of naive smiles and trivial aspirations, they are hopefully as sluttish as their father.

Peter de Rome

I Loves You, Porky

from *The Erotic World of Peter de Rome*
(Gay Men's Press, 1984)

My first orgasm coincided with my first seduction. He was fourteen, I was eleven. His name was Brian Hartman, my brother's friend. It was one of those eternal summers of one's youth. Cabbage butterflies on the purple spikes of the buddleia in a buzzing, overgrown orchard in Kent. Large, straggling old fruit trees dropping their meagre crop into the long grass where the wasps were having a field day. The almost classic setting of a tool shed at the bottom of the garden.

He had lured me round on the pretext that his parents were out and that he had something to show me. It turned out to be a ferret that he had bought to go rabbiting; I didn't particularly like it or the smell. I had noticed Brian's hand moving around in the pocket of his long grey-flannel school trousers, and now that he took it out there was still something protruding. He saw me gazing at it, and said: "Do you want to see something? Promise not to tell?" I nodded.

He unbuttoned his fly and withdrew his cock. I was impressed with the stiffness and size of it and the luxuriant dark pubic hair around the root. He played with it a little and then said: "Here, feel it." I put my hand around it and it felt good. He proceeded to masturbate, and suddenly the semen spurted out onto the dusty floor. I had no idea what it was, even wondered if there was something wrong, as if his urine had become thick and cloudy.

"What's that?" I asked.

"It's what makes babies," he said with a laugh. "Here, why don't you try? It feels good."

And he reached over to put his hand in my crotch, where I certainly had an erection, but not nearly as impressive as his own, and not a sign of any pubic hair. I remember the almost unbearable sensation of my first orgasm as Brian continued to jerk me off beyond the point of endurance to the moment of exquisite agony when the fluid appeared. Rather transparent and thin as I remember. Not the thick and creamy substance that soon developed, nor with that force of trajectory that later was to prove such a turn-on.

* * *

That was nearly fifty years ago, although I'm sure it's still happening in very similar ways today. Only the circumstances and the expressions change. I remember at the time the phrase was 'toss off' or 'rub up', just as a hard-on was a 'beat' or 'the horn'. As in so many other areas, the American sexual vernacular sounds more forceful, more exact. 'Box' or 'basket' sound stronger than 'packet' – a fuller, rounder image. Just as 'buns' so effectively describes the cheeks of one's ass ('arse'), and 'blow-job' sounds more nearly exact than the strange phrase we had at the time of 'giving a gam', presumably from the archaic French slang word *gamahuche*. Even the completely blunt phrase 'wanna fuck?' or an invitation to 'get down' are less euphemistic than the rather prissy way we would then have of asking: 'Would you like to play?'

I did in fact continue to play with Brian Hartman periodically all through my school years and, surprisingly enough, well into middle age, long after he was married and had a family. Even more surprisingly, as I never really liked him. He was one of those boys – there must be one in every class – who is universally unpopular for no clearly definable reason. Somehow one just didn't trust him, his motives or his sincerity. I never had the least bit of affection for him, and yet there undoubtedly was a sexual pull. I wasn't attracted to him physically even, except that his cock was big and straight and he was always ready for sex.

On the subject of size, many people claim that it is the quality and not the dimensions that is important. I don't agree. Size plus quality is the yardstick, to employ a suitable analogy.

A *certain* size – usually referred to as 'household' in my immediate circle, and in which group I would class myself – has always seemed mandatory to me. Bigger is better ('large economy'), although biggest is not necessarily best, and can be – and usually is – a definite drawback. Whilst on the subject, I would also add that I believe that on the whole the black penis is definitely larger than the white. This is not to equate size with virility, but simply that in my experience the average black penis is larger and fleshier than the white. The eternal search is, of course, for the perfect prick, and as with most other things, there aren't too many around.

In fact, it is extraordinary just how common imperfections are; either they curve to the left or right, or they bend downwards, or they bend *and* curve, or they are too pointy at the tip, or the head is too big; or the skin won't pull back, or the head would be better covered... there is no end to the list of possible defects, so that the faultless cock truly is 'a thing of beauty and a joy for ever; its loveliness increases', and, to continue the quote, it will give us 'a sleep full of sweet dreams'. Though I wouldn't be certain that Keats had a cock in mind when he wrote those words.

Brian and I would play 'doctor and patient' at his house during those long summer afternoons of our youth, and I can still remember the particular smell of his crotch – which hadn't changed when I met him almost thirty years later in the New York Hilton. He was now with a large tractor-trailer corporation, and on his way back to London. He had invited me round and in no time at all was hinting at sex. He apologized for not being able to offer me a drink – 'running short of cash and only get this small allowance, you know' – and somehow that gesture, or lack of it, seemed to sum up Brian Hartman as I made my excuses and hurried out for the last time.

But the three-year difference between us at school was quite a lot at that age, and I found myself becoming much more interested in boys of my own age. Snow, Lewis, Wellman, Mullaley, the crushes came thick and fast, and I didn't waste much time between the conception and the consummation. I was fortunate in that I had been put in charge of the 'Store Room', where all the exercise books and stationery supplies were kept, and whenever I decided it was time to make my pitch I

would simply invite him along to the store room after school, there to indulge in a little mutual masturbation.

It was perhaps the busiest time of my life, sexually. The fantasies were often generated by pictures of male movie stars I saw in the fan magazines of the time – *Picturegoer* and *Screen Romances* – and these were translated into their closest parallels among my peers. Richard Arlen, Richard Carlson, Richard Cromwell all had their counterparts among my close acquaintances, and I tried to invest each of my 'copies' with a little of the aura of the original. The full-page portraits were, in fact, pinned up on the inside of the sloping wooden roof of our beach hut (along with a few discreetly chosen females to allay suspicion), and on rainy afternoons I would lure my not unsuspecting prey along to the deserted cabin where we would lie on a mattress, and I would gaze up at one Richard after another – and occasionally, when the guilt pangs became strong enough, at Hedy Lamarr or Lana Turner – until that awful moment arrived when I had to choose which one would share my orgasm. And when the fan magazines came up with semi-naked pictures of Wayne Morris in *Kid Galahad*, or Bruce Cabot in *The Last of the Mohicans* or Ion Hall in *Hurricane*, the choice became even more impossible, with eyes darting frantically from one to another in a flurry of indecision and later self-recrimination for those to whom I had been 'disloyal'.

My collection of masturbation material – a must for every homosexual household – dates from about this time, and I still have some of those faded and tattered portraits torn from the pages of the movie magazines of my teens, supplemented through the years by the latest hot arrivals on the scene, and despite the inadequacies attributed to him by his ex-wife, a bulging file on the young Marlon Brando.

And then there were the names written on the toilet roll as I sat on the lavatory and masturbated all over it. And bike rides to Canterbury with sex on the way in a convenient Kentish hop field or orchard. And the image of Paul Robeson on the sheet music of 'The Canoe Song' from *Sanders of the River*, which was to have a greater significance than I could have possibly foreseen at the time.

And riding home on our bicycles after school and long chats outside the house, standing astride the crossbar, and the

almost imperceptible movement until one glanced down at the unmistakable 'beat' and the inevitable, collusive giggle.

Oral and anal sex didn't start until a little later, but there were many variations to be practised on the technique of masturbation. I have often thought, in fact, that someone should write a piece on 'Masturbation with Imagination'. Maybe someone has, but I haven't seen it. The various methods of arousal alone are worthy of documentation, and might be helpful if more generally shared. Even a round brass doorknob can be strangely gratifying pressed firmly into the crotch while one grasps the door and moves one's hips around as the spirit surges and swells. It is almost the reverse of that sensation in the barber's chair, when one's hands are grasping the ends of the arms as the barber moves around and presses his crotch into your fist and... is he doing it on purpose or not? It's never worked out for me, but I feel sure it must have done for others.

But there was one boy who took precedence over all the others and who became my biggest affair and my best friend during my last years at school. His name was Patrick Roberts, or Porky as he came to be known for no very good reason, particularly as he wasn't in the least bit fat. I seemed to become aware of him only gradually. Although we were on the same level, he took Latin as his second language and I took German. This meant that our paths crossed only occasionally, perhaps in gym class or art. But my dearest recollection is of seeing him in his green school blazer and grey-flannel shorts (we didn't get into long pants until about fourteen), his red and green house cap and a leather satchel slung around his shoulders.

I don't know what it was that attracted me to him, but once it had happened I couldn't take my eyes off him. I would do anything to be near him, 'scheme just for a sight of him, dream both day and night of him'. Until that inevitable day when we finally started to talk to each other and became friends.

I do remember very clearly our first sexual contact. We had spent the afternoon at the large outside swimming-pool on the beach (the Marina, named after Princess Marina who had come down to open it, and which invested it thereafter with a sort of glamour for me it in no way ever possessed) as the alternative to playing cricket which both of us loathed. I had been quite impressed by the size of the bulge in his swimming

trunks, but no sexual reference had been made by either of us. At the end of the afternoon, when we returned to the changing-rooms to get dressed, I was doing up my shoes when I called out to him: "Are you ready, Porky?"

"No, not yet."

So I stood on the seat to look over the partition to see what stage he was in. It wasn't the one I had expected. He was standing there quite naked playing with his thick, hard cock. I just gazed on in silence as he looked back at me with an easy smile. He was uncircumcised, but the skin pulled back easily to reveal a well-shaped head as his hand gently travelled to and fro. I continued to watch in silence until I could bear it no longer. I climbed down from my seat and found that the partition did not go all the way back to the wall, but left a space of about five inches. I gingerly slid my arm through and opened up my palm. In a moment I felt the warm flesh cradled in my hand and I began to explore its texture. After I had played with it for several minutes, he knelt on the seat in his cubicle and masturbated through the space where my arm had been. He shot all over my wet bathing trunks.

There had been a wonderfully carefree quality about growing up in England in the thirties which would never be captured again. And in this last year of the decade it would reach its apotheosis before the whole frail facade came crashing down around our ears. But while our parents continued to talk about Munich and Chamberlain and Hitler's plans to take over the Sudetenland, I continued to sack and plunder my unopposed way through the fifth and sixth forms of Chatham House.

Porky and I had become the very closest of friends. Our names were hardly ever mentioned apart. We would go to the movies together (hands under a raincoat), go on bicycle rides together, play billiards and pingpong together, climb the cliffs together and trespass through the network of smugglers' caves with a lighted candle, always with sex at the back of our minds.

We were also both avid fans of the popular music of the time. Porky was forever buying new jazz records, and would spend hours in the local music shop listening to the new Ellington, Bechet, Fats Waller, Grappelli or whatever. In those days the leading record companies would issue a small leaflet every month listing all their new releases, and the only way to find out if you

liked a certain side was to play it, the amount of jazz heard on the radio being strictly limited.

I had been taking lessons on the piano since I was ten, and although I was being taught only classical music, I much preferred playing popular songs. I would stumble through all the latest Porter, Kern, Berlin and Gershwin, usually accompanying myself by singing the words; sometimes my parents would ask me to sing a song when we had visitors and I would put up a mild protest before gladly obliging. It was so much more fun than listening to all their boring chat. When it came to a song like 'My Heart Belongs to Daddy', they would all laugh at "those perfectly ridiculous words", without having the least idea just who the 'Daddy' in the title really was.

Gershwin was probably my favourite composer; those strange new chords, those exciting original rhythms. The sheet music would usually appear at the same time as a new film was released: *Shall We Dance*, *A Damsel in Distress*, *The Goldwyn Follies*. But one day I remember seeing music from a show I had never heard of: *Porgy and Bess*. What a strange title, I thought, and who was in it? Little matter, I had to have it because it was Gershwin. But when I got home and started feeling my way through 'Summertime', 'I Loves You, Porgy' and then 'It Ain't Necessarily So', I wondered what on earth it was all about. I had never heard of the book, *Porgy*, on which it was based, and at that time could have no idea that it was a story about black people on Catfish Row, South Carolina. But slowly the melodies caught hold of me, began haunting me, although it was to be years before the first production of the opera ever reached London and I finally saw what all those wonderful songs were really about.

* * *

As Neville Chamberlain made his fateful announcement over the radio, Porky and I were enjoying a sexual reunion in our chalet on the beach. I had really missed him, and felt I could demonstrate my feelings and new-found sophistication by giving him a real kiss for the first time. To start with he resisted. But as I persisted he slowly opened his mouth and it wasn't long before he discovered the newly erotic experience of kissing. Finally I

was able to tell him in song: "I loves you, Porky." And I meant it. A little embarrassed by my intensity, but nevertheless touched by my genuine emotion, he softly said: "I think I love you, too."

Almost instinctively but also as if to offer proof, I lay on my back facing him and put my legs over his shoulders. My look must have signalled my message, for he responded without any further coaxing. And in spite of the pain and the lack of lubricant, Porky slowly and gently penetrated me...

Then we lay naked in each other's arms listening to the end of Chamberlain's speech. We had absolutely no inkling of how totally and irrevocably our lives would soon be changed. It was inconceivable that in only a few short years Porky would be a Spitfire pilot and I would be going back to France as part of the biggest invasion force ever known to man.

But for the present we lay there gazing out at the shimmering sea, not knowing quite what to expect. All we really cared about was each other and the wonderful, carefree relationship we enjoyed. Neither of us had anything much to say, anything much to think about except satisfying our own inordinate sexual desires. It was one of those timeless moments, so hard to recapture, so impossible to plan.

Ronnie Chapman

Diary of a Sex Offender

It's the late 1950s, and I'm eleven and a half. I'm still very keen on stamp collecting; that's why Roger became my best friend. Roger and Ronnie — not quite as similar as our names, but both of us left a bit outside of the other boys' more boisterous games. Roger was bigger than me, not exactly fat, but kind of lumpy. He had bright blue eyes. When he got excited about something, his face would light up, and he'd stumble over his words.

I almost always went to Roger's house; he had his own bedroom, and a table where we could pore over our stamp albums. On a Tuesday my parents let me stay for supper, and we'd listen to the 'Goon Show' together. Our favorite characters were Bluebottle and Eccles, silly schoolboys like us, and one of their jokes somehow stuck in our minds: "What is the shape of a kiss?" "A lip-tickle..."

We didn't give each other lip-tickles, but sitting side by side it was nice to rub our legs together, and Roger soon invented tickles of other kinds. The first one we played was 'ver-tickle'. I had to stand up, legs slightly apart, and Roger tickled up under my grey flannel shorts. When he'd finished doing one leg, it was my turn to do the same to him, and so we'd go on.

Right from the start, there was a certain seriousness in our fun. The idea was to give each other a really nice feeling, though we didn't need to put it into words. We'd finish up flushed and glowing, and then it was time for me to go home.

A few weeks later Roger thought of another game. He answered the door with a manic grin on his face, and spluttered as he explained it to me. This was called 'horizon-tickle'. I had to lie down on his bed, on my back of course, while he tickled me in this position. The advantage of horizon-tickle was that as well as my legs, he could tickle my tummy. I had to keep my hands behind my head, to give him free rein. We undid our S-

clasp belts and pulled our shirts out of the way, but our shorts stayed buttoned up, just allowing fingers to creep an inch or two below the waist.

We had to be a bit more careful with this game, in case Roger's mum popped upstairs and surprised us. And while I could enjoy Roger's 'ver-tickling' without getting ticklish, he soon found where to press his fingers on my tummy to provoke giggling squeals. When I tried the same on him, though, he just grinned all the more and rolled his eyes about.

At home in bed, my dick seemed to give more pleasure with each passing month. That was something different from tickling, though, something you did in private by yourself; to do it with Roger, I knew, would risk serious disapproval if we were found out.

Did our pre-pubescent dicks stiffen from the start of our games? Did we each realise that we had this effect on the other? Certainly by the time we went on to play 'horizon-tickles' and 'tummy-tickles', neither of us made any attempt to conceal it. After a couple of sessions of the new game, we agreed that shorts buttons could be undone to extend the playing surface, though a kind of invisible barrier still marked off the most sensitive territory as forbidden.

But rules are made to be broken, and I didn't see why Roger should always define our games. One day, after Roger had to put his hand over my mouth to stifle my squeals, his eyes locked on mine to say: "Look what I can do to you!", I told him I'd thought of a special tickle to try out on him, and bet I would make him squeal this time.

With Roger's hands behind his head, and his shirt pulled up over his chest, I started pulling his shorts down his legs, against spluttered but ineffectual protests. "It's okay," I reassured him, "you can keep your underpants on." Roger's dick made an interesting bulge in his aertex underpants, but I didn't dare start giving him a 'dick-tickle'. I focused instead on the top of his thighs, working my fingers up under his pants until I met the soft skin of his balls. Roger didn't squeal like I did, more an excited puffing and wheezing as if he was getting an asthma attack.

At that moment the door opened and Roger's dad came in. I wasn't allowed to play with Roger again.

* * *

It's a few months later, soon after my twelfth birthday. After the fiasco with Roger, there was no other boy I tried to get close to – at least in a physical sense. Certainly I kept playing with myself, and though still hairless and spunkless, I would reach every night a dry but breathless orgasm – or an even better soapy one if it was bath night.

Our school had very few facilities, and we changed for games in the classroom. I think we were getting dressed after football, school clothes back over muddy legs, when I saw for the first time another boy's hard-on. Some of the boys had started grabbing at each other's balls, which I liked to watch but not to join in. Colin already had his pants back on at this point, when his stiff pink dick popped out through the fly. A couple of boys jeered, then turned their attention elsewhere. To my amazement Colin didn't immediately tuck it away, but stood there on show to the world, facing right towards me in fact.

* * *

I had my thirteenth birthday a few weeks ago. In the last few months, I've got hair on my crotch, my dick seems to grow like Jack's legendary beanstalk, and I spunk off at least twice a day. It's now summer, and we're dressing after athletics practice. One of the younger and most innocent boys, Michael Wilson, is standing on his desk stark naked, a clean-limbed, fair-haired boyish beauty quite ignored by the other kids, but a fascinating contrast to my own self-image. Mr O'Connor, the sports master, enters the room, looks appreciatively at Michael, and then to my embarrassment catches my eye. A look of complicity passes swiftly between us. At thirteen years and two months, I am recognised as – a boy-lover!

* * *

I've started to see a few more hard-ons. Two of the rougher boys, Gareth Howes and Jeff Burton, regularly compare length and width, hairiness and other desirable properties, watched by admiring – or incredulous – prepubescents. A rather dumb kid

called Spike, always sat at the back of the class, sometimes gets his dick out and plays with it in geography lessons, held by a rather ineffectual (and short-sighted) teacher on Thursday afternoons.

Every time I spunk off now, I think of Gareth's dick and imagine more crazy things I could to it. Sometimes I think of Jeff's as well.

*   *   *

The unimaginable happens. It's that geography lesson, and Gareth's sharing with me one of the double desks we have. What gave him the idea? I know he caught my eye when he was showing off his dick the other week, and I was trying not to look. Jeff is off school with chickenpox.

Gareth nods to me to look under the desk, and I can see his hard-on sticking up in his trousers. He takes my hand and lets me feel it. My heart's thumping nineteen to the dozen. He reaches inside his belt and makes an adjustment, then nods to me again. I put my hand into his pocket, and can feel the soft-skinned hard flesh through the thin silky material. I forget everything but the magic feel of his dick.

At the end of the lesson he whispers to me, "Come back with me after school." He lives in a little terrace house, unlocks the door, there's no one else at home. I copy him in throwing my satchel down in the hall and taking my shoes off. He doesn't say much, and I can't speak at all, my mouth's too dry. I just want him to nod to me and give me the go-ahead.

"I like to get my school clothes off," he explains. There's a pair of jeans and a cotton sweater over the chair beside his bed but he doesn't put them on. He lies on the low divan in his singlet and underpants; it's almost like I imagine it when I wank.

He grins at me. "'S'all yours, Robbie." I go straight for his dick, reach into the leg of his Y-fronts and let it flip up free. I'm exploring it gently with my fingers and when I stroke the purple bit it twitches like anything and I hear him breathe in. Then I'm rubbing the juice all round, just like I do on my own dick, and he really likes that. I'm kneeling on the floor beside his bed, and he reaches to tousle my hair.

"Good kid," he says after a couple of minutes. "You want

me to do you?" I swallow hard and nod, stand up and struggle out of my trousers and shirt. Gareth pulls his Y-fronts off over his feet before pulling my underpants down. His grin reminds me a bit of Roger.

He's kneeling on the bed now, so I can carry on playing with him while he pulls on my dick. He stands up against me, and squeezes our dicks together. "You wanna help me spunk off?" he asks. I rub the top of his dick all wet and sticky while he pulls on the shaft till he spunks all over his tummy and mine. He reaches for a towel he keeps under the bed to wipe himself, but I rub his spunk over my dick and shoot only a few seconds later.

"You're a dirty little bugger," he says playfully, and tousles my hair again.

* * *

A few days later I go back with Gareth again and we really get to work. Amazingly, he was a bit shy with me last time as well. He shows me how you can do a kind of wrestling, and slide your dicks together between your tummies. Fantastic! I thought we could spunk off like that, but Gareth has a different idea.

"You heard of dicky-licking?" he asks.

I hadn't heard the word, but it was one of the things I'd imagined doing with him. A few seconds later I'm working my tongue round his foreskin, then my lips over his glans. I let him wank into my mouth till he's getting ready to spunk. He puts his arm round my head to try and keep me in position, but I pull away. He aims his dick so that he spunks all over my face.

* * *

Next week Jeff's back at school, and I catch him and Gareth looking at me and nudging each other. I bet Gareth's told Jeff what we did last Thursday.

On Tuesday afternoon Gareth invites me back again. This time Jeff comes along too; I'm not sure if I like the idea or not. Upstairs in Gareth's room it's a bit awkward what we're meant to do. The two of them seems to like the idea of taking my

clothes off first; they feel me up, then struggle to get their own things off. "Go on, Jeff, tell him what you want," Gareth eggs his friend on.

"You gonna lick my dick," says Jeff; I'm not sure if there's a question mark.

Of course I lick his dick. He can pull his foreskin back up even when it's hard, and I try and get my tongue under it. Gareth is telling me what to do; he seems to know what Jeff likes. I'm kneeling over Jeff, who's lying on the bed, going crazy on his dick, when Gareth goes round behind me and reaches between my legs. He's wanking himself with one hand and playing with my dick with another. Then he works back round my balls, and one finger starts brushing against my arsehole. That's something new for me, and I have to stop work on Jeff to think about it.

"Okay Jeff, let me have a go now." Jeff's a bit reluctant to move, and Gareth and him wrestle around a bit, like I liked to do, before Gareth takes his place on the bed and I'm sucking his dick again. Jeff doesn't waste any time and starts right away where Gareth left off on exploring my rear end. I feel his dick against my balls and squeeze it between my thighs. I'd like him to start wanking me, but he seems to have other ideas. He pulls back, spreads my arse apart and pushes his dick against my hole.

There's no way I can let him do that, so I let go of Gareth's dick and wriggle away. Gareth sees what Jeff's trying to do, but just laughs. "C'mon kid," he says, a bit impatient. "I can feel something's getting ready to shoot out." If Jeff hadn't been there I'd have let Gareth spunk in my mouth this time; but I'm not doing it with him watching. Anyway, I put my mouth back where Gareth needs it, and right away Jeff tries the same thing again. I pull away in a hurry, and it seems I've hurt Gareth's dick with my teeth. He swears and clouts me on the head, I huddle in a corner and want to go home.

"You stupid bugger," Gareth calls Jeff. "It's all your bloody fault."

Jeff just shrugs. It's funny to see them quarrelling, their hard-ons haven't even gone down. Then Gareth is tousling Jeff's hair like he did to me last week. They're both ignoring me, and the next thing they're down head to tail on the bed, and both wanking into each other's mouths. I hadn't quite worked out you could do that.

Jack Robinson

The Egg and I

from *Teardrops on My Drum* (Gay Men's Press, 1998)

On my first day in school after being transferred from the infants'
department, I met a boy named Eggy. We were to share a two-
seater desk in Standard One. The school had seven classes
numbered from one to seven. If we turned out to be bright lads
then we would miss Standard Seven and finish up in Standard
Seven A, a special class for those with a promising future.

"My name's Jack," I informed him as we sat down. "I'm
Tim," said the boy, "but everybody calls me Eggy." "Stop talking!
shouted Mr Free, and threw a heavy blackboard duster. It hit
my desk mate on the shoulder and left a big white chalk mark
on his nice blue blazer. "Get out here and clean the blackboard!"

Eggy picked up the wooden eraser, walked to the
blackboard and wrote the word 'Twat!' in huge white letters.
To the kids in St Jude's this meant a girl's sexual organ.

Mr Free stood with his back to the roaring coal fire, his
piercing blue eyes searching among the faces of his new class and
his hands behind his back. He wore a smart grey suit, polished
brown shoes and a neatly tied bow on his neck. He couldn't see
Eggy, which was fortunate for the bright-eyed boy with the curly
black hair. Eggy gave the board one final rub and then returned
to our desk. A slight murmur of suppressed laughter ran through
the class. From that moment on I knew that I was going to like
my new desk mate and the rest of the kids at St Jude's.

"Keep quiet!" roared the teacher. He left the warmth and
comfort of the glowing coal fire and examined the board,
suspecting something. He seemed satisfied, picked up a piece of
chalk and wrote the words: 'Knotty Ash'. "How many of you
can play football?" he asked. Most of the hands went up.

"How many of you think they are good enough for the

school team?" was his next question. All the hands dropped, with the exception of a scaly, pumice-stoned extremity belonging to a bright-eyed lad named Stanley Marsden and the eager hands of myself and my desk mate Eggy.

Mr Free then wrote the words 'Margaret Street' on the blackboard. "How many boys can swim?" he asked. There were about thirty boys in the class and only three hands went up, the same three as before.

"Right! Settle down," said Mr. Free. "Margaret Street baths is where you will swim. Those of you who think they are good enough to swim for the school team will receive free passes. That means you can go in any day of the week. How many of you want to train for the swimming team?" A dozen hands shot up and Mr Free allowed a faint smile to grace his thin lips.

"Knotty Ash is five miles from here," he went on. "St Jude's owns a piece of land out there. It is our football and sports training ground. Members of the football team will get a free pass on the tramways and can get out to the training grounds in their spare time.

Cowboy Donaghue raised his hand. "I'm a good footballer," he said. "I'm a good swimmer too, but I have no football boots and I don't have any swimming togs." Mr Free just smiled, wrote down the names of his budding athletes and handed out passes for the tram cars and swimming pool.

Mr Free had two canes. He showed one of them to the class. It was four foot long and made a whistling sound as he slashed it through the silence of the classroom. "This is for those of you who do not pay attention," said the old devil, then produced his other cane. It was burnt black, hardened at the end and twice as thick as the other cane. He brought it down with a crash! The inkwell jumped from its little hole in the wooden desk and a cloud of dust arose. "This is for the bad boys," he smiled, thin lipped. I decided right then and there that I would be a good boy and pay attention to the words of Mr Free.

My new friend produced a packet of sandwiches at lunch time and shared them with me in the playground. "Will you walk home with me after school?" he asked. "I'm going to watch the men flying kites and I don't like going by myself." I'd never taken any particular notice of the kite-flying unemployed and thought it a very childish thing for grown men to do. However,

my friend seemed to be a nice lad and I could see no reason to refuse his offer.

He took me to Margaret Street reservoir: a park built high in the sky alongside a gigantic water tower. "Don't go into the lavatory," said my friend. "The last time I was here, a man offered me some money to do something for him." "What did he want you to do?" I asked innocently.

"I don't know," replied Eggy. "I didn't stop to find out. He scared me so I ran away." We stared up at a tiny dot in the sky.

"Look at that one!" said Eggy. "I bet it would pull you off your feet." A cheery-looking young man about thirty was paying out the string. "You can hold it if you want," he said, offering me the taut white twine. I took the line in my hands and discovered the thrill of kite-flying. It was fantastic! The guy could see the look of surprise on my face, the strain on my arms and knew the kite was pulling me off my feet. He took the kite string from me and returned to his little wooden box-like seat. We strolled around, got quite involved in the flying and spoke to the depressed and shabby men reduced to such childish pastimes. There were hundreds of them; they sat on little home-made stools, rigged up quaint looking kite tails and talked about the kites as if they were aircraft. They were indeed great kites; they were not toys by any means. One of the men had travelled as far as Japan to a kite-flying exhibition. He told us that they sometimes flew kites in Japan that could carry a young man aloft.

When they decided to pack up for the day, Eggy turned to me. "Let's go!" he said. "They'll be here all evening winding up the string. It takes hours. Come along and I'll take you to see the kite man."

The kite man smiled at us when we walked into his workshop in Breck Road. "What do you want?" he asked cheerfully. "Tails? Balls of string? Kite stools?" "We want to see you making kites," replied my friend. "We might buy one at the weekend when I get my pocket money." I knew then that Eggy was going to be my true friend; he included me in all his conversation.

Some of the balls of twine in the kite man's workshop were as big as footballs. The kites were made from greaseproof

paper stretched over a thin, octagonal bamboo frame and decorated with colourful stickers. Each sticker was in actual fact a strengthener. A tiny hole in the star-shaped strengthener allowed the string through from the bamboo frame. The eight strings met and were tied together about twelve inches from the skin of the kite. Some of the frame strings were of different length. The secret, explained the strange old-fashioned man, was to tie the strings in such a way as to get the correct angle for the airflow. When we left the quaint old shop I was a kite-flying enthusiast and intended to fly a kite so high that it could not be seen by the naked eye...

So ended my first day in the big boys' section of St Jude's. It had been pretty good. I had a new friend, a new hobby and was a member of the football team. And being a member of the swimming team thrilled me! I had a pass to the swimming pool! Showers every day! I could keep clean for the rest of my life and it felt like being born again!

The months passed quickly. The public library beckoned. Eggy joined the library with me and the first books I took away were *Grimm's Fairy Tales* and *Robin Hood*.

Spring came and the blossoms fell from the trees in Shiel Park. The hard stony ground turned to rich green grass and I joined the school cricket team with my friend. We went down in the history books as the only team to score a century and clean bowl the opposition for a duck! Cowboy Donaghue said in his gorgeous, Anglo-Welsh-Liverpool-Manx-Irish accent, "We wundem eezy! Darrell be in dee *Echo* ternite!" "Worrell be in dee *Echo*?" asked Stanley Marsden, the back stop. "A hundred fuckin' nil," replied Cowboy. "Dale gerrit in da buke a fuckin' records!"

* * *

Fortunately, during my early years with Tommy Lawless, I'd been impressed by his nicely formed words and easy manner of speech. His grandmother had insisted that we read poetry aloud and she had helped me with my diction. I was only a poor, ragged kid but I did not intend to remain one all my life. True, I could eff and blind with the best of them but I tried my very best not to speak like a 'buck'.

The difference between a buck and an everyday scouse is this: The buck is aggressive. He says, "Warra yew luken at?" The scouse replies, "I dunno, the label's fell off." The buck threatens to hit you with a brick; the scouse says, "Gowome, yermum's got cake!"

A stranger, on asking a buck a simple question like "Where's the urinal?" would be given a surly look and the words, "Fuck off, wack!" The scouse would reply to the same question, "How many funnels has she got?" Verbal badinage comes natural to the scouse but one gets only abuse from the buck.

Eggy spoke nicely and he was always friendly and witty. If it had not been for the lunch he shared with me every day, and the empty bottles that I got from Teddy Kirkwood, then I would not have survived. Teddy and Joey Kirkwood stole hundreds of bottles of pop from the mineral water lorries but wouldn't return the empties and claim the penny deposit. I felt no guilt when I returned them. I bought fish and chips with the money and that's what kept me alive.

"'Ow's yer father... all right! Sitting in the ale-house ...all night! 'Ow's yer mother... okay! Standing at the pawnshop... all day!" That's a little snatch from a skipping rope song.

Someone, some body or organisation, actually cared about the poorest of us; we could get free dinners and free milk at school. This meant a trip to some place called the 'dinner house' and the carrying of a pink ticket in order to claim the right to such things.

There were times when I was sorely tempted to apply for a pink ticket but some kind of inner pride prevented me. There were only three or four kids in the whole school who went to the dinner house. Five minutes before lunch break, the teacher would call out: "Those of you who are going to the dinner house can get away now!" Not a single lad in my class moved and I don't think any one of us even knew where the dinner house was situated.

No morning sunshine shed its glory through the rich green trees and no birds sang when I awoke, dragged my ragged grey shorts on and ran to school unwashed and barefoot.

There were no trees, and the streets were thick with fog and lined with horse manure. Fog horns blared on the Mersey as huge cart-horses pulled their heavy loads along the miserable

roads, slipping on the square stone setts, dropping a few more loads of steaming manure and adding streaming yellow stinking urine to the mess for other cart-horses to trample in and slither on.

Nevertheless, I enjoyed my morning journey to school: St Jude's Church of England. Good old St Jude! The patron saint of lost causes...

Bottles of milk stood cold and lonely on the doorsteps of the wealthy. I had never tasted real milk in my life and I liked the condensed milk which always graced our table. Its colourful tin and jagged-edged lid were the only things worth looking at, as the table was usually piled with dirty plates and dirtier-looking cups and saucers. But always amidst the jumble of unwashed crockery stood a dish of brown-stained lumpy sugar, a cracked saucer of margarine and the good old tin of 'conny onny'. I could grab a slice of bread, dip one of the dirty table knives into the tin and spread the sticky, sweet mess on the stolen staff of life which was my breakfast.

It was one of those days when everything was going to be just fine and dandy and you knew it instinctively. Joey Kirkwood had pinched a big bunch of bananas from the greengrocer shop and couldn't eat the whole lot by himself, so he gave me two and I wolfed them down. Eggy invited me to his home and promised me a load of comics. And it was swimming bath day: a chance to get clean and have a good time into the bargain. Swimming and running – how I loved those two sports!

We lined up outside the school and the deputy headmaster said: "Right! Lead on you lot, and don't pinch anything from the fruit stands on the way or you'll all finish up in the Bridewell." Nobbler, one of the smart-arsed kids, had a special overcoat with no lining in the pockets and a draw-string bag tied around his waist which his mother used when she was out shoplifting. As we passed the fruit stands, his long lapping overcoat brushed against the luscious-looking goodies and his unseen hands grabbed and filled the 'knock off' pouch with apples, oranges and plums. We reached the swimming baths at Margaret Street loaded with fruit and one or two bottles of pop for good measure. He was quite a specialist at that sort of thing and he was generous to his hungry mates.

None of us had towels and only one boy had a pair of

swimming trunks. He had reached the pubescent stage in life; thick red hair sprouted from his pubic region and the headmaster had bought him a pair of trunks to spare the lad's blushes. The rest of us swam naked and, as the sexes did not meet in the swimming baths in those days, this was the norm. The corporation supplied us with hard, rough towels and we shared two to a cubicle when we changed.

Eggy and I dried our skinny bodies in the privacy of the cubicle, and for the first time in my life I felt slightly embarrassed with my friend. My dicky stiffened up and Eggy laughed. "You've got a hard on, Jackie." "I can't help that," I said blushing. "You get one sometimes, I suppose."

He pulled back his pointed-looking foreskin and a small red end appeared. His pigeon got hard and stiff and he played with it in front of me. "Let me do it for you," he said excitedly, "and you do it for me." I had seen other lads do it together so I agreed and we pulled our stupid organs until the sensations overcame us and we had to stop. Neither one of us could produce the mysterious fluid but we certainly tried hard enough. I was tempted to tell him about my adventure with the stranger in the cinema but thought better of it. I knew he would not believe me if I told him the guy had sucked the damn thing like a gobstopper.

Eggy was a nice respectable boy from a good clean home. Unfortunately he had no father, but his mother adored him and she rather liked me for some reason or other. When we reached his house, he invited me in. His friendly mother kissed him and rumpled my hair, laughing. "My goodness, you do smell nice and clean. What have you been up to?" I blushed like a schoolgirl, thinking about the things we had been up to and going a bright red.

"We've been swimming," said her son, laughing and tossing his black curls. "Can Jackie stay to tea with us?" "Certainly, darling. Go and play and I'll call you when it's ready." We ran up to his room and he pulled out a pile of comics. They were all my favourites and I wanted to devour every one of them, so I sat cross-legged on the warm, carpeted floor and opened up a *Hotspur*.

Eggy ran his hand up my shorts and felt me. "You can read them any time," he said, taking my penis between his fingers

and making it stiff. "Put them away and let's play dicks."

We were not exactly mealy-mouthed kids and we came from a rough neighbourhood, but swearing in your friend's house was taboo, almost as bad as smoking in front of your parents or swearing in front of a girl. But sometimes it just came out and this was one of those times. "Fuck off! Fuck off, Eggy, and leave my cock alone. What's up with you anyway?"

He simply smiled at me and said, "Sorry. I thought you liked pulling off! Don't fall out with me!"

"Okay, Eggy. I don't want to fall out with you. You know I don't. Let's read the comics; your mother will be calling us down for tea in a minute."

He piled up his comics and arranged them in alphabetical order. Then he turned to me and smiled, saying, "You can take this lot home with you when you go. I've read all of them and they're no use to me." It was very generous of him because he could swap them for others he had not read and it would save him quite a lot of pocket money.

"How would you like to spend the weekend with me?" he asked. "Mom won't mind and we can play with my Meccano set."

It seemed like a good idea and I wanted to stay in his comfortable home because I didn't have much, and the thought of eating his mother's home-made cakes made my mouth water. However, I had not stayed with anyone before and was not quite sure what my mother would say, apart from "Dirty, friggin' gett".

"Jesus, Eggy! I'd love to spend a weekend with you. Are you sure your mother won't mind?"

"Of course she won't," he laughed. "She likes you and she thinks you're one of the best kids around here." We fooled about laughing and joking until his mother called us downstairs and the three of us sat at the table. It was spotless! The food was delightful and his friendly mother smelled of home-made cake and crushed violets. I think I fell in love with her, and wished I had someone like her to give me a few kisses and a smile like the ones she continually showered upon her handsome young son.

She invited me to spend Saturday night and all day Sunday, and when I reached home laden down with comics I thought it must be Christmas.

Strangely enough my mother did not object and I waited out the rest of the week patiently. Thinking about Eggy and his continual sexy advances kept me awake at night, and when Saturday morning came round I was standing outside the Royal Hippodrome at ten o'clock wondering if the strange man would keep his promise and take me to the zoo.

* * *

The comic books we shared and swapped, the visits to the park, the swimming and running together – all took on a very minor role in our young lives. The only important thing now was the secret love that developed between us. I remember coming home from the public library with him, going to his house and finding a note from his mother. "Mam's gone to the pictures and she won't be back till late," he announced. "She says here: 'Make some tea for you and your friend, and get something to eat from the chip shop for both of you." Obviously we were very happy at the prospect of being alone bur we had not planned it.

Their home had a new radio by this time and we sat together listening to the music. At six o'clock we went to the chip shop, bought our tea and ate it in the comfort of his home, discussing a match between Everton and Liverpool. Our headmaster Pat Kelly, who was chairman of Liverpool Boys', had given us free tickets and we were very interested as we were good footballers and played for the school team.

"Come up to my room," said my friend. "I've got a scrap book with all the players' pictures in."

Perhaps it was the intimacy of his room, sitting together on his bed, or simply strong physical attraction. Whatever it was, it united us, brought us together in a new way. We jumped into bed naked. I had a few pubic hairs by this time and was past twelve years of age. We searched in vain for hairs on my lovely friend, but he seemed happy enough stroking mine.

We must have played dicks a hundred times but neither of us had ejaculated as yet. This time however, we tried something else. I am not quite sure who started it first, but it worked! It was the most exciting night of my life. Unfortunately, I did not see the magic fluid because it vanished into the young body of

my gentle schoolfriend. He was equally successful and we became much closer.

Every morning on our way to school, my friend bought sweets, crisps, comic books and all the things that schoolboys buy. He shared everything with me because I never had any money during the week. At weekends Eggy had no cash, but I had money from a small part-time job and I shared it, paid for visits to the cinema, football matches and days out in the park.

We planned our love-making intelligently... we had to, because we liked to undress. It wasn't too difficult; the nights when his mum went to the cinema left us with the opportunity to lie naked on his single bed. We no longer played with our fat little pigeons or searched for growing pubic hair; we simply cuddled, held each other warm and close, kissed, watched the magic wands grow hard with desire and moved our warm young bellies together until we were slippery with clear fluid. Strangely enough, we knew it was quite natural for us and had no feelings of shame or guilt when we entered into our secret cave, filled it with little pearls of love and wonderful satisfaction.

Then we would lie side by side, looking into one another's eyes, kissing tiny boyish nipples, lips, eyelids and small freckled noses. Words of love never passed our lips and I don't think we spoke about our feelings, but we were in love and knew it well.

We made sure of well-timed little jobs like baby-sitting by volunteering and never accepting any payment, usually for his married sister and her young husband who enjoyed the temporary release from a couple of very young children who always slept soundly enough. This was our house of utmost pleasure, because they had a car, went out for the whole evening, and could be heard returning noisily. Here we indulged in the most beautiful love-making of all: looking into each other's eyes as one of us entered the magic circle.

The first time it happened was quite an experiment. "Let me try it like this," said Eggy. "Lie down on your back, lift up your legs and show me your bottom. It'll be like a boy and girl."

It was tender and delightful; Eggy stroked my smooth cheek with the back of his nice clean fingers, kissed my belly once or twice and then entered me quite easily. It made me feel like a young girl being seduced. Seeing his handsome smiling face above me gave me almost as much pleasure as the firm young penis in

my bottom. My lovely friend had always been the driving force and seemed more masculine than me. He moved a little faster and a lock of soft dark curls fell upon his forehead. His lips parted and I saw his pink tongue and gleaming teeth. His eyes opened very wide and he stopped moving. I knew it was going to happen immediately. My dickie throbbed, stiffened just a little harder, quivered springy on my belly and fluid shot from it like silver pearls, landing on my chest.

"Did you enjoy it like that, Jackie?"

"I can't believe it! It's better than bumming you!" He used one of the baby's napkins, cleaned the sticky goo from my belly and threw the napkin in the wash.

Unfortunately, it didn't affect my companion in quite the same way. When I caressed him, looked into his eyes and made love, it was beautiful for both of us. I filled him with my shooting stars, but he still had to take me in turn to fulfil his desire. As time passed I became the gentle one, accepted the handsome boy willingly, and finished up with a sticky belly from my own squirting spout and a slippy wet bum from his. We played our separate roles and set a fixed pattern: Eggy, the masculine lover, and I, the happy, nuttering, young sweetie beneath his firm thrusting young muscles. It just seemed natural and we liked it that way.

Things were much different on the streets. I worked very hard. Nobody could find a job of work in the whole city but I cleaned windows, trimmed hedgerows and pulled a handcart, loaded up like a donkey, for a grocer shop that stayed open until ten at night.

My schoolfriend didn't need to work and I'm sure his charming mother wouldn't have allowed him to slave like me. He was a real true friend, looked after the money I earned, the odd clothes that I managed to buy and the few shillings I managed to save.

* * * * *

The sequel to Jack Robinson's *Teardrops On My Drum* is *Jack and Jamie Go To War*, which Gay Men's Press hopes to re-issue in 2001.

Chris Anderson

Twelve and Thirteen

from *Four to Fourteen*, a memoir

TWELVE

We all met up again through Scouting: Andrew, Peter and I all joined the troop where Phil and Stephen were members already, one year above. That summer, 1979, we prepared for our first proper camp.

The new boy, Peter, had arrived in our street and into my year at school two years before. I had been smitten straight away. I even pretended to take his sister as a girlfriend – she was so like him in looks and in character.

They came from over the county border – almost as exciting as coming from abroad. Peter was cute: small for his age. And he was pretty. And he was sweet. The first time we played we played hopscotch – a bit feminine, I feared, but a contact point.

The night that Andrew and I made out under the stars, we discussed whether Peter might ever have "diddled". We decided that everybody had at some time, and that Peter most probably had with the over-the-border childhood friend that he had had to stay – a butch and gruff and hunky male for his age. Evidence in favour of the thesis was the night the three of us shared a tent on an adventure to a campsite a long cycle ride away, when it was Peter who began a live commentary on the waxing and waning state of his erection – a conversation which we had both joined in, but which had no momentum to lead to anything more.

The year before, as a Scout troop, we had had just a one night bivouac camp: build your own shelter from what you could

find. I had latched on to Phil as my partner in this, and hidden us away behind a dry stone wall. I had it all planned, but sod him, he slept like a log, and there was no quiet of the night in which to play, as several others – and I joined them – spent the whole night awake by the campfire. The plan failed – and I had felt like he owed it me too.

As far as Stephen and Phil were concerned, Scouting was acquaintanceship renewed – no more. In terms of watching the boys, I was actually most enchanted by the camaraderie of the older boys – fourteen and fifteen – with their authority, their deep voices, their mischief, their cigarettes and their near adult forms. I longed to be a part of their group, but could only aspire to their approval – any occasional hint of which was sure to make my week. I was besotted.

The time for the first proper camp came around and the first night set the tone. The camp was divided according to age to sleep eight to a decent sized tent (all new). That meant that there were only three "extras" for padding in a tent which was occupied by Andrew, Peter, Stephen, Phil and me. And strangely it was not us, but definitely the three, who led catcalls and wolf whistles and strip tease music as people tried to discreetly undress and to get into bed. And there we slept, eight parallel boys, in our bags, on our mats, on the floor, one tent, with dirty jokes and rude talk and unlikely bragging into the night – from the three.

Night two, Phil rose to the strip tease challenge, being last back to the tent, after a pee, the rest of us ready in bed. "Give us a flash," yelled one of the three, and Phil decided that he could oblige. Teasingly turning his bum to us all, watching us over a shoulder, he pushed out his arse and gave us a flash – just one corner – to cheers and applause.

I was watching dumbfounded, not only entranced by the sight, but wondering how he knew how: how he knew how to be so seductive, how to enslave me with one glimpse of flesh.

Phil stood there glowing with pride at the heart of the cheering and the applause. "Again!" A bigger flash, and more cheers.

"More! More!"

"No. Somebody else."

"Show us the front!"

This he did: smiling coyly, he lowered his pants, revealing a boy erection – hairless flesh of smooth white crotch, boy size cock standing to attention, small balls hanging in the crumpled sack below. And this was not a flash. He held it there. This was a show.

"Turn round!"

This he did. Playing the seductress again. Once. And then once more. Then he pulled them back up, but remained on his feet: show girl, or prostitute, or ring master, of this circus of captivated boys. "Someone else show us now," he said.

First was one of the three, then another. Nobody stood. We crowded around them, they sat on their bums, they pulled away covers. Four or five torches picked out the details of one boy erection, then another: tall stiff small but sexy dicks against white flesh of stomach.

Phil still standing, master of the game; his boys back in their places.

Me now: "Someone give us a bumming demonstration."

Multiple calls of approval: "Yeah!"

"Who'll do it?" I would have loved to, but I just did not dare – for the shame of it. Perhaps someone else could be persuaded. I was happy to be the voyeur – at least at first. So who will do it?

Enquiring eyes shot around the tent, looking for the likely showmen. This went on for a while, these enquiring, pleading, persuading looks, an eyebrow raised, a dirty nod and a jeer and a grin. Phil, the showman, was giving them time; then perfectly timed: "I will," he said.

It now needed only one more volunteer. The first suggestion had been mine. They were calling my name now. They wanted for it to be me. "No!"

"Well show us your dick then. Come on!" And they crowded around.

Peter on my left was faking sleep. "Come on Peter, you're missing all the fun," – but he said no. Andrew on my right had been sitting out as well, silent, staying in his place; but the prospect of my cock now brought him fully into the game. Stephen was behaving like a half detached elder statesman, looking on, peering over other's shoulders silently to see.

And so my cock had a formal audience of six, as I climbed

out of my sleeping bag, sat on my arse, and pulled down my trousers properly for the viewing. Cock pointed away from me, still smooth, still boy size, a textbook model of foreskin, glans and shaft – for a boy. Someone reached in and lifted it, assuming a cock should point to the sky, but found it fully stiff and staying right where it was. "Any hairs?" asked one, and more than one hand stroked where they might be found, examining and then proclaiming the presence of several colourless sprouting bristles, quite distinct from the down around them.

"Andrew, let's see yours." And six boys with hard ones peered at another; and then, for near completeness, at the third of the three.

Peter slept. Stephen kept silence. Seven boys had seen six cocks as six boys had displayed them, each one erect and hard and fleshy and stiff and fully aroused and straight and hairless and uniformly – it must be said – prepubescent.

Attention returned to Phil, still standing, who gave us another strip tease and a twirl. One of the three met the challenge to copy with the fastest pull down and quick turn he could do (buttocks flat like two bags, but precious none the less). Thinking him a likely candidate now, the cat calls returned for a demonstration of bumming, but he protested: no demonstration was in store.

As encouragement and erotic entertainment, I told of my fantasy of Planet Zog where the species had only one sex: male organ in front, and receiver behind, and orgies conducted upstanding in lines – or even in complete circles. "Shall we all do it here?" No!

The evening was fading but one treat remained. Stephen finally spoke. "Come look at this."

We gathered around the top of his sleeping bag and torches lit up the inside.

There against his lower belly was a sight which left every one of us breathless. Its base emerged thick from somewhere out of sight between his legs, via a wide and spacious sack of crumpled flesh containing two huge accompanying balls. It continued long and thick and white and wide and deep across a large round nest of thick black curls of hair. It ran on and on towards us, both deep and broad and hard inside and sheathed in soft ripples of illuminated smoothness. Still in full proud girth it

carried on past his belly button, arching above it by its own rigidity, and it carried on fearlessly towards us, on and on. Somewhere near the softness of his lower chest, it swelled in a great ridge to its incredible utmost maximum girth, and then peered out huge through a foreskin ring to taper to a slotted point, one end of a phenomenal bright heavy thick stiff soft-coated cylindrical mass, running nearly a foot engorged from his deep crotch to its point.

There were gasps.

I had seen the promised land.

Six erect boys looked on, looked on at this man cock. The night was concluded.

Predictably unpredictable, the next day Stephen tried to provoke a reaction from his respectable older brother by telling tales, in public hearing: "Phil did a strip tease last night; showed us his dick and his arse."

"I thought Phil was a nice boy." Or used to.

Several weeks later, again in a public place, Stephen mentioned that night to me. "Did you like my willy at camp?" Could it have been a come on? Could it have led to more? Or was he just playing, saying anything at all, for a reaction? "All those hairs, they all come out when I'm sitting on the loo. Ping, ping, ping." I was frightened by his raising it: fearful at the potential for an awesomely pleasurable replay as much as at the potential for an awesome humiliation. Stephen was dangerous to know.

I had seen the promised land. But like Moses' spies, I was frightened of the giants. Needlessly, of course – like them. Another needlessly celibate winter ensued: forty weeks wandering in the wilderness.

* * *

Over the next nine months my penis grew from boy size to man size. It was so gradual that I was hardly aware of it happening, but the total change over the period was astonishing: from the 'before' state of all boyhood to date, to the 'after' state of manhood for ever thereafter; from a thing the size of a pen cap to a thing the size of a hammer handle.

If I was aware of what was going on, it was because of the

pain: the pain of having an erection with trousers on. My cock still pointed directly away from my body. It would make as though it was trying to bust out of my flies, directly forward, making itself frighteningly evident and hurting as well because it wanted to go further still. During the day I would just be cripplingly embarrassed. Alone in my room in the evenings, sitting at my desk or behind the bed, I would unzip and let it out, and hold it there, heavy like a third leg, throbbing with heat and swollen to the point of pain. I would handle it and watch it as it evidently demanded attention, but I had no idea what attention it craved, no idea what to do with it, no idea what I could do with it, as I sat there alone with it delicately balanced in my hands. I would just look at it and hold it as it lay there, radiating heat, so far extended out of my body that it really did seem to be a thing with a life of its own, an offspring which I just could not understand, a companion which I was failing. I felt helpless, and melancholic.

The one thing which I knew that both it and I would love to do was bumming. I dreamed of someone lying prone beneath me, myself prone on top: I lay a pillow in my crotch, partly to play the part of arse, partly to relieve the pain of lying prone with that erection.

One thing about an arse fixation is that there is no shortage of tempting sights around. The principle of western 1980 clothing cuts seemed very simple: cocks and cunts to be hidden, boys' bums to be on prominent display. At school, still carrying the faith of the divinity of arse – renewed now by the new dream liturgy 'to bum' – I was throughout the day surrounded by grey-clad gods. So much temptation, absolutely no hope. I felt useless: the failed parent of my new grown cock, unable to provide the one simple thing that it desired. Ever. Even though they were all around.

My reaction to these grey-clad gods was hardly changed in type from my reaction to the blue clad boy in 1T, so many years before: desire, lust, attraction; a longing to see, to worship, to possess. It was modified only in that bumming was now the final goal: to lie fully prone, full body to full body, with my penis lying along the bottom of the valley of his arse. But whilst the reaction was virtually unchanged in type, in sheer magnitude it was totally transformed – by the same proportion as my newly

grown cock. Every boy's arse was a target. And hints of torso under light summer shirts. And smooth 'porcelain' legs in shorts. And those occasional extra special sights would now disturb me not for minutes but for days. The memory of one makes me sigh even now: Colin, only two years above me, widely acknowledged as the coolest boy in school, and genuinely sublimely cool rather than just popular; detached, self-sufficient, blond, and gorgeous. I saw him every day at the bus stop, and he had the world's most perfectly rounded arse: high, slim, deep, firm, and wrapped in tight fitting grey felt trousers which left nothing to be imagined. Every day I stared and felt helplessly breathless. And then one day the gorgeous Patrick, also popular, blond, and cool, a national swimmer with the perfect swimmer's build, totally desirable as friend and lover, my own age, my own year, came and leaned over the desk next to mine, his arse virtually in my face, fully exposed except for a clinging film of light grey felt. I suspect from his grin that the bastard knew exactly what he was doing. But I certainly did not know what was happening to me. It felt like a panic attack. My internal organs were in flight. I did panic. I had no idea what was going on. It felt like a medical emergency. I thought I might die at any moment. I had no idea what was happening, but I certainly knew what was causing it, and I knew I wanted to possess that cause more than anything else in the world.

The French call orgasm The Little Death. But I did not know that then.

I was in awe at these new reactions as much as in awe at my newly re-sized cock.

And I lived every hour of every day with this wholly unattainable dream, ashamed of my past, ashamed of my present, overwhelmed with desire.

I was twelve. Winter passed. I turned thirteen.

Thirteen

Life was dominated through every day by lust and by shame. My body and my visual mind knew exactly what I sought – it was all around – but my power of speech refused even to contemplate forming the words in my mind, let alone imagine

ever speaking them aloud. I was walking around in a fog of lust which shame forced me to spend the whole of every day concealing. Fully adult emotions and fully adult shame had arrived together, and dominated the day.

It was Scout Job Week in the Easter holidays. I happened to be in town with Andrew. He, my cloud of lust, and I, happened to meet Phil there. The three of us talked Scouting things: that was our point of contact now. I said I might get the tent out for the first time that year: Andrew and I could sleep out again. Andrew turned his nose up at the idea. I then made a suggestion which had genuinely not occurred to me, until that moment, in the thirty months since the end of that previous summer – when Phil and I had tried and failed to bond our friendship in advance of an enforced parting of the ways: "Phil, why don't you come and camp out?"

"Yeah, OK."

And even before he had spoken I knew. I knew that I was going to get my wicked way with him that very night. Even before he had spoken I knew. His smile confirmed. I knew.

He turned up late evening. We pitched the tent, put in mats and sleeping bags and torches and the rest. We took a bedtime drink and turned in for the night. He was more well built than the year before, pretty close to adult height and build. It turned out that it was his birthday the next day: he was to turn fourteen at midnight. I did not dare any glances at his nakedness whilst changing for bed. His night clothes were an old wool jumper and shorts: my bit of rough. I wore clinging brushed cotton winter pyjamas, made like thermal underwear, all elastic cuffs and a dreadful sky blue. We hid in our sleeping bags to talk into the night.

There was chat at first about schools and friends and what we were both up to. And then about Scouting things. And then about last year's camp. I mentioned the night when "you did a strip tease."

"Yeah, that was fun wasn't it." Then a pause. And then this: "Have you started wanking yet?"

"What do you mean?"

"Wanking yourself until you come up."

"No. What do you do?"

"Well, you know the sign for wanker," – he demonstrated

with one hand. "You do that on your knob until you spunk up."

"What – just like that?" I made the same sign.

"Yeah. And the sign for knob-head," – he demonstrated – "it's just the same."

"Will you show me?"

"No! I'm not showing you!" He managed to look genuinely appalled at the suggestion, though it had not seemed at all unreasonable to me, given that he was presuming to tutor me in these mysteries.

"Why do you do it?"

"You have an orgasm when you spunk up. It's the same as when you have sex. You get this tingling all over and it's really excellent."

"How long have you been doing it?"

"Ages."

"And it's like having sex, yeah?"

"Yeah."

"So it's something to be proud of." My mind was working this one out.

"Yes."

"So when people say Wanker as an insult, it's them who's stupid."

"Yes, I suppose it is. I'd never thought of that."

Yet again. Censorious playground idiots in the wrong, boys in tents with their dicks out in the right. Wanking Is Good. Playing With Your Dick Is A Good Thing.

There was a pause. We had been sitting up, talking animatedly. I lay back. He followed suit. We were both staring up at the canvas, hands behind our heads.

Me: "Do you remember three years ago when we spent two nights out together?"

"Yes."

"Did you enjoy it?"

"Yes."

No point suggesting anything here and now. He had just given a confident and unexpected No for tonight.

"Have you ever done anything else like that?"

"Have you?"

"Might have done. You tell first."

"Last year at camp was fun. And then I've done a lot of snogging." And he listed some girls. "What about you?"

"I've done loads of stuff."

"Tell me about it."

"No."

"Go on. Confession is good for you."

"No."

"Go on. I've told you. I won't tell anyone."

"Oh all right." A pause, like a sigh. Then I began. "We used to have a Rood Club. There were loads of us. It went on for years on and off. We used to look at each others' dicks and bums and stuff."

"What else?"

"Promise you won't tell?"

"Yeah."

Enthusiastic now: "We used to sniff bottoms. It's incredible. You'd think it'd be horrid but it's not. It's like this really sweet ... it's just amazing."

"Oh!"

"There were lots of us. Andrew. Stephen. My Brother. We all did it."

"Huh!"

I was wallowing in confession, somewhere between pride and a gloriously redeemed sense of shame. There was pride because I had done sex things that other boys – who considered themselves better than me – had not done. They were virgins in this realm. I was not. Sheer pride. Just like I now knew it was good to be a wanker, and they didn't: proving themselves to be idiots and virgins with their own attempts at ridicule. I knew better. Arses smell good. Ha Ha Ha. And the shame that hung around me in a cloud was suddenly glowing itself. This was like playing in the mud, throwing it around, mud glorious mud, talking dirty, pride in filth, utter filth, pride in human extremes, pride in that supposedly shameful thing, sniffing arse; pride precisely because Phil would think it shameful, but I had been there, to this human extreme, and he had not.

Phil: "What else did you do?"

"No – you tell some more first."

"There isn't anything else to tell."

"Well I'm not telling any more."

"Go on."

"No."

"Go on. It's interesting. And it's good for you! Confession is good for the soul."

Half reluctant, half keen. "OK." Stop.

Phil: "How did it all start?"

And he got the whole story, into the night. Concluding with Andrew at eleven, in great detail. The whole story. Concluding with Andrew. At eleven. Just two years before. It took a long time to tell. I enjoyed telling. He encouraged me to include every detail, every event. He made it clear that he was more than enjoying the tale.

"And then last year there was Scout camp." And that was that.

Then Phil: "So you still haven't wanked then?"

"No. Will you show me?"

Trusting now, fellow conspirator: "OK."

He sat up. I sat up. He was looking down at his own crotch. He let his sleeping bag fall right down around him, and pushed it down so that he was sitting cross legged on top of it. He pulled out his dick through the wide front opening of his boxer shorts.

It was not the same now as the year before. It was a man cock. An entire thick fist full and then a knob on top as well. It pointed upwards without his stomach actually being in the way. It sprang from a thick root surrounded by curls of brown hair. Stubby, circumcised, it was twenty times the size of last year by volume. He took his fist off it to let me look. He paused like that a while. And then he wrapped his fist around it again and began to wank: tiny vertical movements on the shaft.

"You haven't got a foreskin."

"No, I had to have it cut off when I was little."

Pause. Watching. "What does it feel like?"

"Pretty good."

Silence. Watching.

I suppose, looking back, he had had plenty of dirty talk to build up a good head of steam. But that night I knew nothing. I just watched this sight.

It did not take an unpleasantly long time. Certainly I was still captivated by the sight when something began to happen. His movements deepened and he was gasping. Then they

quickened as well. Finally he was jerking more than rubbing, and his free hand flew behind him to stop him falling back as his cock starting kicking and spitting out high spurts of white spunk.

Silence.

I watched.

He recovered himself after a while, and sat up, and began mopping up with his sleeping bag.

"It's a sort of mucus," he said, "like snot really." Then: "It's all the little swimming jobbies I feel sorry for. Millions of them." Still mopping.

"Do you do it at home?"

"Yeah."

"Where?"

"In bed."

"What do you do with the stuff?"

"I usually wipe it on the blankets or something."

Pause.

Phil: "It's better if you use a lubricant. I usually use some of my dad's motorbike grease. It gets it going better. Feels better."

"And you just wipe it up afterwards?"

"On tissues or something."

I was spellbound by the whole thing. I sank back into my place, hands behind head, staring at canvas.

Me: "What would you do if we had Scout camp like last year again?"

"I don't know. What would you do?"

"I don't know."

Pause.

Phil: "What would you do if Alison was here?"

"I don't know. I'd tell her to get all her clothes off." Pause. "What would you do if the sisters were here."

"Snog them both. And then perhaps have a wank."

OK. This was a new game: a game of What If. I could find out all kinds of things. And it would cost me nothing: he was seeking entertainment and titillation, not humiliation. It was all hypothetical. I could reckon to have said it just to tease him, if I had to.

And so we played What If into the night. What would you do if your school burnt down? What would you do if the four minute warning went off? What would you do if you saw a flying

76

saucer?

I wanted sexual information: to find out what was going on, to rate my chances. I could not tell what game he was playing: his questions became more and more tedious, less and less interesting. I would ask what he would do if he met a naked woman in a forest: he would give a totally non-committal answer and then ask what I would do if an elephant came in to the tent. I would ask what he would do if he met a naked man in a deserted beach hut: he would give an even more non-committal answer and then ask what I would do if the tent started leaking in the rain. It was becoming increasingly hopeless. I felt that he was bored, and I was only carrying on because of the thrill that it gave me to be saying outrageous things to him, all of which he took without flinching, almost without any reaction at all. So eventually, very Stephen-like, entirely for the rise, purely to see whether he could be made to flinch, knowing that his answer would be "I would say Get Lost", or words to that effect ... imagining us snogging and rolling naked in the hay ... I said ...

Actually, at that very moment, he said he had to pee and started to get up. So it was as he moved towards the tent door that I said: "What would you say if I said Let's take all our clothes off and roll about on the floor."

And without flinching, and almost without pausing on his way out, he looked me in the eye and said, "I'd probably say Yes," and he disappeared to pee.

I was all a quandary. Now was the moment. The moment was now. I hadn't actually asked him. I had only said What If. He had not actually answered. He had only said I would. He had only said I would probably. I still had to ask him. It was only the last yard of the two thousand mile journey. It might still fail. But it was certainly in sight. I waited paralysed, terrified, for his return. As soon as he appeared at the tent entrance I asked him, as he moved back towards his sleeping bag: "OK: let's take all our clothes off and roll about on the floor."

"OK."

Arse imminent!

Practicalities. Principle agreed: but now what? He was actually back in his sleeping bag. I was in mine. He was awaiting further advice. I asked: "What do you want to do?"

He had already decided what he wanted to do. It was

something that he had never tried before. It was something that had kept me sexually stimulated for eight consecutive summers. It had been my favourite thing from four to eleven, and now he wanted a try. Knowing it sounded an odd thing to do, he nevertheless began at least half confidently, and certainly fully expectantly: "Well, you seem to have spent years on end smelling bottoms."

I was horrified. That was a disgusting shameful thing. Wasn't it? In a life completely dominated by lust and by shame, shame had won the day on this one. I actually interrupted him, real bossy style: "No, that's child's play." A withering rejection: he must have been hurt. And a pointless self-denial: I was a fool! But for something adult, something respectable, something serious, my goal, without a hesitation I made my alternative proposal, the one thing I desired so much: "Have you ever tried bumming?"

"No, I haven't."

"Do you want to try it?"

"Yeah, OK."

In fact, the only part of him to touch me was the conical top of his thick circumcised cock. And it was touching me somewhere that nobody else and nothing else had ever touched me. Ever. At all. And it was not just touching or caressing there, where nobody, nothing had touched me before. It was pressing there. Pressing hard. The conical top of his thick circumcised cock was in the conical hollow at the very centre of my arse, the entrance portal of the arse hole itself, that sacred place which my many partners had reverently worshipped whilst drawing its addictive scent but which none had ever touched – with nose or hand or anything at all. And theirs, also, I had worshipped and revered, but never touched. The soft folds of that most beautiful point were virgin folds for myself and for all my partners, too holy to be anything but adored. And Phil was touching there. He was touching the whole of there, the whole of it at once. He was touching, pressing, the whole of there with the conical tip of his cock, a perfect fit to the conical hollow of the very central heart of my arse.

I had never imagined this. I had imagined instead the whole cock swallowed by the whole valley floor. But I realised what he was trying to do. He was aiming to have the whole of his

cock absorbed through that entrance way – through that entrance way so that the whole of his cock would be through it and into the inside of me, his cock inside me, his cock, inside, me. And nothing had ever even touched me there before. Absolutely nothing had ever gone through. I had never even imagined it, let alone considered whether it was possible or not. Now I could certainly imagine what he was imagining, and with some urgency, I was considering whether it was indeed possible. One of us was fundamentally wrong about bumming. Was it me or was it him? I thought it best to find out by letting him try it his way – which if it worked ... wow, what a concept. Into. Into. Into the holy of holies. Into the arse. Into the Sacred Heart. Through that holy entrance way. Through it. Into the unknown but deeply desired beyond. Into. Cock. Into. Me. My. Arse. Hole. Him. At the centre. Pressing. Trying. Now.

After a while, pressure released, Phil: "This isn't going to work."

He knelt up and pulled on my hips. "Perhaps if you come up, like, on all fours."

Logical. My arse flesh would be tighter, my arse hole pulled apart. I went up on all fours, sky blue shirt still in place, sky blue trousers still round my thighs. He knelt behind me. Another touch, another push. The heights were all wrong. Cock height had to match arse hole height. Plus he wanted to lie over me, as though I was the corner of the bed and someone wanted his arse behind him. With shuffling and moving and pushing and pulling, angles were altered at back and at hips and at knees until things were very roughly lined up and the pointed tip of his cock was once again pressing hard on the softest virgin folds of my heart of arse, not laid gently in the valley, but with an unprecedented, unimagined, perpendicular push for entry right into me through the sacred mark itself.

Was it possible, was it possible, was it possible? I wanted it to be so. It began to move in. A fourteen year old cock was moving in to my thirteen year old arse. Conical tip first: my arse hole widened to take it. The rim of his glans, the widest point, was against the outermost part of my arse hole. The tip had gone through. Holy of holies. Inside me now. I felt that widest point moving through the untouched sacred channel of my arse hole. My arse hole closed tight round his shaft behind it

and held him in there by a firm grip: I had him by the cock, clasped inside my arse, where nothing and nobody had ever been before. He was lying on top of me now. His penis was inside me. Inside my arse. Inside my body. Inside me. He was holding my cock.

He was holding my cock. At the time I had no idea why, but he seemed to like it. I understand now! On reflection I realise now that he had still not seen it since Scout camp the year before. Since then it had become a very different thing. I do remember that his fist, wrapped around it, covered not even a third of its length. His cock, meanwhile, was pushing deeper in my arse, my arse was swallowing his cock: that made sense even then. Supreme sense.

He pushed and pulled a bit, juddered a bit, pushed and pulled some more, sighed or panted deeply once or twice, the pressure seemed to peak, and then he lay there quite still. The pressure eased. He had one more push and more went in – to more swallowing movement at my arse hole. It was fantastic. Not just a dream, but a dream of a dream, because I had never even imagined.

That one last push, his balls against my lower arse and balls, and he finally let go of my cock, leaned up, and withdrew, in one continuous movement lying down prone by my side, then on to all fours, and crawling forwards, shorts round thighs, arse exposed, to go where I had been: "OK, you go." The invitation at last. The dream of years.

He was fully grown, for goodness sake. We both were: adult stature. His arse was broad and white, the valley no more than a dip in its landscape, and there was the centre, a clear circular mark in the breadth of the plain. Below were the tops of legs, with dark boxer shorts asymmetrically lodged around thighs, and above, an old wool jumper: nothing exposed but the arse – and cock on the other side, I presumed, to little interest.

I did not pause to examine his arse (more's the shame). I knelt up and manhandled my monstrous cock to point its tip at that circle, and pushed. For the first time in my life I was touching that sacred place. There was sight, there was scent; now there was touch, and thorough touch, a conical tip touching every part of the surface of those folds.

It was placed there and pushed but nothing moved inwards.

I shuffled awkwardly and tried a few different angles. The heights were all wrong, the angles were all wrong, nothing was going to move, to give. I wedged it in place and lay myself on top of him, one arm and then the other wrapping around him, round chunky-knit wool. Sky blue shirt to old wool jumper. Sky blue waistband to cotton boxers, tying together and keeping apart our four parallel thighs. Still fully dressed, only cocks and arses exposed between night wear pushed aside. Cock up arse. It was moving. A half inch. It was moving. Now. An inch. Glans moving in. An inch and a half. Glans swallowed. Two. Two and a half. Swallowing shaft. Three. Stop. A tiny fraction of the whole, but how much could he take? Dry and sore, no more right now. I lay there, cock in arse, legs tied up in clothing, arms round wool jumper. I lay there.

I lay there.

I lay there, my cock right inside Phil's holiest place. I had never imagined. Anything. Like. This.

He moved a little. I moved a little, my cock in his arse. My mind went blank. I lost track of time. Time passed. I came to with a shudder, as though I had dozed off and come to, though I was most definitely wide awake up till then. Then I suddenly felt completely exhausted and totally unable to balance at all, I did not know why. But it did clearly if mysteriously feel as though the liturgy was concluded, had reached some goal, some end, some life achievement. I now withdrew my cock from his arse and fell stumblingly off him and on to my side. When I looked up he was lying on his side, propped up on one elbow, with a certain look: the whole picture I knew said 'seductress': take me I'm yours. This I knew because on a paper round one Sunday the *Sunday Times* flagged an article on seduction, and the picture of the woman looked just like this. He wanted me. But there was no me left to have. I had to let him down.

I pulled up my trousers from my thighs and over my worn erection. I crept in to my sleeping bag and there I slept. Not a word was exchanged.

Next morning I hated him. This was not because of what we had done. By the morning I was ready to affirm and celebrate all that we had done. I was ready for a little encore, or at least a more than knowing smile, as a seal of approval on the night, and as a promise for the future, for more of this. But Phil was not a

morning person. Nine tenths asleep, grunting, grumpy, incognisant, he disgusted me. Perhaps if he had been different...

I went to the bathroom alone. It spurted a bit as I took a shit. It was very cheesy behind my foreskin, and not just white but a browny white paste. I showered.

At the non-verbal level, that fuck became my life. At the verbal level, shame overtook lust yet again – though both were huge. It was a close run thing. In the tent that following night, Phil was still sated and took no lead, proffered no encouragement, except to note no objection to the night before. My lust wanted fuck, but shame had overtaken. Strangely though, shame had decreased in the Rood play department, perhaps because of Phil's positive reactions and even his positive request the night before. But the words in my head were all over the place, speaking shame and guilt one minute and lust the next. Phil must have been bewildered – or more likely just bemused. I know now that he lived then on the simplest of pleasure principles. I must have sounded like a head case.

That night I did hold his cock. And he held mine. Awkwardly, reaching into each other's sleeping sacks both at once. And that was that. The end of the holiday week. That was that. The end.

I dreamed, oh how I dreamed. "Thou shalt not commit adultery" – the only prohibition on sex in the top ten: so I reasoned that as long as we only fuck each other that's OK. We could pledge our troth for the teenage years. We could camp every weekend. I could pitch the tent on a Friday evening and we could fuck for two whole nights before the school week started again. This year, next year, the year after that, for the whole of our teens at least, and then anything. Oh how I dreamed of those fucks but I just did not dare. Phil was out of sight, out of contact, but that fuck was never out of mind.

* * *

There remains just one more story to tell. The astute will have noted that Peter's arrival had spoiled my unbroken record – of having had every contemporary boy's arse in the street. Peter's arse I had not yet had, and he had been there now three years. With both of us now thirteen – all three of us counting

Andrew in as well – the score chart was now about to be made complete once again. And that most dramatically.

Late summer, and Andrew and I somehow decided a tent night would be an idea. And Peter was to join us, even though we had hardly kept in touch. We never met Peter now outside of Scouting. We all went to different schools. But there he was, right next door, so for the first time in a year, we knocked, and we invited him to play. He said yes.

My motive for this was singular lust. Andrew's – who knows.

In the tent that evening it was Peter who started strip poker. Read that again, because it is true. Let's play cards, let's play poker, let's play for strips, said Peter. Said Peter. Said Peter. It was him. Strip poker, he insisted. My third arse messiah. My new, my latest saviour.

Strip poker – is foreplay for beginners.

When is strip poker supposed to end? When one person only is naked? That would be so unfair! It would lack even the simple conspiratorial justice of "You show me yours and I'll show you mine." And it abandons this brilliant game right at its most exciting point. No, it is only fair – and it correctly reflects the momentum of the game and the level of fun – to play on at that point, until everyone is exposed. It's only fair, between naked or virtually naked compassionate friends.

And so, late in the night, as Peter was the first to lose his very final cover, exposing his confident erection at the centre of his naked frame, the game had more momentum than at any time so far. The three of us being good friends, all naked or not far from it, full of the excitement of the moment, wanting to be fair, it was entirely inevitable that we would play on. Three boys wore between them only two pairs of underpants and one pair of jeans. So close already, surely we would all be completely naked soon, surely we would all have our erections exposed as Peter now had. It's only fair. And already so close. We dealt again, one cock naked, one in just a cotton slip, one in jeans. The rest was already bare flesh. It was only right, three boys, three garments, we three.

Peter's cock, standing there, naked and erect as we played another hand, was boy cock still. I was so disappointed. I wanted more. And I already knew that Andrew's was still a boy. So this

night was not to be the night of nights: just another marker on the way. But this was still my first sight of naked sexual Peter – freely offered by Peter himself – and it was truly very pleasant. Bare arms. Bare feet. Bare legs. Smooth chest, smooth stomach, smooth hips, smooth crotch. Cock. Plenty of foreskin. Solidly upright. Softly sheathed. Desirable. Definitely the best. The best boy cock. Definitely the best one.

I was very aware of the monster that I was still hiding. It was only a matter of time. But what now if naked Peter lost again? A forfeit of some kind was required, just in case. His cock had been examined, and so it was agreed: the forfeit was an inspection of his arse.

With three of us playing, each round took for ever. The anticipation was extreme. I lost next and Peter had his first sight of something very different. But after the inspection there was still no doubt about what was to happen next: another hand would follow. The momentum was undiminished. And with the next hand – Peter and me completely naked, Andrew still in jeans – Peter lost and willingly knelt on all fours for the inspection.

Andrew in jeans was even keener than naked me to examine naked Peter's arse. Examine we did, most thoroughly: touching, spreading, passing comment; four eyes, four hands, on one proffered arse. My first sight of Peter, bumping heads with Andrew, pleasant odours around; firm curves, pink heart.

Score chart once again complete. Full house. Every contemporary boy's arse in the street. Every single one had been offered to me as part of some deliberate and pleasure seeking game, and every single contemporary boy had taken mine in return, deliberately, playfully, seeking pleasure. Every single one. Every single boy. Not a single one had missed out. Not a single one had I missed. I had had every single contemporary boy's arse in the street in play. Score chart completed again at thirteen. With the arse of a third messiah.

A half hour later, Andrew naked at last, and Peter already inspected again, they were both peering in to me – "lots of hairs" – and with the momentum to play undiminished at all, further forfeits were now required.

We decided a menu of forfeits was good: the loser would have to choose.

"Give a wanking demonstration." – Peter's suggestion, first item on the new list.

"Pretend to bum someone. They get to choose who." – That was mine.

"How about running naked round the outside of the house." – Andrew's idea.

"Or a pile up." – Me again.

"What's a pile up?" – Peter.

"One person lies on the floor, face down; the next one lies on top of him; the last one lies on top." – My simple explanation. Nakedness assumed. We were all sitting round playing poker with three erections and not a stitch on. "The loser decides what order."

"OK."

More cards were dealt. It all took time. Nothing could be hurried. Each one of us, stark naked, had time to plan what we would choose if the lot fell to us.

As the night went on, only two of the forfeits were taken up. Twice, Andrew ran naked round the house. Every other game ended in pile up.

With three of us, there were six permutations, and every one was tried. The dream place was in the middle. Peter and I soon had no shame in requesting it. We were getting into sex and into each other. So the dream place, the middle: first an arse below, between the cheeks of which to place one's cock, tip perhaps touching the actual hole; and then, that still in place, the cock of another above, slipping gently between cheeks, perhaps with its tip in turn deliciously found right on one's sensitive entrance way. Cock and arse both stimulated, both an arse and a cock possessed. All six permutations, several times.

And whilst Andrew was out running, a shared conspirators' thought from Peter: "We could have a wanking competition. Everyone has to stand up doing this till they come. I've come before. You'd win but I'd come second. Andrew'd be here till next year."

Getting very late, momentum finally flagging, it was time for more items to freshen the menu. Ideas all mine: "OK, you can choose from these. Pretend bumming's already on. Or you can choose real bumming, and choose who with, or dick sucking, and who with, and which way round, or a pile up but with real

bumming instead of pretend."

Peter: "But hang on, if the loser gets to choose which way round, he could make someone else suck his dick, and that's like getting a prize, not a forfeit, like it was something they wanted."

"No, its horrid whatever way round, surely. They just get to say what."

"OK. Yeah." A pause, and then: "I'm not gay or anything. I just want to see what it's like."

In a new and concentrated silence, the cards were dealt again. Andrew lost and ran. Then I 'lost' a hand and it was time for something new. I chose to suck: to suck Peter. He assented, of course; leaned back, elbows behind him, hard boy cock high in the air. I leaned over and closed my lips around its very base, so that the whole of it was in my mouth, and from there, with my lips, I gently pulled soft foreskin upwards over the tip, and then closed my tongue on to it inside my mouth, feeling its whole form against the roof of my mouth, sucking gently, then pulling away. Another life achievement, I guess. Peter said "Wow."

It fell to me again. I requested the reciprocal. It was clearly within the rules, no matter how outrageous. I asked that Peter suck my cock. He did not object. I leaned right back on my elbows, cock tall from my crotch and vertical up in the air. He did not touch with his hands. He lowered his mouth over the top, only just able to open it wide enough. The whole glans disappeared into the cave of his mouth, but nothing touched: then he closed his lips into an 'O', making one full ring of contact round the shaft: nothing more. No softness of tongue or inner cheeks round the glans. Just that sealing ring, and then off. It was new. It would do.

Peter next took the middle of a pile up, Andrew below, myself above, and then it fell to me again, and I announced real bumming. But with whom? I knew who I wanted: I lusted for him, but I had to pretend not to care. After all, none of us was gay or anything. So I said not him but Andrew. Andrew lay prone on the floor, surprisingly willing tonight to give it a try, perhaps even charmed to be chosen. I knelt over him and tried and failed to push it in, though he wriggled to try to help.

Peter, watching our efforts: "You could try it like this."

I looked around and there was another surprising sight. Peter was lying on his back and with his arms he was holding his

knees up by his shoulders, arse hole exposed in a way I had never imagined. Rather than begin negotiations with Andrew about going up on all fours, I simply turned round and pushed the tip of my cock hard on to the inviting hole of inviting Peter's arse. Still it would not go.

Andrew, behind me: "This is fun." I turned around. Another surprise. Andrew was copying Peter, doing the same, rocking on his rounded back. I shuffled over and pressed on to him, also now inviting, peering down: cock on arse hole, but nothing would move.

"It won't go in," – my complaint.

"Never mind." Peter. "We'll let you off this time. Pick something else next time."

Glumly for me, cards again. It took so long but the game dictated it was Peter's turn to choose.

Peter had already made his choice of forfeit, and solemnly now he announced it: "OK, real bumming, with..." and he said my name.

I wanted this. I so wanted this. It was a total surprise. I had not even dreamed to expect it. But now here comes naked Peter. And he wants me.

I played by the rules as thus far established. I lay fully prone on the floor. Peter mounted me, making like pile up games, only this time he was working his cock with one hand, working it into the very hole at the heart of my arse. There was prodding and pushing and little achieved, but he was not going to give up. He persevered. He pulled foreskin forward and positioned again, his dick on the opening at the heart of the heart of my arse. And he pushed. It went in. And some more. And some more. A tiny prepubescent thing, a boy thing, tickling around, his balls touching down. He held it there as deep as it would go. I could feel its entire length, right through my arse hole and into me. I think he came. At least he moved around, and then shuddered, and gasped.

And then slowly he withdrew. Naked Peter had fucked naked me as naked Andrew looked on. And Peter was satisfied. Fantastic.

"OK, let's call it a day. Let's get some sleep." That was Peter.

Peter was gone before Andrew and I woke up. It reverted

at once to how it had been: we only saw him at Scouts; and then not at all, when I left the next year.

But the score card was complete once again. Every contemporary boy's arse in the street. Every single one. At thirteen.

Boris Davidovich

My Best Friend

from *Serbian Diaries* (Gay Men's Press, 1996)

I dreamt of Vlada last night. In my dream, he phoned to tell me to come on over to his place, which was not the house where he used to live, but another one with marble staircases and iron banisters. He waited for me in front of the front door, with a smile on his face. He was young and beautiful in the dream, wearing his famous hairstyle which made him look like a bristling cat, just like a long time ago, when we went to school together, not as fat as he is nowadays. We greeted each other, talked for a while, and then he started showing me his new apartment. He took me to his bedroom which contained a large bed. He took his clothes off, sat on the bed, spread his legs and told me to suck his cock. When I began to do it, the dream was over – it's always like that in dreams, they finish at the very moment when the most beautiful things are about to happen.

I met Vlada when we were in the sixth grade of primary school. That's when I moved with my parents to Cvijiceva Street from another part of town. I also had to go to another school. Vlada and I made friends quite soon, and we shortly became what people call best friends, not only because we attended the same classes and lived pretty near to each other, but also because we had many common interests, plans, and shared the same teenage dreams. My first memories of him reach all the way back to the time when he had short, bristly blond hair and freckles on his face. He used to wear yellowy-brown velvet shorts without a fly, T-shirts and sandals (that's how I remember him most of the time). I liked him more than any other in my class. He was one of the cleverest and most restless children in the class. I was attracted to him physically as early as that but I was

not particularly aware of it. He was taller, stronger, cleverer and more handsome than me. He got A's, I got B's. Everybody liked him and adored him in a way, schoolkids as well as teachers, whereas I was an average lad who lived in his shadow. His father died when he was just a baby. He lived with his mother, a French teacher, and his sister, on Stanoja Glavasa Street, but his windows faced Cvijiceva Street.

I cannot remember the exact moment when we met or how we became close friends, but I can still recall some of the episodes of our life together. We both hated our country, the communist system, the mentality here, school, etc., and we both planned to flee to America one day and get rich there. We wanted to become famous Formula One racing drivers. He infected me with his love of cars. We used to buy all the Yugoslav car magazines and, when we could, the rare foreign ones too. We used to read them for hours with awe, like we were leafing through the Holy Book, and fantasised about sports cars we were unable to see around us. Later we started frequenting car races, first the ones held around Kalemegdan, then those held in Usce. We dreamt of visiting Monza or Le Mans one day.

As we wanted to go joyriding so badly we decided to steal a small Fiat 600. We went out armed with screwdrivers, pliers and wires, although we really had no idea of how to use these tools. We'd heard how you could steal a car, but neither of us had any first-hand experience. We picked a car, but whenever a passer-by came along, we'd run away. The idea of stealing a car on New Year's Eve was very silly because the streets were more crowded than usual. Of course our plan failed and we didn't manage to steal any car.

Once, we decided to flee to Italy. We persuaded our parents to let us go to the seaside by ourselves. We said that we were going to Istria and would take a couple of day trips to Trieste. This was our 'official version' but in fact we intended to emigrate and stay in Italy. We wanted to buy a cheap car there – we knew what the prices were from an Italian car magazine – and to roam the Italian autostradas. The fact that we were minors and had no driving licence didn't bother us much. We didn't realise any of our grand plans. We hung around Trieste for a couple of days, bought some clothes – T-shirts, jeans – mostly in the Ponte Rosso open-air market and the shops nearby, and having spent all our

money returned home to Yugoslavia.

We were inseparable in Belgrade, we saw each other every day. Our class teacher even called our parents to tell them that we spent too much time together, neglecting the rest of the class, and to advise them to forbid us to see each other so often. Despite this we remained inseparable, going out together to the cinema, and on day trips to Topcider, Avala, etc. I liked going to the airport most of all because aeroplanes were the second-best things in our hearts. To us they seemed miracles of high technology connecting us to the unreachable, faraway world we constantly dreamt about. We would watch the planes take off for Paris, London or New York, dreaming of going there ourselves one day.

We often went to the airport to watch the planes, Usually we went along the motorway so as to admire the foreign limousines. Sometimes we hitch-hiked and quite often sameone would pick us up. We even got a lift from an English diplomat who was driving a big green Vauxhall. We sat back on the soft leather seats and enjoyed ourselves. We especially liked a dim green light which lit up the dashboard.

The new airport in Surcin seemed to us like a foreign enclave – a window through which you could view the whole world because of all the foreign planes, limousines and foreigners arriving and departing. We used to walk around the airport building observing planes from the terrace. During the summer we often sat on the haystacks placed near the fence along the runways. There we were able to observe planes taking off and landing at close quarters, recognising different types of planes and the liveries of different airline companies. Most of the time we wore only our slips or were stark naked. This added an erotic touch to our adventures though I was unaware of the full implications at the time. We also used to go to Ada island in the summer. We would find hidden places and strip off. To start with we were each a bit ashamed to take our clothes off in the other's presence. But as I got more and more interested in seeing him naked I started posing naked before him whenever I got the opportunity so as to set an example and give him the opportunity to do the same. That worked. From then on we saw each other naked quite often.

I have the most pleasant memories of our first physical

contacts and sexual experiences. To start with, we teased each other by tugging at each other's zippers – attempting to feel what was inside with our fingers. We even tore each other's trousers once by doing that. The naive story we made up for our parents was that we'd been attacked by older boys. We also used to wrestle to see who was strongest – though we both knew he was the stronger and he always won. First we would wrestle with our clothes on and later when alone at home we used to strip and wear just our underpants. While wriggling around the floor our naked bodies would touch and our arms and legs would intertwine. I wanted to stay in that position, snuggling up to him, for as long as possible. He noticed this once so he asked me if I wanted to wrestle just to be able to touch him. I cannot remember my answer though I probably denied it. He never asked that question again although our wrestling continued.

We started taking baths together whenever we were alone. We used to light the fire in the old steam boiler with old newspapers – there were no electric heaters at the time – fill the tub with hot water and get in together. I remember the time I took a snorkel and put my head into the water while he sat facing me. I pretended I was a sea-bed explorer. I examined his body closely under the water, paying close attention to his cock. I played with it imagining it to be a fish. Finally, at a more mature stage in our sexual relationship we took up masturbating. Most of the time we would masturbate each other or just help each other by rubbing each other's balls or the perineum. We both liked that very much. I tended to initiate our mutal masturbation more often than not. Once we were laying on the bed and simulated intercourse between a man and a woman just for fun. He knelt over me and placed his cock right in front of my mouth. At the time however I was ignorant of sexual techniques and not at all familiar with oral sex, so nothing happened. That stage of our teenage sexuality was the most beautiful sexual period in my life. Never again have I felt such a joy and excitement with sex.

I remember us shoplifting together. On one such occasion we stole a bottle of Racke whisky from a supermarket on Cika Ljubina Street. While he was attracting the shop assistant's attention I took the bottle and hid it in my jacket. I managed to leave the supermarket without being noticed. When he joined

me outside we were overwhelmed with joy – we had triumphed, we had won. To us our shoplifting was not immoral or dishonourable but an act of courage and revenge on the society we both hated. My other motive was to gain his respect for my bravery. Once we wanted this small plastic racing-car model displayed in a kiosk. We made elaborate plans on how to steal it, we loitered near the kiosk thinking what to do. Then I decided to act all by myself. I asked the assistant to let me see the toy. As soon as I took hold of it I ran as quickly as I could. The assistant cried out, "Thief!" and I was even chased by someone for a while, but I managed to escape. As Vlada was the one who initiated and planned our thefts while I was a mere accessory or a perpetrator, this action, thoroughly conceived and performed by me, really made me more respectable in his eyes.

I almost depended on him, I adored him without being aware of it. I felt really bad every time we quarrelled, especially when he was mad at me for days and he did not want to see or phone me. I was also very jealous of all the boys and girls he spoke to. I wanted him to be all mine. During sports lessons when he removed his T-shirt I experienced real seizures of jealousy because others would see his body. I wanted to be the only person privileged enough to see him naked. I was desperate, not wanting to share anything of him with anyone else. I knew many girls in our class were in love with him. He didn't care for girls for a long time, regarding them as a sort of 'lower species'. However, his attitude gradually changed and he be came quite interested in them. I grew desperate and regarded his behaviour as a betrayal. Now, he started using his stripping off during physical education as a means of seducing them. Those in love with him started to write him poems and love letters, sending secret messages and so on. Nevertheless he was still inseparable from me and he still despised the girls in our class. I managed to keep him by my side until the third grade of secondary school. Then he fell in love with a girl called Maja, who went to another school and was even older than him. He was proud of being with her whereas to me she seemed like a cheap whore. I found her repulsive the first time I met her – a coquette and nympho-maniac. It was the beginning of the end of our close friendship.

In Freudian terms he had left the so-called homosexual stage of development behind him, while I stayed in it for my whole

life. Gradually we got more alienated from each other and stopped seeing each other so often. We enrolled at different universities and I went abroad with my parents, spending four years out of the country. He dated Maja for almost six years. He was completely nuts about her at first as she really charmed him. She had full control of him, wrapping him around her little finger, and he followed her around like a little dog.

Later they switched roles, he gradually became colder to her so she tried desperately to keep him by her side. She cried, begged, tried to slash her wrists, but he eventually left her. He studied film and joined a theatrical company. He became a real Don Juan, but took up drinking and became quite fat. He wears a beard now so there is no trace any more of his boyish good looks and slimness. With his beard he reminds me of Hemingway. We corresponded for a while when I was in Switzerland, and we saw each other on my short trips back to Belgrade. However we were completely alienated from each other and so gradually we lost contact. I heard he'd married a woman from Dubrovnik and had settled there. They had two sons. I never knew if he was sober for long enough to ever graduate from university and then, during that period, the last time I saw him he was fat, bearded and his face was swollen with alcohol.

Richie McMullen

Joker's Wild

from *Enchanted Youth* (Gay Men's Press, 1997)

I sucked in the glorious evening anonymity of rush hour in the bustling concourse of Euston station and let out a whistle of absolute schoolboy delight. I'd never seen so many people, not all in one place before. If this was London, I already loved it, for, not one person paid me the slightest notice and that's just the way I wanted it to be. I needed merely to melt into the place and become part of it. Why had Joseph feared that London would chew me up and spit me out? No way! He obviously didn't know just how streetwise I was. I mean, I'd arrived in London with more than I'd set out with, and I had his address, and, most valuable of all, I had met Alexander. London! A piece of cake!

I bought a packet of cigarettes, a box of matches, a pen and a pocket-sized notebook from a kiosk. In the back of the notebook I wrote Alexander's name and telephone number, not because I might forget them, there was not a chance of that. I just wanted to see his name in writing. Below that, I copied Joseph's name and address, because there was every chance I'd forget them. Why are some things easier to remember than others? Turning to the front page of the notebook I wrote in my best handwriting:

Alexander

Alexander, I believe I
Love you;
Even though I am a
Xen in your world.

Any place you are, I
Need to be, however
Dichotomously.
Ever yours,
Richie.

That one page contained two very special secrets; my love
of a dark-haired boy and my love of the sounds and shapes of
words. Although I wasn't the most outward-going or gregarious
person in the world, I did have an inner facility to create pictures
in my mind. This facility was born out of necessity, as a way of
getting away from the harsh realities of my father and his drunken
violence; I would travel inwards to a world more beautiful. A
world of colour and enchanting words. A world where I could
use words in any way I wanted to. As I would find out later,
these words were considered, by others, to be poetry. Yet, I'd
always hated 'poetry' and usually when I spoke to other people
I was almost monosyllabic. Why should that be? I'm sorry, there
I go again with my 'why' questions. I can't help it. You know
what I mean! Perhaps you can work things out better for yourself,
than I could then.

I closed the notebook and placed it carefully in my inside
coat pocket, next to my heart. I was too thrilled to think straight
but I did know that I didn't want to get on another train so
soon, even if they did call it a 'tube' and even if it did only take
a few minutes to get to the West End. I needed to walk, to feel
the air, to get into wider space. So, having discovered the general
directions to Soho, from a prissy woman in a fur coat, I set off in
search of what it had to offer. I would telephone Alexander
tomorrow.

There was no mistaking Soho. All life was there, an
international blend of laughter, colour and strange behaviour. I
was instantly addicted to the place. Time and order had no
meaning here, it was heaven-sent adolescent anarchy. Flashing
lights and strip joints; restaurants and card sharks; provocative
girls and theatres; every language and every fantasy; wealth and
money; coffee bars and jukeboxes; and still more money! I was
in paradise!

Cold, hunger and tiredness took me into a coffee bar called

the 'Two I's' in Old Compton Street, where I drank frothy coffee for the first time and where I made my first mistake. That is, I paid for myself! Time would teach me not to do that very often. As I drank the strange and enjoyable mixture I reminded myself that months before I'd written, *'Watch for punters, learn the score, money first, then his pleasure, make the punter want you more'.* I let myself off the hook, however, telling myself that it was my first night, and besides money was all around, just waiting to be picked up. Convinced of this, I ordered a hamburger and another frothy coffee and sat back to listen to a song, which had been released just a couple of months before, on the jukebox. It was the new rock 'n' roll idol, Cliff Richard with The Drifters singing 'Move It'. Whilst listening to the record, I overheard the folks on the next table excitedly telling each other that Cliff Richard started by singing in this very coffee bar, as had Tommy Steele. I really was in paradise. Cliff Richard was the first British 'pop idol' to attract me, and I realised that it was more than likely that he would have sat as close to the jukebox as I now sat. Perhaps, in the same seat. Paradise, indeed. Why is it, do you suppose, that so many adults fail to understand a boy's adulation of his favourite pop idol?

Reluctantly, I left the 'Two I's' and followed my nose through streets which I would come to know well, down Old Compton Street, into Brewer Street; turn left into the fabulously narrow and packed Great Windmill Street, then, right onto Shaftesbury Avenue. There, before me was the object of my journey, Piccadilly Circus!

Having walked around it at least a dozen times, taking in its magic, I settled myself against the railings, under the arches of Barclays Bank, by the number one tube exit and lit a cigarette. Without realising, I'd landed, somehow instinctively, on the place known to all as 'The Meat Rack'.

It was a natural choice. The arches of the building above gave protection from the November cold and rain, whilst the warm air, rising from the underground railway, gave one a marked advantage over the folks on the other side of the road. Why 'The Meat Rack'? Because boys hung around the railings waiting for punters, like marketable produce in a butcher's shop. Body posture and eye contact being the 'for sale' signs.

There was no shortage of boys out tonight. I stood between

a cute-faced kid of about sixteen and a boy in a motorcycle jacket, who I guessed to be about eighteen. They seemed to know each other. Too many for business! I initially thought so but no sooner had I lit my cigarette than the punters took notice, my sign was up. Men moved purposely from boy to boy sounding out their sexual preferences and price. I turned down three offers because they were too kinky. One wanted me to spank him, another wanted me to dress as a girl and the third wanted to drink my piss. I wasn't shocked, I'd had such offers back home. It just wasn't my scene. The cute friendly-faced kid went off happily with the piss drinker, throwing me a wink as he went. Minutes later the boy in the motorcycle jacket went off with the guy who wanted to be spanked. I waited.

Suddenly, the Rack emptied of boys and punters alike. I was completely baffled. I'd made my second, and what could have been a very costly, mistake. That is, I stayed. The sight of the blue uniform enabled me to put two and two together quite rapidly, however, and I made tracks. When the blue-bottle was out of sight, the Rack resumed its normal activity once again. I knew I'd been lucky and thoughts of being dragged back to Liverpool made it unlikely for me not to spot a policeman ever again. I took up my place and waited, but I must have been sending out all the wrong signals for punters stepped cautiously around me. Experience would soon instruct me that a punter can smell a nervous and frightened kid a mile away. The agitated nervous signals the kid sends out are like signs to prison, easily avoided. Why risk a kid unsure of himself when the Rack is full of willing boys?

By the time I'd regained my composure the cute-faced kid was back on the Rack, smiling and chatting to the other boys. It was clear that he was was very popular and was taking an interest in me, so I smiled. He quickly saw the invitation and came directly up to me, as though he'd known me all my life.

"Watcha! You're new right? Not seen you around before. How's business! There's a nip in the air, ain't there? Do you know what Baden-Powell said when he started up the Boy Scouts! He said, and I've got to talk like Churchill to get this, he said, '...I have seen thousands of boys and young men, narrow-chested, hunched up, miserable specimens, smoking endless cigarettes...'"

I laughed at his marvellous performance. He went on, "He

should've come round here, right? Can you imagine it! We'd all have bleedin' funny hats on an' uniforms, an' short trousers, bleedin' punters would go crazy for it. You don't say much, do yer? What's yer handle? What do we call yer! Can't live without a bit of a laugh, right! Do you like Skiffle? I think Lonnie Donegan is fantastic. Come on, say something."

I was still laughing. I offered him a cigarette and we lit up.

"My name is Richie, what's yours?" I asked, eager to know this cute kid.

"Blimey, you are new ain't yer?" he scolded.

"What do you mean?"

"No names, no pack drill, know what I mean? They call me *Joker*."

"Sure, I'm Scouse."

"See yer round, Scouse, that punter over there, the one with the raincoat over his arm, he's taken a shine to you, say no more, don't do anything I wouldn't do, see yer later, okay!"

"Okay," I agreed.

The punter was a shy American businessman, lonely for the company of a boy. He was staying at the Regent Palace hotel just across the street and he smelt of money.

"I have yet to eat. Are you hungry?" he tested.

"Growing boys are always hungry, you should know that."

We ate a magnificent meal at the Chinese restaurant which overlooks the Meat Rack. He skilfully sidestepped any talk of himself other than to say he was a businessman, and brought the conversation around to me. He seemed keen to know all about my life. Why should that be? I lied about everything. I told him that my name was Mark Crosbie, that I knew London well, that I was staying with friends of the family near by, that I went to public school in southern Ireland and that I'd spent my allowance all too quickly. He asked if I would object to him helping me out with a small gift. I blushed, out of guilt that he was falling for all the bull, but which he took as embarrassment. He apologised for offending me and assured me that he meant no harm. I thanked him for his generous offer and told him that under the circumstances I'd accept, but only if he'd have coffee with me at his hotel. His face lit up and he placed the money for the bill on a side plate and pushed a further twenty pounds across the table towards me. I folded this with care and then slipped it

in between the pages of my notebook, inside my jacket pocket. We understood each other perfectly.

On the street, as we neared his hotel, he suggested that he go in first, to 'order coffee', and for me to follow in ten minutes. We could then enjoy it in the privacy of his room. I agreed, saying that I had to buy some cigarettes anyway. I lefl him on the corner and never saw him again. As I watched him going into the hotel I rejoined Joker.

"Watcha, Scouse, how'd it go? He was a Yank, wasn't he! You know what Henry Miller says about Yanks don't yer? He says, "...The American ideal is youth — handsome, empty youth..." But is he right, I mean, who's empty! The Youth or the Yank! Is the Yank's wallet lighter or not? And, is the handsome youth full? Which is it! You may speak."

"I don't know where you get it all from," I said, spellbound by his seductive charm.

"'Tis but a sign of a good education. So! Which is it!"

"I got a meal and twenty quid!"

"Not bad, not bad at all. But one must learn whether to collect the stuff or spend it. I've got a tenner, what do yer say we go to the pictures? Then, a bleedin' feast of hamburgers, an' then you can doss down at the flat afterwards. Speak, northern mortal, speak."

"Terrific," I enthused, eager to spend as much time with Joker as possible. "You've got your own flat?"

"No, I share with a bunch of others in Kangaroo Valley. Don't worry, it's sound."

"Kangaroo Valley?"

"Forget it, you'll soon know yer way around."

At the cinema I produced my notebook and took the money from it. Joker's keen eyes spotted my piece on Alexander, as my eyes too were held by it.

"Did you write that!"

"Yes, today." I said, slightly peeved that he was looking, but pleased at his interest.

"Can I read it!"

He sounded sincere and I'd warmed to him. I gambled and let him see it.

"That's sound. Real sound."

"Keep it to yourself, please, Joker!"

"Leave it out, what do yer take me for! I'm telling yer, it's sound, ain't I! Is he a scouse too?"

"No, he lives in London. I'll tell you all about him one day, okay."

"Sound. Yeh."

Joker let me pay for the tickets and I let him know that I was treating him, this time, after all.

"You're the one who spotted the punter."

The changed expression on Joker's face told me to put my brain in gear. It then dawned on me that Joker had set me up with the punter and could just as easily have had him himself.

"You're something else. You set me up, right?"

Joker was pleased that I'd seen his generosity at last, and shrugged his shoulders, as if to say, "So what?"

"Thank you, Joker."

"Don't get all serious on me, it was nothing, forget it, enjoy yourself, okay!"

"Okay, but I pay for everything, right," I insisted.

"Now, you're getting the picture." He laughed, letting me.

"You crafty son of a bitch."

"Consider it a lesson from a master, me old mate. You'll learn, yet. Put it down to experience!"

And that's just what I did. I liked Joker, who could fail to? His cute open face; his warm and friendly laugh; his knowledge of the street; his constant quotes — from God knows where; his caring; his roguishness; his ability to survive. I admired him greatly, and told him so, as we took our seats to watch a Hammer horror film.

"You're okay, yourself," was all he'd say, and he never spoke another word until the film was over. After hamburgers and bottles of Coke we took a taxi to Warwick Road in Earl's Court. In the cab, I asked Joker how it was that he was always so cheerful. He paused, looked at me and then quite seriously he said, "That poem, you know, the one you wrote about Alex something or other..."

"Alexander," I corrected.

"Yea, that's it. Anyway, you love him, right?"

"I think so. I'm not sure."

"Take my word for it, you do! At least, somewhere inside you, you do. Anyway, he's not here with you, is he? I mean,

something keeps you apart? Well, it's like that with me."

"I'm not sure I follow you."

"It's simple, look, I love happiness, but where the friggin' hell am I going to find it on these streets? Nowhere, that's where! So, I make my own, it's simple."

He pulled a small book from his pocket and showed it to me. It was a book of quotations.

"Keep this to yourself, right? See this, this is my passport out of here. I learn one of these a day and one day I'll go to college or something and kiss goodbye to all this."

"I follow you, but how do you make happiness?"

"The same way you make mistakes, by being yourself. Look, no one gives a toss about the likes of you and me. They think we're toe rags, right? So, they expect us to be like toe rags all of the time. Well, I mess up their biased expectations, don't I? I'm never like the way they expect and I'm dead chuffed about that. It's the same with you, ain't it? I mean, a rent boy who writes poetry, see what I mean?"

"Yes, I think I do. There's more to you than meets the eye. You're something else Joker, I'm real glad to know you," I said, sincerely, offering him my hand.

"Understandable, perfectly understandable," he teased, shaking my hand warmly and returning to his former self.

Joker confidently instructed the taxi driver to stop the cab on the corner, by a pub called 'The Lord Ranelagh', and waited for me to pay, which I dutifully did.

"You'll need a couple of things, to pave the way, kind of thing, with the others," he instructed, leading me like a pupil to the corner shop.

"What kind of things? Do all the shops stay open this late?"

"It's not that late, I guess they do, never thought about it. Keep it simple, coffee, tea, biscuits, milk, that kind of thing. Here, do you shave?"

I didn't, but blushed at the memory of trying to do so once, about six months previously. Having found nothing to shave on my face, I'd shaved off my pubic hair and luxuriated in the prepubescent feel of my body.

"No, I don't shave, not yet."

"Me neither, thank Christ. Just get some soap then. You can use my towel. Oh, an' get some sweets for Angel."

"Angel?"

"You'll see, he's okay, but watch him, he can be a right son of a bitch when he wants."

The shopping complete we headed for a house on Warwick Road, near to Earl's Court Square. Joker led the way down the basement steps, fished around under some plant pots and brought out a key, which he used to open the door.

"Here, stick that back will yer," he said, handing me the key. "It's always there, so you'll know yer way in from now on, okay!"

I put the key back but was tempted to turn on my heels for I felt anxious about what I was getting myself into. Why should this cute-faced kid take an interest in me? Perhaps I was being set up to be rolled! Joker kicked the door closed and, seeing my face, said, "Come on, relax, it's sound."

"Then why the hell am I shaking?"

Joker had no time to answer. Out of the kitchen came the prettiest boy I'd ever seen, dressed in a white bathrobe and looking exactly like a twelve-year-old choirboy, a piece of toast in his hands. Looking at me but speaking to Joker, he asked, "Who's he?"

"This, Angel, is the *Poet*. He's one of us an' he's staying."

I looked at Joker in blank amazement. The 'Poet'? Was this to be my new name? Surely, he wasn't going to speak about Alexander?

Angel's eyes were now on the carrier bag. "Sure, there's space. Hello Poet, been shopping?"

"Yes, just some essentials. I thought, well Joker thought, that perhaps, that you might like these," I said, nervously handing Angel the sweets.

Angel was aptly named. He was strikingly beautiful, angelic, with soft white skin. He held the packet of sweets to his chest, as a child would hold a precious toy. Joker's warning about this gentle child must have been a total lie. Why would he lie? Perhaps they were lovers. Perhaps, this was Joker's way of saying, "Hands off." Angel thanked me and silently followed Joker and I into the kitchen, where I unloaded the other bits of shopping onto the crowded work surface.

Whilst Joker made a pot of tea, Angel asked me how old I was.

I told him fifteen, which delighted him for some reason. He wanted to know precisely when I'd turned fifteen and danced with joy around the kitchen when I told him last month, October 28th. Joker explained as Angel went dancing through the flat. It transpired that the Joker was sixteen, that Angel was fifteen, and until my arrival had been the youngest in the flat. As things turned out Angel was two months older than me.

Carrying mugs of tea, I followed Joker through the flat, as he explained things to me and introduced me to the others.

The flat, it seemed, belonged to Actor's sugar-daddy. Actor was a kind of vague soul, lost in his own world of Hollywood and dreams of becoming famous. He was nineteen, good-looking and could do what he liked with the flat, and himself, just so long as he didn't have 'it' off with anyone else. He chose to surround himself with those he felt familiar with and superior to, rent boys. His stage career, seemingly, was held back only by his voice and he worked hard to try to get rid of his Birmingham accent, which amounted to him putting the word 'actually' at the beginning, sometimes in the middle and always at the end, of every sentence. His first words to me were,

"Actually, you may stay, it's one pound a week, actually, paid on Fridays, in cash, there's a spare bed in Joker's room, actually."

I was to share a room with Joker, Angel and seventeen-year-old Magpie. Magpie, apparently, was not expected back for 'quite some time' because he'd stolen anything and everything which hadn't been nailed down, though not from the flat; he was currently doing time.

The other room was shared by Biker and sometimes his girl, Flyer and Banker. I recognised Biker as the boy from the Meat Rack, the one with the leather coat, who went off with the guy who wanted spanking. He pulsed aggression and 'fuck' proved to be his favourite word.

"Fucking good to see a friendly fucking face around here," was his welcome to me.

He scared me but I, nonetheless, sensed that he wasn't such a bad person. He was eighteen, the same as Flyer, who was out trying to score a fix. Flyer, it seemed was into just about any drug he could lay his hands on, and would do anything he had to in order to get high, to fly. Banker, the oldest in the flat, at twenty,

kept himself to himself and struck me as being kind of weird. He saved every penny he could get, for what? That it seems was his secret.

Actor had his own room, into which no other person was ever invited whilst he was in the flat. When he went out, the room had two huge padlocks fitted, which were securely tightened; and, which, according to Joker, were the biggest talked about living problem in an otherwise sound arrangement. Biker, it seems, had more than once threatened to 'smash the fucking door down' to see what the big mystery was.

The rules of the flat were simple, there weren't any! Except for one, 'no punters'! Otherwise, it was an open house. Do as you like. Sleep as long as you wanted, when you wanted. If you could afford it, you were expected to buy food.

None of the flat sharers questioned my new-found name. To them I was the Poet. This embarrassed and amused me. Based on one piece of writing, I'd become a poet. The instant and unquestioning recognition was, however, a boost to my confidence. Perhaps Joker was right, perhaps one could create one's own world, simply by being oneself. The trick was to make constant and consistent choices to be whatever it was one wanted. Joker, more than anything, wanted to be happy. Whilst I wanted to run away from violent rejection. Was there a difference?

Back in the kitchen, and more relaxed that the unknown wasn't so terrible after all, I listened, along with hovering Angel, to Joker's latest impromptu performance of Churchill, with eager ears:

"You should write about rent boys, Poet. For, as Henry Miller once said, '...The poem is the dream made flesh, in a two-fold sense as a work of art, and as life which is a work of art...' And we are dreams made flesh. We are the dreams of tired and lonely men, mostly married, who seek to recapture, or discover for the first time, the beauty of being a boy. We do a great public service when we melt our lives into their dreams. The rent boy's life is a multicoloured work of art, a tapestry, but alas, there are many weavers and only one boy, one piece of fine sculptured cloth. The rent boy is a living poem and the poet must find the words hidden within him. You think I jest?"

"I jest think you're bonkers," laughed Angel.

I shared Angel's laughter, but secretly wished to learn more

from Joker. I applauded his performance and told him that he was a real artist, that he should go on the stage.

"I'm already on it!" He laughed, bowing to the applause. "Come on, let me show yer where you're kipping."

The 'beds' were four mattresses, one in each corner of the room, each with a couple of sheets and blankets simply arranged on top. As we prepared for bed, and no doubt infected by Joker's humour, Angel told me that he knew some poetry, and proceeded to recite:

'She stood on the bridge at moonlight,
Her lips were all aquiver.
She gave a cough,
Her leg fell off
And floated down the river.'

We groaned and hissed our way between the sheets of our separate beds and Joker put the light out. Ten minutes or so later, Joker whispered, "Poet, you okay!"

"Sound, Joker, thanks."

Sleep came easily after that, despite the sound of Radio Luxembourg coming from the next room. Bad dreams, however, came just as easily, and it wasn't long before my mind was full of violent confrontations. I was fighting with my drunken father and was shouting at him to leave my mother alone. He was cursing, throwing plates of food into the back of the fire, screaming at my mother that she couldn't cook as well as his mother. Just as he's about to hit her I pick up a knife and throw myself between them. The knife, about to enter his chest for the second time, is dripping blood. I sit bolt upright in my bed, wide awake, sweating profusely, heart racing, eyes full of tears, and me, terrified of my own violent potential. How many times must I have this dream? Why do I cry so? In the shadows, I heard Joker snoring and saw, coming towards my bed, Angel, as naked as the day he was born.

"You need some company," he whispered. Was he asking, or telling me? Whichever, he wasn't waiting for an answer, he climbed in beside me. My very soul was crying out to be healed of violent dreams; my body longed to be held. I opened my arms to his and kissed his voluptuous full lips as we fell inevitably back into the pillow. My tears fell on his face. His response was instant. Soft coiling limbs surrounded mine in gentle healing

movements. His hands explored and stroked my tear-stained face. He comforted me with his own need to be loved. His erect boyhood pressed against the hollow in my belly. He tugged at my underpants, and together we managed to get them down, without our lips parting. Kicking them loose, I became free to allow his smooth hairless boy flesh to move mutually over and against my own naked consent. Our erections danced a sliding, slipping dance. Unaided, we reacted as we should, with spontaneous electrified tactile combustion. There could be only one conclusion. With words, superfluously transcended, the senses came alive.

I touch, hear, smell, taste and see the boy in my arms. What will follow, must follow. There's no order or plan to it. It is what it is. Nothing can be better, surely! He licks my chest, my belly, my thighs and then the full length of my cock. He opens his mouth, and takes me in. Oh my God, I'm ready to explode, but then, perfectly scripted, he moves his attention to the cheeks of my bottom, his body asking mine to turn. He's licking, gently biting. Never have I felt a tongue do that. Moving, so that his body covers mine, I feel his erection slide between my legs. He first senses my delight and then, using nature's lubricant, he enters the mystery within me. I can not hold back, I have to let go. I must erupt. I am erupting. With the knowledge of rhythm, he pulses his shared harmonic melody into our one joint reconciled, inestimable, climax. We gasp for air, not wanting to move. We stay like that, unspeaking, content. With him still inside me, my own belly wonderfully covered, we pant, still in rhythm, for breath; he kisses my neck and we sleep, as one.

In the morning we are two again. Very close, still wrapped in each other's arms, but two. The oneness, a dream, a memory. I wake and look at Angel's face and I want to cry again. Can there be any more beautiful sight than a boy sleeping, so contentedly? I know, deep in my soul, that it can't last, it never does. It can't. As Joker so wisely reflected, our lives, the lives of rent boys, are but a tapestry, woven by many weavers, and we are in their hands. But, what was it he also said? Something, yes something about defying their expectations? My head wants none of it. I can't make head nor tail of it. I want only to be loved, and to love in return.

I hold my breath and begin to count. If I can count to a

hundred before taking a breath, if only I can hold my breath long enough then perhaps, I might slip into that dream sleep where Angel and I were one, reconciled. I make it to seventy-three, and my gag for air wakens Angel. He rubs his chest, then the sleep from his eyes. When he takes his hands away his face has changed. The new day challenges him to survive. His eyes narrow. His thoughts are elsewhere, and he's not far behind. I say, "Good morning."

He looks around, reading the daylight as precisely as only a street-boy can do and says, "What's the time! Shit!"

"I don't know, I don't have a watch." I apologise.

"Joker! Joker, what time is it?" he screams, as he jumps from my bed, letting the cold air rush between the sheets in a gust.

"Time? Every bloody day, every day for years, you ask me the same damn question. Get a watch, can't you!"

Angel is pulling his clothes on and becoming more and more agitated.

"Come on Joker, don't piss about, please." He pleads.

"Time? You're obsessed. You're either too early or too late for everything you do. You're never there! You're never on time. It's half eleven," he concedes, and snuggles back down.

"That's a flippin' untruth, and some people know it, right Poet?" he answers, looking directly at me. "Sometimes I'm right on time!"

I blush at the eye contact between all three and watch him dash from the room, in triumph.

"Don't worry about it Poet. He always kisses and tells. He can't help it, he just has to tell people. God alone knows why. He's a bit like that boy Holden, in Salinger's *Catcher In The Rye*. You know, he promises not to then does it. He says, '...I keep making up these sex rules for myself and then I break them right away...' Well, Angel always intends not telling, and always does, without fail. Besides, I heard you at it, you noisy pair of sods."

I make a mental note of the book Joker's just mentioned and ask him where the nearest library is, so that I can borrow it.

"Biker's got a copy, somewhere around the place. You can look for it when you put the kettle on."

"Very subtle," I acknowledge, and drag myself from the warm blankets into my cold clothes; and into an even colder

108

kitchen. What a mess. Why is it that teenage boys never wash up after themselves, ever? Waiting for the kettle to boil, I look into the other room. It's in darkness, figures move in fitful sleep. The door to Actor's room is closed and padlocked. He must have left early. Angel dashes from the bathroom, punches my shoulder, winks and is out of the flat, all in a matter of hyperactive seconds.

Joker sits up for his tea and pulls a blanket around his shoulders. I return to my bed and do the same. I risk a direct question. "You know what you were saying, to Angel, about the time? You said he'd been asking you the same question for years? I know it's none of my business, but how long have you known each other?"

Joker, far from being offended at my probing question, put me at my ease. "We aren't lovers, or anything like that, though, as friends, we have sex, but it doesn't feel right. We're like brothers, see?"

Their brotherhood, he went on to explain, had grown through their meeting in a children's home. From which they were both on the run. I sat silently and listened, transfixed. Joker was an only child but had never known his real father. His mother married again when he was about ten years old. His new 'father' had taken a special interest in him from the start, lavishing time and effort on him. He was a really nice person to have around. He took Joker to the cinema, swimming, everywhere. After a short while Joker had become unashamedly dependent on the attention. Increasingly, however, the attention became sexual. That is, his father would bathe him and linger, with soapy hands, around Joker's genitals. Joker felt no sense of guilt or shame for what happened, since he knew that his father 'loved' him dearly. He told him so many times. By the time he was twelve, Joker was secretly sleeping with his father, when his mother was out, and the relationship had become much more sexual. It was on one of those fully sexual occasions that they'd been discovered, by his mother. The police were called and Joker was taken into 'care' and sent, with all the guilt he could carry, to a kids' home. His father was sent to prison and his mother blamed him for breaking up the marriage, which ended in divorce.

At the kids' home he was befriended by another new

arrival, Angel, who'd been sent there after setting fire to his school having tried to blackmail a teacher. The blackmail had never come out and Angel was sent to see a psychiatrist, who thought he was dangerous. Every week after that, he had to see the trick-cyclist who was assigned to the kids' home. It was a crazy situation. The teacher had been touching Angel up for years and Angel had tried to regain his own sense of power and control, in the only way he knew how; he asked for money. The teacher, with access to hundreds of other kids, had refused and, from then on, shut Angel out. That's when Angel broke into the school and torched his classroom, and the fire got out of control. Angel was arrested watching the blaze. No one ever asked him why he did it simply assumed that he was an emotionally disturbed kid who'd become a danger to society.

Angel learnt his lesson quickly, get the money first in future. He learnt, too, that his seductive pretty face was his greatest asset and soon he had one of the care workers wrapped around his finger. Money first, then his pleasure. Angel was never short of money, smokes or sweets, which he shared only with Joker. He also came to share the care worker, who became putty in their hands. When the other kids began to put two and two together Joker and Angel went 'on the run'. They'd been undiscovered in London for nearly a year.

James Beresford

Peter

from an unpublished memoir

Imagination was my sanctuary in the bleak moments of childhood and was a never-ending source of wonder and mystery. The design in the carpet became buildings, and layouts of magnificent cities; the pattern of the wallpaper was a fantasy-land, where strange people, carrying odd-shaped bundles and wearing still odder shaped hats, made long treks though jungle or over mountainous terrain and along the craggiest of ravines. For the most part I merely sat and stared into space, creating great adventures in which I either travelled alone or with one or two friends (often imaginary) with whom I shared unquestioning loyalty: our thoughtfulness to each other would be unparalleled.

Then there was the enacting in my mind of meeting a great hero, who, upon first noticing me, would immediately accept me as his confidential companion, becoming my mentor and allowing me to be his apprentice.

My fantasies were wide-ranging, covering not only tales of epic proportions, but also simple events and tableaus. Mostly they championed good-heartedness in people and the wonders of nature. It is from these dreams that I confirmed myself to be an inveterate lover of beauty; always dwelling on anything expressing charm, attractiveness in natural shape and design, or having less artificial content.

When allowed out to play I did not so much attempt to live-out my fantasies as use their experience in support of whatever I was doing. The few friends I had soon learned I could be relied upon to generate as much fun as possible.

As a rule I did not invite other boys back to my home, for the prim surroundings seemed to make them uneasy and subdued. Admittedly, many of the more exciting characters with

111

whom I was friendly had little time for the niceties of life, and in my mother's eyes, were quite despicably beneath our station. Mother was quite efficient in running down the virtues of almost everybody I knew, so I dreaded her finding a sticky smear from their alien hands, or a petal dislodged from one of her precious arrangements. I much preferred to visit my friends, or meet them at a place where we could play outside.

And not long after my first few months at Roehampton, I met eight-year-old Peter. Knowing instantly that he would not be accepted by Mother if she knew of his background, certainly in Mother's eyes well and truly beneath our station, I would need to invent a social status for him and his remaining family of a mother and an older brother. As Peter's father was dead – he had been a private killed in action towards the end of the war – everything fitted in well as far as invention was concerned, for I could elevate the man to a necessarily accepted status. Thus, Peter's late father became a captain – I thought something like a colonel or a general might be stretching things a bit too far! So, despite my new friend's decidedly unkempt hair and scruffy appearance, Peter was reluctantly allowed to enter my home and my relatively new life in the magnificent grounds of my immediate and exciting world.

Mother's sympathy for the boy? No – his father had been a *captain* in the army!

Living at Roehampton provided one specific advantage: immediately adjacent to the college grounds, in which my home was situated, and within a short walking distance, was a golf-course, set out in splendid parkland. There I spent many hours, often with Peter, my accomplice in the 'Lost and found ball business'. Not that the object of our endeavours was the return of the balls to their owners, paid or otherwise: a large collection of anything is the envy of any small boy.

Peter, despite being almost two years older than me, was my closest friend and confidant and we shared the same sense of adventure, Peter seeing in me something of great appeal to his every sense. We could rely on one another for complete and active support in any actions of daring or mischief in which one of us had embarked, dropping into suitable character-roles in the blink of an eye. Our base camp was either the grotto, a folly built around the pump-house for the artificial lake, or a wendy-

house in the college grounds, where we hatched our conspiracies, or just daydreamed, free from the outside world.

It was the wendy-house also where, being free from the gaze of adults, Peter and I added much to our knowledge of personal matters through detailed physical examination of each other, including appropriate comparisons. On one occasion, on our return from the golf-course, I had acquired a scratch on the back of my upper leg. A bramble had painfully found its way up the leg of my shorts, as I forced myself, bottom first, into a thicket to retrieve a ball, and attention was needed.

Back in the wendy-house I was endeavouring to twist to inspect the damage, whilst Peter described what he could see. "I think we'd better take a look at that, Mr Smith. Just to be certain," he pronounced in his sternest clinical voice. It seemed that all patients went by the appellation of Mr Smith. I snapped immediately into the role he had set for me and complied with his command, "Yes, Doctor..." and downed my shorts and pants in manly fashion.

After appropriate, and some not quite so appropriate proddings, together with incomprehensible medical terminology, the Doctor authoritatively declared he did not think the condition was life-threatening, but felt it best to play safe on such occasions and give me a full examination – just in case! With the atmosphere of solemnity maintained, I completed my disrobing and mounted the examination couch – the carpeted floor in this case – and submitted to meticulous, professional administrations. Everything was examined at least three times, and with the nine-year-old Doctor concentrating on certain areas of my anatomy, the particular intimacy taking place was not quite what was expected. A more open horseplay ensued, with less pretence about the fun we were having, with Peter making a full and purposeful contribution to the anatomy on display as we changed roles. With the two of us giving way to a far more intimate pursuit, I was both envious of Peter's knowledge of such matters and of his physical development, better in all departments than mine.

Having discovered much earlier that our camaraderie extended to curiosity of intimate issues, Peter and I pursued our mutual interests with each other on a number of occasions, each having full confidence and trust to submit to the other's every

enquiry and ingenuity in experiments. However, our studies were brought to an abrupt, but by no means permanent, end one afternoon at about the time I was seven. Peter and I had ensconced ourselves in my bedroom whilst my mother and a neighbour chatted over tea in the lounge, and quickly becoming bored by driving Dinky-toys around the pattern of the carpet, we decided to continue our personal experiments by way of a diversion. Having checked that my mother was otherwise engaged, and that we were safe from disturbance, considering that discovery would be quite unlikely by dint of my mother's usual penchant for prolonged discussion over Earl Grey and Royal Scot biscuits, we removed our clothes and took advantage of the comforts of my bed.

Mother's ill-timed discovery of both Peter and I, stark naked, my rump in the air as I knelt there in readiness for nine-year-old Peter's second bout of joyfully thrusting away deep inside me, was devastating. When I explained to my mother later that afternoon that we were only playing a game called 'bums', and only wanted to examine each other out of curiosity, the result was Peter's banning from the house. What might have happened, had she actually caught Peter deflowering me, I dread to think. Perhaps, in that instant, there had been a modicum of good fortune!

The consequences of discovering what Peter and I had been up to in the bedroom that afternoon had a lasting effect on me at home, but it did not prevent any association between Peter and myself after school in selected places of meeting. My parents were quite incandescent with rage, and a great deal of which I am still convinced was righteous indignation for their own sakes, rather than any concern for the moral damage I may have caused myself, and had they known that Peter and I had played 'bums' on a number of occasions, there is no telling what Mother might have said, or what extra fate might await me. And had Peter's mother known that Richard, their eldest son of twelve, was frequently having his lustful way with his younger brother, and that Peter was having an affair with a neighbour for money, there is no doubt also that Peter's life would have been in added turmoil from that day.

At no time was there any attempt from them to explain the sexual and moral issues involved. Quite frankly, I had so

frequently heard all the metaphors and comparisons with animals and degenerate people used for directing my everyday behaviour, that I was completely deaf to them then. Neither did they stop to question why I had involved myself in such covert activity, aside from just plain mischief. It passed their comprehension, too, that most children acquire essential awareness from games such as 'You show me yours, and I'll show you mine!' or 'Doctors and nurses', of which my games with Peter were an elaborate version.

This incident marked the beginning of the end of my confidence in the assumption that my parents' clear image of life was unbiased and complete in all essentials of knowledge. My grandfather had already instilled in me that element of well-being whilst receiving his comforting attentions, and now that Peter could offer me that same harmless delight, my mother was obviously wrong!

Allied to this enhanced lack of trust in my parents' ability to recognise what I, on balance, considered to be nothing more than plain good, harmless fun, was not only my grandfather's perspective on things physical, but those other, countless incidents in my early years which I either witnessed, or in which I became a willing participant. And here I speak of that innocent but covert distraction which most children have been consciously involved in. There was never any question as to who invented such games as 'Doctors and nurses', and I never questioned why another boy should want to show me his penis if I showed him mine. It all seemed so perfectly natural, and what difference did it make whether it might be my kneecap, or elbow, or penis? They were all a regular part of my body, and if someone wanted to look at some part of me that was as prominent and thrilling to touch as that which signified my gender, then that was all right by me. If something as apparently innocuous as comparing sizes was to be accepted by those who felt a need for such regular practises, then that more rewarding pursuit of tactility left for many of us a far more memorable and satisfying perception of pleasure.

As children, the moral issues were virtually non-existent, regardless of any parental mediation, and such levels of excitement derived from any form of sexual contact with another like-minded person were equated with the eating of sweets, or

the playing of thrilling games. I knew it was wrong to steal, for that meant depriving someone of a valued possession, and I could easily relate to that. To physically harm another person was also wrong, for this meant suffering of a purely physical kind, and I could relate to that also. But where an activity gave nothing but pure, simple pleasure to both partners, then logic dictated that there could not possibly be anything wrong in it. Thus, Peter and I were in no way deterred, and in seeking pastures new, discovered the relatively safe comforts of an abandoned garage; complete with discarded sofa, frequently taking advantage of the cushions, sustaining our bodily needs, and adding something of intrigue to our enjoyable game of *'bums'*.

For Peter and myself, that which was considered by adults as immoral was construed by us as nothing more than a big naughty adventure. Immorality, like politics or adult social conditioning and mores, meant nothing to us. We were simply not interested. And why should we be? We were two very healthy and energetic young boys, wanting to do what healthy and energetic young boys wanted to do without causing harm to others.

From Peter I learned to take a more profound interest in other boys' penises, comparing sizes, shapes, and whenever possible, actually involving myself in a decidedly tactile furtherance to my growing interest. I seemed to prefer the long ones in those early days, and short, acorn-shaped ones with long foreskins had little attraction for me. Between us, we devised a system of recognising those shapes having most appeal to both of us, ignoring those which came under the heading of basic 'knobs', particularly those which had been subjected to the cruel banality of circumscision, and were left with little more than a small pink wrinkled protuberance. Those boys accorded the accolade of possessing a 'cock'. That was as cylindrically shaped as possible, and like Peter's and my own, such were highly in favour. Only one boy in my school at that time was lucky enough to have one longer than Peter's, and he was my undoubted, although envied, champion, never failing to thrill me with his erections in the showers or toilets, once allowing me to feel it to confirm that it was as hard as it looked. Peter's, however, was, and remained, the faultless shape and size as far as I was concerned, and since it was both long and thick – almost four inches long at

ten years of age – I envied him that superb example of burgeoning manhood. I relished each and every feel of it, not only through the sensitivity of my compliant fingers, but receiving its wonderful firmness when Peter saw fit to use it properly: and in a way which, he assured me, was its real purpose, and not for copulation when reaching adulthood. It all seemed perfectly logical to me. But when fully and solidly erect, it not only displayed that thrilling completeness for me, but enhanced my wonderment of its fascinating and unrivalled exquisiteness. And unlike others I had purposely taken notice of from time to time, Peter's managed quite successfully to constantly conform to my idea of perfection, and few could match either its size, shape or feel. In itself it was a god – a paragon of everything I cherished. I dreamed about it, and often could not wait to either see it or feel its firm, silky smoothness once again. Such was my infatuation!

Had I learned from anyone but my parents, perhaps, that such boyhood appendages were to be regarded as nothing more than a personal and relatively unimportant appurtenance for urinating with only, thus to be consigned to the list of relatively uninteresting parts of my body such as elbows, knees or ears, it is likely my interests may not have been so prominent. But Peter, more than any, however, and a great influence on me, belied any conjecture that might have evolved as such, taking great pains to emphasise the paramount virtues of size in particular, and dwelling in almost animated terms on those he had fiddled with, and subsequently sampled in other ways – at his school in the toilets, on Roehampton Common, in swimming pool changing-rooms, and in particular, with his brother and his friends.

It did not occur to me then that this type of pursuit or interest was so widespread; I regarded it as little more than a necessarily covert, puerile foible, and relegated to the commonly practised 'Doctors and nurses' scenarios exploited by so many children at all times.

So, Peter, having pipped my parents to the post in a far more alluring way, was the one who ignited the flame of significant curiosity within me. He had planted the seed, and the subsequent healthy germination and growth extended to boundless realms.

117

more than about twenty minutes, and once over, it was almost as if we had gone there to discuss our favourite film-star or swap cigarette cards. Such was the casual but rushed effort in indulging ourselves in this most secret act.

During the third month of these Monday-afternoon meetings, however, the simple expediency of them took on another dimension, and was changed. Something which not even Peter was wholly taken with, and later put a stop to the meetings altogether. Richard's friend, Joseph, a thirteen-year-old of stockier build, had been invited one afternoon to join in, having been enlightened as to what went on in the garage, and obviously eager to take part. The same procedure was carried out, but with Joseph insisting that Peter "do me" with both of us standing, and not on the cushions. Neither of us had any real objections to this, but Peter, being slightly taller than me, found the positioning to be somewhat troublesome in order to reach a suitable parity of levels. This, however, was of some advantage to Joseph, for whilst Peter was thrusting away, Joseph delighted in either fellating or masturbating me at the same time.

Then it came to Richard's turn, again with myself draped over the arm of the sofa, and then Joseph in that same position. Unfortunately for myself, Joseph was much larger than Richard in that salient department, and by no means as gentle in his action, forcing me into the padded arm of the sofa and leaving me with soreness and red marks on the tops of my thighs where he had gripped me to aid his thrusts.

The short-lived relationship with Richard and Joseph came to a thankful end one Wednesday afternoon when I was invited to come alone to the garage, Peter not being informed of the arrangement. There I was met not only by Richard and friend Joseph, but another of his adolescent friends who had heard that I was 'easy', and didn't mind being 'bummed'. The result was that I was stripped of all of my clothes, made to bend over the arm of the sofa, and was systematically and painfully buggered by all three of them. To add insult to injury, one of Richard's friends thought it would be good fun to hide my clothes before running off, leaving me tearful, naked, bruised and sore. It was more than fortunate that Peter, somehow having found out about his brother's whereabouts, came to find me, and saw me wandering about outside in the derelict yard looking for my

clothes. That put an end to his brother's involvement with me in particular, but made no difference to the relationship between Peter and myself.

* * *

Who it was, exactly, who led me and others like me, like a bellwether, into that sensually verdant valley of Utopia, where nothing more than euphoria and blossoming aestheticism became a staple diet, I don't really know. It could have been Grandfather; although his particular interest was little more than a means to a self-gratifying end, despite the thrilling tactile- and mouth-seducing attention he gave me, either before, during, or after I had sated his own lust-hunger. This, of course, was combined with the knowledge that I not only thoroughly enjoyed it, but recognised it as part of the loving relationship we shared.

Peter, no doubt, provided much of the initial allure, and undoubtedly opened the flood-gates of my own innate desires, embryonic though they may have been at that early age. Others later personified all that I relished from any form of sex, and it is perhaps because of their unstinted liking for me that I soon associated love with sex. Certainly, those concerted relationships did much to convince me that sex, love and friendship were much of the same thing, despite the anomalous nature of the friendship, and were consolidated to such an extent that I could not have recognised any such anomaly.

Immured within my own cosy, unthreatening, self-protected and self-justified cell of complacency, and one that seemed so inviolable, nothing of that became a real problem. Of course, conscience sometimes reared its chilling embodiment of morality, and so did fear of discovery, but they were usually overcome by reminders of past successes and their cocoon of secrecy. And then there was that element of blissful ignorance pertaining to whatever penalties might arise if one was caught.

As far as I was aware, any punitive measures likely to come my way, should anything of my immoral behaviour be discovered, would be little more than, in my particular case, a sound thrashing – of which I had suffered many; bed without food; incarcerated for whatever length of period within the comforts of my bedroom, and a relatively short-lived but

adequate chastening from both parents.

Considering that I had had 'sex' with Granddad each and every time I stayed at his pub, that added to my conviction that discovery would be minimal, if not unthinkable. Besides, to add to that conviction yet more, Peter and his older brother had been caught not once, but three times, in bed together by their mother, both naked, and both fully erect, and obviously, as far as their mother was concerned, most probably up to no good. And although Peter and his brother had, at those times, falsely but forcedly countenanced their mother's view that: it was not proper to be in the same (single) bed together, naked, with erections, and with Peter on one occasion with his back to his brother, little more was added to the event other than a close watch to ensure such behaviour would not happen again. It did, of course, but by actually catching them in the act – or shortly before, in each case, apparently – any further venturing was safeguarded by awareness.

For the above mentioned reasons, and others, Peter soon became not only my mentor, but, by dint of his apparent immunity to punishment and virtual ascendancy within his family and friends, my guardian angel – or, in my particular fawning case, my guardian god. This raising to an emotional pedestal applied to another older boy in later months. But for differing reasons, that pedestal was extended to perhaps a greater height, for the other boy, David, was a boy prostitute, and had made films!

Had I been aware, at the outset of my friendship with Peter, that his outstanding attractiveness, both in looks and behaviour, would make him one of life's charmed and successful people, it is likely that considerations of my own physical appearance and capacity for friendship would have made me think twice about pursuing some of Peter's exploits. Not that I did not do well for myself in that respect. But whereas I might be rejected as a possible candidate for some clandestine foray or another, Peter would be accepted without more ado.

I cannot remember any jaundiced attitude levelled at Peter throughout our long friendship, but I did, however, envy that gem of character that gained him more friends than I had, and whatever might result from some secret, or otherwise, activity.

All of this, of course, was interspersed with the more

'normal' pursuits of boyhood – which though meeting greater public approval, were often just as rewarding, and could bring an even greater degree of camaraderie.

Our boisterousness and vitality often belied that disguised level of effetism or delicacy concomitant with our double life. For myself in particular, although by no means ebullient by nature, it is unlikely that any chink in my armour would have been noticed. I had soon learned to cloak my predilections and weaknesses by idiosyncrasies of another kind, allaying any potential suspicions. Fortunately, I suppose, there were very few times during my less circumspect early childhood when I was caught during one act or another, but whatever might have been deduced by the revelation was quickly and adequately smothered by a suitable reason or excuse.

Once, when another boy of my age – I was ten at the time – and myself had taken ourselves to a remote and secluded part of Roehampton Common, for an innocuous act of 'I'll show you mine, if you'll show me yours', with both of us knowing that it most probably would not rest with the simple diversion of size comparison, we were actually caught red-handed by another boy three years our senior, and when asked by him, rhetorically, what we were doing, my reply that I had wanted to see what a circumcised penis looked like, because I might be having mine done, was accepted – I think – and passed over as little more than normal puerile interest.

When, some time after our discovery, and the older boy had gone – or so we thought – it left us to carry on with our own lives. And thinking that we were safe to continue, we furthered our interest to the point of far greater tactile efficiency, and both of us soon displayed a superb erection. My inventiveness came to the fore once more and saved the day, for about to sample my friends circumcised member with my mouth, but fortunately, not quite having got that far, we were pounced upon again by the same sceptical – and, as it happened, noticeably aroused – third party.

This time the explanation offered was met with a knowing grin, when I calmly proclaimed all innocence for us both, and disclosed the fact that in order to satisfy myself that by my being circumcised, I did at least need to be assured that I would be able to get an erection. And as that concern had by now been mitigated

by my friend's ample example, I was now happy. When the boy pulled out his own penis and displayed his own erection, asking me to 'give it a suck' I knew that all was well.

* * *

After so many years of studying not only my own motives during childhood, but similar behavioural patterns of others, I can perhaps clearly understand why it was that Peter and I became so close, relying on each other for a great diversity of reasons.

It might, perhaps, be possible to ignore the needs we had from each other – for conformity or for identity, for example – and attribute everything to 'coincidence', of which of course we were very ready to take advantage. That might have been true for other boys, less self-aware than were Peter and I. But for us, I have decided to rule out coincidence as the reason for our shared interests. We both knew long before our relationship began that we would come together, and that we would each find in this the fulfilment of our individual needs.

Peter's introducing me to a neighbour called Wally, confirmed in me that same measure of coincidence when telling me that he had known, even at the age of seven, when he first met him, that the man was interested in him for sexual reasons, thus developing into a spasmodic relationship, and when I first became involved with Wally, I also felt it was a natural condition, and when I first positioned myself in front of him, naked and healthily aroused, it washed away any previous apprehension about modesty or decency, having always reserved such propriety for females only. Although Peter was always the more slightly dominant during our acts of sex, he always allowed me whatever I chose by way of change or foray. I mentioned previously that the event which might have sparked off our illicit interest in each other was the incident with the thorn scratch in the wendy-house. In fact, it began long before then, when Peter asked me one afternoon, whilst we were looking for golf-balls in the college grounds, if he could see my penis. Having no objection whatsoever – after all, he was a boy, also – I pulled down my shorts and underpants, lifted up my shirt, and revealed my small protuberance to him. I was then six and a half. Allowing him to play with it, in a similar vein to Grandfather's tactile interest, it

naturally became erect, thus transforming it to something worthy of being labelled a 'cock', and not an insignificant representation of my gender. Peter was quite impressed and told me that we could have lots of fun together, and if we kept it a secret, I could play with his whenever I wanted to, and he knew how to give other boys 'really super feelings all over', as his brother and a man called Wally had proved to him.

Yes, I wanted to play with his lovely big penis as often as I could. And why not? And from that day onwards, myself not questioning his interest in my penis, or, on occasions in the grotto, my full nakedness, it became good fun, and quite harmless as far as I was concerned. I always enjoyed taking my clothes off when in his company, often letting him play with my 'winky', as I then called it, or letting him rub his own naked body against mine, causing both members to rise up and stand out like gun-barrels on a tank. And he was quite right, anyway: it did give me 'super' feelings!

When I requested that Peter also divest himself of his clothing on occasions, perhaps not having that same level of licentious interest as himself, I nonetheless thrilled at seeing not only his nakedness, but that part of him which soon became increasingly fascinating, especially as it was the biggest example I had seen so far, apart from Grandfather's, and when fully erect, it most certainly put mine – and others – to shame. But what was it, exactly, about that nine-year-old's magnificent specimen that so attracted me? Not just then, but for an eternity afterwards? Had some obscure and unfathomable, yet powerful, curiosity suddenly broken out of its shell; and in my especial case, eagerly awaited the next viewing?

Even at that very early age I was always avid for the chance to see his penis, whether flaccid or erect. And the older I became, that avidity never waned, and neither, so it would appear, did Peter's as far as my or other boy's penises were concerned.

Unlike myself at the age of ten; which was how old Peter was when I first began to notice his other investigative, subtle and improper behaviour, he would often take advantage of other boys' accessibility. Many was the time when I would watch him deliberately entice a more timorous boy into one secluded place or another, myself tagging along to witness his perverse waywardness, and if the boy was wearing shorts, in would go

Peter's hand, take hold of the boy's penis, and endeavour to see how big it felt if an erection was forthcoming.

Peter admitted to me, when I was about eight or nine, that he actually loved feeling other boys' cocks, and if they didn't voice any strong objections, or actually enjoyed the thrill of being felt at the time, then they were 'decent chaps'. But if they did object, then they were 'creeps'. On one occasion, during our respective schools half-term, I watched him pull down the trousers and underpants of a nine-year-old in amongst some trees on Roehampton Common, bring the boy to an erection with his fingers, then fellate him until the boy was begging him to stop: no doubt having achieved an orgasm, he could no longer stand the aftermath sensation.

Age seemed to make very little difference to him, and once asking me if he could bring someone to the grotto where he and I were to play 'armies' or some such game the following day, I agreed, thinking it might be a mutual friend from the neighbourhood, but when Peter asked me to bring a ruler, but would not say why, I was somewhat puzzled.

The 'someone' turned out to be an extremely gormless, thick-set boy of about sixteen, known to me and others from our school as 'Tim The Nut-Case', who, poor chap, was gullible to the extreme. I was nine at that time, and Peter, eleven, and not being used to much older boys, I was at first somewhat sceptical, especially knowing of the boy's simple-mindedness.

Having been told by Peter at the outset that in order to earn a shilling, Tim had to take all of his clothes off and walk around naked in the grotto, the boy did so. The boy was hesitant at first, thinking someone other than us might see him, but when convinced by myself, just as eager to see him without any clothes on, that the college was closed for the holidays, he removed all of his clothes and stood grinning at us like a halfwit. Peter at first sniggered unkindly at the boy's pale body and extremely well-developed genitals, then told Tim that he had to prove he could make his 'cock' grow bigger. Although he had not actually seen it, Peter knew something of the boy's penis size from others, and telling me that it was supposed to be about seven inches long, and wanting not only to see it for himself, but me, also – knowing I would be impressed – suggested that we measure it when fully erect. Apparently, a few other boys had measured it

when taking Tim somewhere to exhibit himself one night on Roehampton Common, with four or five torches all lighting-up the magnificent member as it grew to full priapism.

Tim certainly proved all counts, and I think it even surprised Peter, for it was indeed almost seven inches long when fully erect, and neither of us had ever seen such enormous and pendulous testicles on a boy. I know Peter was quite thrilled by feeling it, and holding it as if it might go off in his hand, examined it like an object not seen before. And when it became my turn to feel it, I was filled with admiration and respect for the older boy. Not even Grandfather's measured up to that, in either size or rigid strength. Tim had what I later learned was called 'A Surprise Package', and although of a respectable size when flaccid, more than doubled its length when aroused.

The end result of what was to be rather a short foray into another aspect of Peter's unpredictable world, was that after the boy had agreed to Peter and myself feeling his full and stupendously large erection, he then masturbated himself to an extremely copious orgasm, ejaculating all over my face and shirt. I was not just shocked: I was totally horrified. I had never seen an ejaculation apart from Grandfather's, and the last thing I expected was one from this boy, and the result of his semen shoot out quite unexpectedly all over me was quite traumatic.

When the boy had gone, promising to return again the following day, and earn another shilling from Peter, I went to the lake to try and wash off the evidence, fearing my mother's wrath and questions.

I learned from Peter later that afternoon that Tim was not only well known as a nut-case, but would do anything for sweets or money, and as he, Peter, had wanted me to witness the boy's size of penis, he thought it was a good idea to invite him, and by Peter giving Tim the shilling it would guarantee another visit from him the next day.

When Tim did arrive, later than we expected, the same procedure was carried out, but with much more time being taken to thoroughly examine the boy's nakedness and arousal. This time, however, Peter himself masturbated the sixteen-year-old to yet another copious orgasm, but with myself well out of harm's way and watching it shoot out against the light-grey of the grotto's false stonework.

Tim wanted to do it again the next day, but Peter had run out of money, and as I had already spent my pocket-money, and neither of us had any sweets to give him, we were deprived of his exciting company.

Through that short-lived exhibitionism at the grotto, Peter arranged for another demonstration, but this time on Roehampton Common, and with a much larger audience of ten or so eight- or nine-year-olds after school one afternoon, and with the boy's eagerness to impress us all, we witnessed the amazing spectacle of his virility.

Taking Tim to some secluded spot in the density of trees, the sixteen-year-old allowed each of us in turn to hold it or feel it, apparently enjoying every second of our exploratory attention; despite one or two of the boys behaving somewhat stupidly and flicking it or pulling it down as far as it would go and letting it ping back to its near perpendicular position. He even allowed one eight-year-old to pull back the foreskin to examine the vast bulbous glans, with Peter urging the junior boy to suck it. The boy sensibly refused.

We were all spellbound, including me, despite having already seen it twice before, and I wanted to stand there and feel it for as long as I could, but I had to take my turn with the rest of them. He was made to masturbate himself to a climax, having been promised about two bob (two shillings) collected from a whip-round between us boys, just for the thrill of seeing not only 'the largest cock in the world', but for the privilege of seeing him actually do what only men could do, and 'spunk up'.

With all of us standing there watching him masturbate himself to an orgasm, the astounding spectacle of his gushing emission was enough to send several of the boys running, some almost retching from shock, and one boy being quite violently sick at the sight. But knowing what to expect, I stood there brave-hearted and giggling, telling those boys remaining in awe and stupefaction that Tim's 'cock' was bigger than my father's. The fact that I had never seen my father's penis was besides the point, but it sounded impressive for Tim, who, quite frankly, was probably quite oblivious of the fact that he owned such a magnificent member.

I learned about six months later that Tim had been taken into care after being found naked and bruised near a pond on

Roehampton Common. Apparently, he had been attacked and subjected to some horrendous activities before being left dazedly to find his clothes and then make his way home. I remember feeling extremely sorry for him, and I hoped that he would be looked after properly.

PART TWO: FICTION

Guy Willard

How I Spent My Summer Vacation

from *Foolish Fire* (Gay Men's Press, 1999)

1

I was up in the Fort with my cousin Bobby. The Fort was a treehouse in my backyard I'd built with the help of my dad. Actually, my dad had started out by helping me build it, but growing impatient with my incompetence, had taken over the job himself, grimly, expertly hammering the boards into place, stepping back to survey his handiwork while I stood off to one side watching it get built. I'd never been mechanically minded, nor handy with tools, and I only felt in his way whenever we worked together on something.

Ever since it got built, the Fort was the place I liked to escape to, especially in the summer. I even slept in it sometimes, feeling like a boy drifting on a raft downstream. Naturally, whenever Bobby came for a visit, we would come up here as much as possible.

Every June, at the start of summer vacation, it was a custom for his family to visit us for about a week before proceeding on to the coast. His mother and mine were very close as sisters, and our fathers had gone to the same college. Bobby and I were exactly the same age. He was the brother I'd always wanted, and we played together like longlost siblings during the one week allotted to us each summer. Every summer we picked up our friendship as if there'd been no interval since the last visit.

Safely ensconced in the Fort's shady solitude, soft drinks and comic books on the wooden floor beside us, we gazed down upon the rooftops of the neighborhood through a shifting curtain of leafy green, pretending we were on the swaying deck of a ship

131

at sea or in the gondola of a fabulous lighter-than-air balloon which was just skimming the treetops. It was easy to shut out the entire world, simply by pulling the canvas flap at the door shut, and sitting cross-legged on the creaking floorboards.

Bobby kicked his legs out over the side. "Guy, why is it that junior high school is so different from elementary school? I mean, it seems that the kids in my school only have one thing on their minds: girls. Yuck."

"I know. It seems like that's all they care about anymore. Last year they wouldn't be caught dead talking to them."

"Everybody's changing so much. Getting so stuck up and stuff. I wish we could go back to the days when everybody was reading comic books and trading them."

"Well, as you get older, your interests change. Just like you yourself change."

"I don't change. I'm never gonna be any different than I am now."

"Personally, there's some changes *I* don't mind at all...."

"Oh? Like what, for instance?"

"You know...."

"No, I don't. What?"

I looked at him. Bobby had always been a late bloomer, a little slow to catch on to things. For all I knew, he might not even have discovered masturbation yet. In order to find out for sure, I began dropping hints, making veiled references to it and watching for his reaction. Without ever coming right out and saying it, I wove phrases like "doing it," or "wrist action" or "shooting off" into my talk, with obvious emphasis. He laughed along good-naturedly, sensing a joke but not quite getting it, with a hint of lostness in his face-and I took a malicious delight in this subtle needling.

"Come on, Guy, what are you laughing about? Are you making fun of me?"

"No. It's just that you're so damned innocent."

"What's wrong with that? Why should I feel ashamed because I'm not as smart as you? Good grades aren't everything, you know."

"No, dum-dum. I'm talking about the facts of life. Sex and that kind of stuff."

"Oh." He fell silent. "You mean like dirty jokes and stuff.

If you want to know the truth, I just don't like those kinds of jokes."

"Maybe it's because you don't get them. If you don't understand the punch line, it won't make any sense to you."

He shook his head vehemently. "No, I mean they're all so stupid. Like this one joke about a man with a ten-foot long dick. It's so long it reaches all the way up to the ceiling. He trains his pet monkey to climb up it but the monkey keeps slipping down. Or something like that. It's a dumb joke." His voice trailed off and he looked truly lost.

"Don't worry, Bobby, it'll come to you someday."

He made a face, then turned to me with a serious expression. "Guy, what's all this about 'beating off?' I heard some guys talking about it once, but they wouldn't tell me."

My suspicion was confirmed: he knew nothing. And it made me feel so superior.

"You mean to tell me you don't *know*?"

He shook his head, big-eyed. "What is it?" he whispered.

I smiled mysteriously with the smug look of one who knows all the secrets of the universe. "Boy, are you dumb."

"Come on, Guy, tell me." Then with a suspicious look on his face: "Do *you* know?"

"Of course I do."

Obviously he was still very much in the dark about something which, for me, was the ruling passion of my life. It was delightful to savor the immense gap I felt suddenly yawn between us. Leaning back, I laced my fingers together and cupped my palms behind my head. After peering up through the cracks in the primitively constructed roof at the patterns of leaf and sky beyond, I hesitated for a moment, then said:

"You know what? I don't think you know anything about anything."

A worried look crossed his face. "What do you mean?"

"I mean, about sex. Where babies come from. And how babies are made. That kind of stuff."

"Oh, I know all that. We saw a film about it in hygiene class."

"Yeah?"

He shrugged his shoulders. "The woman gets pregnant when the man puts his dick inside her. There was a cartoon

explaining it all."

"Yeah, we saw the same thing. What a laugh. The cartoons made it all seem so mechanical, like pieces of a machine fitting together. No mention about how good it feels."

"How do *you* know how it feels?"

"Because it probably feels a lot like beating off."

"Oh." He looked perplexed.

I grew impatient. "Listen, 'beating off' is just another term for masturbation."

"Masturbation?"

"Yes, dum-dum. That's when you make yourself *come*. You know what I mean by 'come', don't you?"

His face fell a little. "Yeah," he said evasively, his voice getting weaker. He seemed to sense that the talk was getting into dangerous territory. "Yeah, I guess I do."

"Do you really?"

"Sure I do."

"Then tell me," I taunted. I saw the look of panic which flitted across his face quickly replaced by an uncertain attempt at casualness. I pressed on: "I bet you never even did it."

"Did what?"

"You know. With yourself."

He hesitated, then – as if offended – shot back, "Sure I did."

"Oh yeah? Then how do you do it?"

"The same way as everybody else, I guess."

"How does everyone do it?"

"I don't know how *every*-one does it. You'll have to ask every-one." Then he countered triumphantly: "How do *you* do it, Guy?"

Now it was my turn to hesitate. I was weighing the alternatives: to keep him in the dark and continue to needle him, or to risk the chance of his finding out from another source. My choice was clear...and my stomach shivered at the thought of what I was about to divulge, the mystery to which I was initiating him – every boy's most cherished and wonderful secret.

"Do you really want to know?"

"Yeah."

"Then listen."

My throat was dry and I could feel little shivers trickling along all my muscles. My stomach felt cool and weighty. I could

almost feel Bobby's trembling excitement as if we were linked by invisible sparks jumping across the space between us. I swallowed, then went on in a low voice:

"You know how your dick sometimes gets hard and points straight up, like this?" With my index finger, I imitated a penis coming to erection with a series of short, quick jerks.

"Yeah?"

"Didn't you ever touch yourself when it was like that?"

"I guess so."

"I mean," I said impatiently, "touch yourself in the way they call 'beating off?' You know...."

Ringing my fingers around a phantom penis in the air before me I demonstrated with a rapid up-and-down jogging of my wrist.

Bobby's face blanched. He wore a look of awe and horror mixed with fascination, as if he were witnessing something sinful and forbidden. In the silence we could hear the children in the next yard calling and squealing to each other.

I tisked with scorn. "God, I can't believe how dumb you are. All the kids do it. That's what they're talking about. Didn't you *know*?"

He remained silent with a look of queasy stoicism.

"You keep doing it like this, and pretty soon it starts to feel real good. That's when it shoots out."

"It *shoots* out?"

"Yeah." I made a rasping noise with my lips and traced the arc of a trajectory with my finger, landing on his lap.

"Gross!" He drew away in disgust.

"It doesn't feel gross when you're doing it. It feels good."

"How does it feel? Sort of tickle?"

"I can't describe it. It...it's just the best feeling in the world. There's nothing in the world like it. Nothing even comes close." Then with a suggestive grin I added, "Why don't you try it?"

He shook his head and backed away a little. "No way. Forget it." He looked shocked and embarrassed, even slightly sick – and I felt a twinge of cruel delight.

"Do it tonight in the shower," I urged confidentially. "No one can see you."

"No way. I'm not a sissy like you are."

"What do you mean? Everyone does it. Besides...I thought

you said you did it, too."

"Not like that," he said in a last desperate attempt to regain his dignity. "I do it different."

"Sure you so...."

"If you don't believe me, I'm leaving."

"Don't worry, I believe you. Who said I didn't believe you?" But the look on my face must have clearly indicated skepticism, for his expression turned defiant. "Okay, Bobby, forget it. I was just needling you. Come on, let's read these comics. Just like the old days."

"All right."

2

That night as I sat on my bed, Bobby came running from the bathroom where he'd been taking a shower. With a look of wild joy on his face, he came bounding over to me like a playful puppy, almost bowling me over in his exuberance. Dancing, laughing, he threw playful punches at my face, slapping and pounding my back so happily that I had to fight him off.

"So you did it, huh?" I said in a low voice.

He denied it vehemently, but his attitude gave him away. He couldn't keep from jumping up and down.

I pushed him away. "Cut it out." Then I asked in a whisper, "How did it feel?"

"Great!" he shouted. Then in an excited whisper he described how he'd panicked initially at the onset of the strange new feeling, but remembering my words, had continued on until he'd been overwhelmed by the most delicious feeling in the world.

"You should have seen the shower wall! But I didn't even care!"

In his zeal he began illustrating by pumping his fist furiously in front of his pelvis.

"Stop it!" I hissed. "What if someone sees you?"

"Ooops!" He slapped a hand over his mouth and put on a comically contrite look.

"Nothing in the world feels as good, right?"

"Yeah." After he calmed down, he began to talk seriously about certain dreams he'd been having for the past several months. Though he couldn't quite remember their contents, he did have vague, half-forgotten memories of melting bliss. That was what his experience in the shower had reminded him of, and he'd felt an eerie sensation of recapturing that dream feeling.

"It's called a wet dream," I said. "You were coming in your sleep even before you knew what coming was."

"Why does that happen?"

"The pressure builds up if you don't let it out every now and then. It's nature's way of relieving you."

"I always felt a little scared. I didn't even realize I was wetting my pants. It was always dry in the morning."

"At first not much comes out. Then more and more does."

"How come you know so much?"

"I read it in a book called *What Every Boy Should Know*. That book tells you everything. And it's right in the school library, too. Me and Jack are always peeking into it."

"Is that where you learned about beating off?"

"No. I discovered that by accident one day."

"Guy, where do you usually do it?"

"Right here on the bed. About where you're lying."

He quickly shifted away from the spot and I laughed. Then he asked me with a straight face:

"What do you do with your come?"

"When I'm ready to come I roll to the side of the bed and do it onto the floor."

He glanced downward.

"Don't worry, I always clean it up."

"If you do it tonight, be sure and wake me up. That way I can jump out of the way when you're ready to shoot."

"Get lost!"

He laughed and jumped over to his cot. He imitated the motions of jerking off frantically, his face contorted like a monkey's, his throat emitting simian grunts.

From that night on, Bobby's quick pantomime of a jerk-off became a secret signal between us. We did it at each other whenever we thought no one was watching – in the hallway, in the living room, outside. It became a symbol of our giddy, shared joy. And when we were safely unseen, we attacked each other

137

with the gesture, making sputtering noises with our mouths, dirtying each other with the imaginary ejaculate, and afterwards breaking down into helpless, howling laughter, giggling until our sides ached. No one could guess why we were acting so strangely.

Whenever Bobby returned from a trip to the bathroom, I accused him of beating off. He did the same to me. At first we both denied it, but then confessed that the thought of being suspected of it only made us want to do it.

On the fourth day of his visit, we went to see a movie at the Sunnyside Mall. We were sitting in our seats waiting for the feature to start. I was feeling bored and restless, not at all interested in the movie, and I could tell that Bobby, too, had other things on his mind. We fell silent for a long time. Then suddenly we looked into each other's eyes and smiled. Not a word was exchanged. As if at a pre-arranged signal, we rose to our feet and walked up the aisle, back toward the men's room. By the time we got there we were both skipping, barely able to contain our excitement.

The men's room was completely empty, and we took two stalls, side by side.

I'd done it often enough alone in here, but there was something about Bobby's physical proximity that heightened my excitement this time. I was acutely aware of him in the next stall like a twin or alter-ego. His sneakers and a bit of pant leg were visible in the lower gap of the partition between us.

"Are your pants down?" I called to him softly.

"No."

"What are you waiting for, damn it?"

I heard the rustle of his pants dropping to the floor, the clink of his belt buckle hitting the tile.

"Okay, I'm ready." His voice echoed slightly in the high-ceilinged restroom.

"Are your briefs off, too?"

"Yes! I'm sitting here buck naked, with a hard-on fit to bust!" His voice trembled, though it was kept discretely low. "What about *you*?"

"I've *been* ready." Indeed I was already fondling myself.

"I can't believe we're doing this, can you?" he whispered. "This is crazy. What if someone came in just now?"

"They wouldn't know what's going on – unless they can see through walls. What are you afraid of?"

I could hear faint sounds from outside, but the roaring in my ears dimmed it out. The speakers installed inside the men's room suddenly crackled into life; the feature was starting, but we didn't care. I heard Bobby smother a giggle, then catch his breath.

It grew silent but for the sound of our breathing – breathing interrupted by our mischievous giggles. I listened to the sighs and catches in Bobby's breaths, timing my own beat to the tiny slaps I could hear whenever his fist hit his groin. It was soon hitting in a steady rhythm. I felt as if we were mentally linked, caught in the same psychic web, our two separate pleasures becoming one. The heightened intensity of the moment made the pleasure almost excruciatingly sweet.

Then I heard a quick gasp as he sucked in his breath. After what seemed a long, tension-filled interval, I saw, accompanied by the sound of his grunt, the sudden quivering appearance on the floor of the adjacent stall of a small white gob...then another, another – like drops of hot tallow from a candle someone was shaking.

At that sight, I felt my vision get blurred. A heartbeat later, my own offering, identical to Bobby's in every way, joined the floor down between my feet. My heart was pounding furiously, as if I'd just run a sprint. As I tried to catch my breath, I could hear Bobby on the other side of the partition breathing just as hard, a staccato soughing punctuated by the catch of nervous laughter. Amazed at what we'd just done, I gazed down at the irrefutable evidence that Bobby and I were one: we had done the same thing, had felt the same ecstasy at almost the very same moment. And the scattered drops of white on the floor were the perfect seal to our boyhood bond.

3

It was the last night of Bobby's stay. We were talking about what we'd done at the theater.

"I can't believe we actually did that, can you?"

"We would probably be locked away if they found out."

"Who's gonna find out?"

He was sitting cross-legged on his cot with his back against the wall, and I could tell he was aroused. I could see the thick lump of his erection under his pajama bottoms, a hardness like a jackknife. I wondered if he realized how obvious it was. Despite myself, I found my glance stealing downward at his crotch, and he, noting the direction of my glance, brought his knees up in embarrassment.

Inevitably, we found ourselves growing keenly aware of each other's excitement. I saw a trapped look come into his eyes and he began to stammer and swallow a lot. I tried to ignore it even though I knew exactly what it signified. And his excitement seemed to fuel my own.

I grew dizzy from the desire to masturbate yet attempted to turn my thoughts elsewhere, trying to dampen the urge, hoping desperately that it would go away. And I knew he was probably feeling the same thing. The tension built as this mutual awareness tickled our arousal to greater heights. It became almost a competition, an endurance contest. Neither of us wanted to admit to the urge. I was waiting for him to weaken and give in, and with a guilty look on his face find some excuse to go to the bathroom... earning my knowing grin – the grin of a victor for the vanquished.

I knew it wouldn't be long now. He had a troubled look on his face. A faint aroma of semen wafted in the air, and I didn't know if it was from him or me. It made me slightly queasy. Then, his eyes glowing, he swallowed hard.

"I have to use the bathroom," he muttered suddenly, getting to his feet.

I grinned.

"It's not what you think," he said. "I really do have to go."

"Sure you do," I said pointedly. "You'd better *go* before you do it in your pants."

His hand was resting on his crotch, unsuccessfully trying to hide the mound thrusting up beneath his pajamas.

"It's not that," he insisted, dropping down to his knees, then onto his stomach, hiding it. "That's all you ever think about." He sounded peeved.

"Why don't you just admit it?" I pressed. "You wanted to beat off, right?"

140

"Why don't *you* admit it?" His ears were turning red.

I stared at him then made motions of a boy beating off. He kicked me in the leg. For a long moment we were both silent. When he finally spoke, his voice was little more than a croak.

"Listen, I don't want to talk about it, okay?"

I looked at him. "Maybe you wanna do it right here?"

He flushed.

I grinned at his discomfort then went on: "Why are you afraid to admit it, Bobby? I know what you wanted to do just now. You really felt like doing it, didn't you?"

"So what if I did? Didn't you?"

"Me?"

"Yeah, you. Didn't you feel like it?"

I felt my ears burn.

"You probably wanna do it right now," he said.

I felt as if I were at the start of a roller coaster ride, inching slowly up to the top of the first big hump where the roller coaster is poised briefly, almost at a complete stop, just before the steep, rushing, mind-numbing decline. The roaring in my ears wouldn't go away. My voice sounded funny as I heard myself say:

"Okay, then, I'll do it if you do it."

He looked at me in surprise. "What, here?"

"Yeah. What's wrong with that?" Emboldened by the way he flushed scarlet, I pressed on, "Come on, how about it?"

He remained silent. A doubtful look crossed his face. I changed my tactic to one I knew would have a greater effect. "Ah, you're just chicken, that's all."

His face colored some more and I felt my own excitement rise.

"I should have known you'd be too scared," I taunted.

"I'm not, either!"

"You are!"

"I'll do it *if*..." He looked up. "...if you go first. How's that?"

I felt my scalp prickle. The thought of seeing Bobby naked – and not just naked, but with an erection – was getting me excited.

I'd never seen another boy's hard-on, though I'd often noticed the semi-rigid state of some of the boys in the PE showers – a condition which, given the intimacy of the situation, probably

couldn't be helped. Such teasing intimations had only made me yearn to see a boy's full erection. My stomach felt heavy and my knees were weak and trembly.

It seemed a long time passed before either of us spoke.

Finally, in a strained, weak voice I said, "How about if we do it together?" I shot a silly grin at him.

Looking a little scared, he nodded.

For a few moments we felt weighed down by the heaviness of our decision, unable to say or do anything.

"Well?"

Not wishing to appear scared myself, I initiated the action. Getting to my knees, I slipped my t-shirt over my head, then hesitated with my hand on my pajama bottoms, waiting for him to follow suit.

"Do I have to take my t-shirt off?" he asked.

"Yes." I knew that for him, baring his chest was a major hurdle of inhibition.

Self-consciously, with an expression of reluctance, he slipped out of his t-shirt, then waited a moment, scratching at a spot just below his left nipple.

"Well?" I said, suddenly nervous myself. "What are you waiting for?"

"I'm not going till you go."

"We'll do it together, then."

Our hands hovered uncertainly about the waist bands of our pajamas. Then, stealing shy glances at each other, we slid our pajamas down and stood bashfully before each other clad only in our white cotton briefs. We snickered nervously, neither willing to take the final step – even though our mutual excitement was outlined in bold diagonal relief under our shorts, only held in check by the elastic waist bands.

"Go ahead," I said breathlessly.

"No, you go. You're first."

"Chicken."

"You're chicken. It was your idea."

"At the same time, then."

"All right."

"One... two... three... go!"

As if racing, we wriggled out of our briefs, kicked them away and straightened up again. At first we both found it difficult

to look at one another, to gaze directly at what most drew our attention. Yet neither did we make any attempt to cover up our nakedness. Now that the last barriers of modesty had been removed, we were struck dumb with shyness.

There was a special feeling of intimacy in seeing him naked now, and it was quite different from watching a classmate in PE. In the locker room or the showers, nudity was taken for granted. But here in the privacy of my bedroom another boy's body became also imbued with the 'idea' of nakedness, a condition necessary for intimacy; baring your genitals was the prelude to the most private acts a boy could perform: bathing, defecation, or masturbation.

"Well?"

I thought his penis was the biggest one I'd ever seen in my life, and felt my chest shiver. At the same time I was relieved to see that it looked so much like my own – even down to the swollen veins. It was just as I'd imagined it.

Poking up flat against his stomach, its bulging glans was glowing a deep reddish purple. At the base of the shaft was a wispy patch of light brown hair much sparser than my own. And hugging the groin tightly were the balls, small and close together, almost as if enclosed in a single sac. A few isolated hairs poked out from them.

My mind was in a daze. I felt light-headed, as if all this were happening in a dream... in some naughty daydream as I sat doodling at my school desk or reclining in my backyard hammock.

"You ever notice how much alike everyone looks?" I said. "I mean, alike in a way, but different in a way."

"Yeah. There's a guy named Mason in my class whose dick is shaped a little weird."

"How do you mean?"

"It's curved a little. All the guys make fun of it behind his back."

I laughed.

"Hey, Guy, is it okay if I touch yours for just a second? I just want to know how it feels."

"Go ahead."

Shyly, he reached out his hand and touched me. At the brush of his finger there was a twitch. We both giggled.

"I can't help it." Under our staring eyes, I felt myself swell up even bigger and stretch to the limit.

Giggling nervously, he continued his exploration. With his mouth slightly open, he traced a vein with his finger. I felt a faint tickle and shut my eyes. When I opened them again he had shifted around, kneeling to examine me closely, his face lowered in eager investigation.

"If you don't watch it," I laughed, "you're gonna get it right in the face!"

"You'd better not!" He jerked his head back, but then brought it cautiously forward to continue his fascinated study.

After a moment I spoke up. "Now let me see yours."

In his turn, he lay back, submitting himself to my exploration. His penis had gone a little soft, but at my first touch, it swelled out again, stiffening with a series of short, quick jerks. I rubbed the glans, marvelling at its smooth velvety feel.

"Hey! Don't do that."

It was slightly damp and warm, and I noticed for the first time a tiny clear drop of liquid quivering like a dewdrop on the very tip.

"What's this?"

Curiously I touched it, thinking it was a drop of urine, but when I withdrew my finger it clung and stretched out, following my movements like an elastic goo. I'd never noticed it before on my own.

"Stop it," he said breathlessly.

"Why?"

"You know."

I flushed. Then, to get over the awkward pause by turning it into a joke, I grasped his shaft and began pumping.

"Is this how you do it?"

My heart was pounding so hard I could barely hear my own voice. The feel of Bobby's hardness in my palm was exciting me beyond anything I'd ever felt before. It was a curious, reversed sensation; the familiar jogging grip in my hand, but with no corresponding visceral response of my own. It was a telescoped, remote excitement, knowing only with my mind what my touches were doing to him.

"Don't."

His face looked flushed and troubled. He shut his eyes and

his breathing became disturbed.

I stopped but kept my hand where it was.

"I said cut it out."

I felt his hand push mine firmly away.

"Then touch me again," I commanded in a strange, broken voice.

His startled look showed that he immediately understood the urgency of my request.

Seeing him hesitate, I urged, "Come on." Taking his hand I placed it on my penis, felt it shy back. Then I closed my eyes as I felt the fingers delicately place themselves into position.

The movement was almost imperceptible at first.

"Like this?"

I nodded. "Harder."

My command was obeyed. To my delight I felt him stroke me briskly with the same motions of the wrist, the identical encirclement of the fingers, the exact rhythm I myself employed. The same information had mysteriously been transmitted to each of us through nature's magical network... without the aid of human communication.

A clump of resistance seemed to melt away as my pleasurable sensations grew. I became a fawning slave to his stroking hand. All the muscles in my body went limp and slack, but like distant peaks being tinted by the dawning sun, separately grew tense.

My resistance broke down; I gave voice to my desire, begging softly: "Take me all the way."

I felt the hand stop.

"Don't stop!" I almost barked, and felt the jog again, the good feel of the jog, and I didn't resist, I couldn't resist, I let go.

"Oh."

Arching my back, clenching my toes, I bucked my pelvis hard against his fist.

Soft warmth kissed my chin... my chest... my cheek....

I lay trembling, listening silently to the repercussions still echoing within my body. When I opened my eyes and turned to look at him, I saw the uneasy look on his face.

"It's okay," I reassured him, "don't worry."

"It's not that..." He was gazing at my body as if seeing it for the first time, a little scared. The expression on his face was

that of a boy ready to crumple into tears.

Suddenly he backed away and wordlessly, without looking at me, knelt on the floor and began stroking his penis furiously. He bit his lower lip with an intent look of concentration on his face. I took note of the subtle way he pumped his hips to accentuate the pleasure of his hand's caresses. Quickly his face softened into a pouty moue. The racing speed of his hand became positively comical. He whimpered, grunted, bucked.

With tiny slapping sounds, a scattering of white islands materialized before him, dotting the floorboards, sprinkled out for quite a distance.

After a moment, he turned to look at me and our eyes met. We were both a little shame-faced, but rather than covering up the awkward moment with jokes, we remained silent. I jerked out some tissues from the box at my bedside and handed him the box. Wordlessly, almost grimly, we began cleaning up our messes.

Andrew O'Hare

Padraig

from *Green Eyes* (Gay Men's Press, 2001)

Padraig and I had just been mutual lust, no emotion involved. We had stumbled into it almost by accident when we were fourteen. Back in school a couple of days after the end of the summer holidays and no one had really settled into the routine as yet. Everyone including the teachers was still getting to know new faces, different classrooms, changed schedules, plus the anticlimax of being locked up again Monday to Friday, nine to four. Renovations to the wood and metalwork department were as yet incomplete, so our class had nowhere to go during the last class period of the day. Luck or bad judgement placed the two or us at the front of the queue outside the door. Mr Swallow grabbed us as he came out of the noise and the dust. "You two! Stay here. The rest of you outside. No woodwork today."

"Please Sir, can we go home then?" from somewhere safely at the rear.

"Those who live locally or come to school on bikes may go now. The rest of you will just have to wait on the usual buses."

"Quietly," in a vain attempt to quell the clatter of feet on the stairs. "You two come with me!"

We followed down the stairs past the Art Room to the Library and the stationery store beside it. When he opened the door and turned on the light we saw stacks of boxes and bare shelves. "Empty all these boxes and put the books neatly on the shelves, make sure you keep all the same sizes and types together" – turning to go – "If you do a good job I'll see that you are this year's stationery and library monitors."

"Thank you, Sir," we chorused as the swing-loaded door closed us in the windowless room.

"I hope we do get the monitors' job," Padraig removing

his blazer.

"Yeah, you get to miss some lessons," I agreed. "If I climb up you can pass them to me," as we set to ripping tops off boxes.

"You'll want to put the smallest ones on the top, Pat?"

"Yeah, let's sort them into piles first."

"Okay."

The room wasn't very big though it was quite high so we tended to bump into each other as we ripped and shoved boxes around. It was also very warm and my blazer soon joined Padraig's on the bottom shelf. All the boxes opened and books sorted Padraig climbed up two shelves and turning awkwardly straddled a corner, feet well apart. His crotch was level with my eyes each time I straightened to pass a pile of books. It wasn't long before my back unused to all the bendings and straightening began to protest.

"God. Sorry but I'll have to stop for a minute," holding my back, eyes glued to his zipper.

"Okay, I need to move some of these along a bit," holding on with one hand and leaning towards me as he rearranged the stacks. I could see the outline of his cock quite clearly. As he abruptly regained his position I noticed that it seemed to be getting bigger. My own was beginning to react and I felt quite breathless. My heart was thudding away and my mouth was unaccountably dry.

"Come on, Shaun, I don't want to be here all fucking day you know." The F word gave me a real twitch. At that time I'd never dared say it out loud.

I couldn't say anything. I know I was beet red. Bending down I passed him a stack of books. Too many all at once. He dropped them. In trying to catch them I inadvertently rubbed my hand up the front or his trousers. It just seemed to stick there. Like a magnet to iron.

My hand on another boy's cock. Padraig didn't say anything, didn't do anything, except continue to grow under my hand. Looking up at his face I slowly pulled his zipper down and slid my hand inside his trousers. Felt the hard hot flesh more freely through his underwear.

"Wait," he breathed and got down. I thought he was going to go as he moved to the door. Looking out he closed the door again, moved some boxes against it. Turned to me with an

expectant look on his face. Little beads of sweat on his forehead staining his white blond hair almost black. With trembling fingers I undid the top of his trousers and pushed them down. My eyes momentarily level with the protrusion in the briefs. Upright again, I stretched the elastic of the waistband and released his cock as I pushed the briefs down his hairy thighs. I was surprised by the amount of hair on his legs, but didn't really take it in at the time, eyes fixed on his jutting cock. Curious the differences to mine. It had a definite twist to the left whereas mine was straight. When we got round to comparisons at a later date my suspicion that his was a little longer proved correct. There was a definite and clearly defined brown patch on the side of the shaft.

That day there was no talking. I closed my fist round him as he reached out and set me free. We had to steady ourselves with our free hand on each other's shoulder. I could feel that we were both trembling violently. Every time I pushed his foreskin back too hard he jerked his arse back, letting me know that his was too tight to retract completely. He appeared totally surprised that mine went back so far and kept brushing the back edge of the head with his fingertips. I felt him sag at the knees and concentrated my gaze on his cock which was beginning to twitch in my hand. I could feel his balls rising against my fingers on the down stroke. He was making little moaning sounds in his throat. As for me, I was rapidly approaching something which promised to be very special in the way of cumming. I gripped him more firmly and increased the pace, hoping he would take the hint. I'll give him due credit. He then and every other time was quick to follow my lead. I moved as close as I could without losing sight of our flying fists. I couldn't decide which to concentrate on, his twitching cock in my hand or the pressure of his fist round mine. I came first in a stomach-wrenching spasm that induced the little bright stars again, my cum landing on his shirt. Then he came with a gasp and almost completely collapsed at the knees. I trapped most of it in my hand though it tended to ooze between my fingers. Continued to stroke him using his cum as lubrication (I'd never thought of doing that to myself, but promised cock an experiment that same night). My hand was getting tired, but already he was beginning to twitch again. A quick glance at his face showed eyes screwed tight shut and lower lip clenched between his teeth, breath whistling through

his nose. Both his hands were on my shoulders now, holding himself up, and I could see that he was on the point of cumming a second time in as many minutes. It came accompanied by a heartfelt groan. His head falling forward just missing my chin to land on my chest. Thirty seconds later, breathing back to normal, he looked up with a smile, pushing his pelvis forward till our semi-limp sticky cocks touched. That was the first time.

"Shit! You got a hanky?"

"Let's get these books on the fucking shelves."

* * *

After the first time in the storeroom, Padraig and I looked for opportunities to repeat the performance. Not though for a week or so after the first time. I think we were both a bit shy with each other for a few days, but we had obviously done well enough as Mr Swallow did get us the monitor's jobs.

A week or so after the storeroom incident we both got off a music lesson when 'Ould Biddy' discovered that over the summer break our voices had broken and we could no longer sustain a steady note. We were packed off to the library to make a start on indexing the new books and shelving them.

No class in the library. A couple of important visitors in with the deputy Head. Head off sick, so no one monitoring the corridors or loos during class time. As we came to the bottom of the stairs opposite the boys' loos I looked at him and realised that he was having similar thoughts. I nodded towards the loos and he didn't hesitate. Closing the door quietly I bent down and scanned the cubicles for betraying feet. None. Padraig opened the door to the showers, looked in and shook his head. "In there then," I said giving him a push.

"Okay," reaching out to undo my trousers, letting them fall and tugging at my briefs. Me returning the compliment until we were both naked from the waist down. We moved together until our upright cocks were touching. I put my hand down and tried to grip them both at once, Not very successfully but it got us both going. Standing back a little we braced ourselves as we had on the first occasion. He gripped my cock and pushed the foreskin all the way back staring at the bulge revealed, a distinct look of envy on his face. Instead of his cock I took his little balls

in my hand and very gently squeezed and pulled them. This was something I'd recently been experimenting with on myself to some quite good effect. He was a bit uneasy at first but soon got into the spirit and began pulling and squeezing me a bit too enthuiastically. "Yeow," I half whispered half yelped. "Here, here, go easy. Go back to this," and relinquishing his balls I gripped his cock. Instead of rubbing or pulling I gripped hard and started a rhythmic clench and release. Fast and then slow as I felt him begin to twitch. He was more interested in the naked head of mine and taking his hand from my shoulder he held the loose flesh right back and traced the contours of my cockhead with his fingers. The tickling scratching sensation brought me off in about ten seconds. Pushing my hand aside he smeared the cum from his fingers onto his bouncing cock.

I found that by holding him quite loosely my fist slid up and down his shaft. I didn't try to push his foreskin back, aware or how much it was likely to hurt. "Harder, Shaun, harder," through clenched teeth.

Leaving him to brace us both with his hands on my shoulders, I took his balls in my other hand and pulled and squeezed trying to keep in time with the stroking of his nearly boiling cock.

"Right. Faster," he was moaning. "Faster. Harder." I gripped more tightly, pushing back very slightly. "Oooh, oooh, oooh, *shit*," I could feel the pulse of it as his balls contracted up to the base of his cock. I pushed my hand between his legs and tickled the shaft behind his balls.

"Oooh, oooh, don't. Please," but not moving or pushing my hand away. As I watched and continued stroking and tickling he shot right into my little patch of pubic hair above my dick.

"Jesus Christ! Oooh, oooh," as he pulsed again landing a small gob on my belly. His head down on my shoulder. He was trembling all over. "Shit, shit, shit. That was great," looking up, breathing beginning to recover. "Can we do it again?" taking hold of my ever willing cock.

"No, not now, Pat."

"Why not? Nobody's coming. I want to."

"So do I," pulling my clothes up. "How about after school?"

"Lunch time," he insisted. And after school."

"Okay then, we'll take a walk up the back of the football

field at lunch time."

"But there's nowhere to go up there," rearranging his cock inside his trousers, trying to hide the telltale bulge.

"Yes there is," as he checked the urinals and cubicles. "Oh, come on, Pat, no one is going to see you and we've to get these books done."

When we got into the library he began to laugh. "What's the joke then?"

"You've got spunk on your tie," and he fell about.

"You crazy sod, why didn't you tell me?" scrubbing furiously with an already cum-stiff hanky.

Lunch followed one of my favourite subjects, history. Joining the noisy exodus we threaded our way across the tarmac playing area onto the football pitch. The field containing the pitch was three times the size of the playing area which was marked out at the end nearest the school buildings. On the far side of the pitch there was a long overgrown five to six foot high mound running almost the full length of the playing field. Soil and debris left over from the building of the school which had been left on site. It now provided an ideal vantage point for watching games. Beyond, running to the low stone ditch which marked the extent of the school grounds was sufficient space to insert another full playing field.

Munching on our sandwiches we gradually left the screaming hordes behind. Although the stone ditch was barely eighteen inches high, there was at one corner a drop of about three feet into the next field. When we jumped down only our heads would have been visible to anyone coming from the direction of the school. Looking the other way, there were just small fields, no buildings or roads.

"See!' as we faced towards the school. "You keep watch and I'll do you," sitting on a lump of granite with my back to the wall. Fumbling with his trousers. "Then we'll swop," pushing his trousers and briefs down to his ankles. Running my hands slowly up the inside of his extremely hairy legs. As my hands travelled upwards so his semi-recumbent cock reared its head. I stopped just under his balls and transferred my left hand to his arse, making him jump.

"What are you doing?" buttocks clenching under my hand.

"Just keep your eyes open, Pat," stroking the curve of his

arse with my palm and lightly pressing the solid root behind his ball sack. It was fascinating to watch from such close range as his balls contracted and relaxed. Everytime his arse clenched his cock jerked, the just visible slit in the head was beaded with a little clear liquid, sticky, when I touched it with a finger. Made him jump again.

"Jesus, Shaun, DO IT. DO IT," taking a hand from the wall where he was bracing himself at an angle and grabbing his cock in frustration.

"Leave off," knocking his hand away. Gripping him full fisted and reaching between his legs to hold his bells. Milking him. Stroking, squeezing and relaxing my hold all at the same time. I'd never seen a cock from such a close viewpoint before and was totally involved in watching it to such an extent that I almost didn't move quickly enough when he twitched, groaned and came. Shooting over my shoulder onto the wall. He couldn't take the continued stroking. "Stop, Shaun" – pushing my hands away. "Holy Shit" – collapsing bare-arsed on the ground beside me. Sweat trickling down his face.

"Don't have a heart attack" I advised, standing to keep watch in the direction of school. Plenty of noise, but no one in sight. Cock had gotten trapped down the leg of my trousers whilst I was bringing Padraig off and the relief when he had recovered enough to undo my clothes and release it was almost sufficient in itself to bring me off as the cool air swirled round my balls.

"Wait, Pat, wait," holding his hand away. "Just a second," letting the tension abate slightly. "Okay, now, Pat, but SLOWLY." I deliberately did not look down as I normally do (or watch myself in a mirror), just gave myself over to the sensations. He wasn't doing it quite right, his grip was too high on the shaft and his rhythm was very irregular, but I didn't say anything. I felt divorced from what was happening, yet at the same time it was just about the most intimate moment in my life so far. I couldn't hold off for long. Muttering through clenched teeth, "Cumming, cumming," my knees started to tremble and I felt myself shoot into the open air.

"Phew," sinking down beside him and watching as he rubbed his sticky fingers through the grass. Trousers still round his ankles.

"Shaun?" he looked at me and down to my wilting cock "Why does your thing go back so far?"

"I just forced it one day," leaning against the wall and rolling the loose flesh back. "And out popped his head."

"Mine's too sore," reclining against the wall looking moody.

"Try it now while it's soft," I suggested sagely.

"It always hurts," he protested, shrivelling up even further.

"No, it won't always," and I leant over taking him in my hand. "Anyway, my Dad says you can get it fixed if it won't go back."

A mixture of shock and fright bugged his eyes and turned his face white. "You TOLD your DAD about..."

"'Do you think I'm fucking thick or something," pulling him down as he made to rise. "I asked him last year and he explained the whole thing."

"Yeah, yeah, yeah. You asked your Dad," disbelief in his voice. "Jesus, my ould fella would beat the shit out of me if I mentioned it," subsiding on the stone again. "What did you say? What did he say?" He glared at me. "You're having me on" – insistent. "Nobody asks their Da things like that!"

"You don't want to believe me. That's okay." I shrugged. "Why should I lie to you? We went for a walk on the beach and he told me. About spunk, babies, wanking and all that." I shrugged again. "And about tight skin on your dick." I pulled my foreskin back slowly. "Mine was just as sore as yours, but the skin stretches as you do it more and more," reaching over to him again.

"You'll stop if I tell you?" through tight lips.

"Surely." He really was tight, and, although he had shrunk almost to the point of non-existence the head was still too large to permit it to come all the way through the hole. It did though, come further than before. It looked a bit odd, even silly, as if it had a belt tied round its middle.

"No more. Stop," seizing my wrist. "Oooo, it's never come that far," looking in surprise at the half-visible bluish tip.

"You're probably better doing it for yourself," easing the sheath back over the bulb. Standing up and turning back towards the school. "Come on, we'd better get back before the bell goes."

"Are we coming back here after school?" – climbing into the playing field.

"They don't like you hanging around afterwards, you know that."

"But we agreed!"

"We can find somewhere else."

He ran and kicked a ball rolling towards us, then returned to me.

"Do you have to go straight home?" He shook his head. "Suppose we walk out the bankhead from the harbour?"

"Okay then," bouncing off towards the scrum. "You playing?"

"Nah, see you later," waving a hand and heading towards the school. I needed a pee.

* * *

Concealed by the long bracken which covered the cliffs on the Newcastle side of the harbour, I encouraged him to show me how he wanked himself off. As he lay back on the ground I opened his shirt, stroked his chest and tummy. "Nuts. Hold my nuts." Propping myself on an elbow I took his balls in my hand and kneading them very gently watched, my eyes flicking from his face to his flying fist. His rhythm varied only in that the speed increased as he came to the point. Just before he came he changed hands, bringing himself off with the left and clutching the back of my neck with his right.

"Oooh fuck. I think I'm going to die," a couple of tears leaked down his cheeks. "Shit, shit, shit" – as the last convulsions of his stomach muscles seemed to pulse in time with the gobs of white landing on his chest and belly. I cleaned him up as he regained his breath and composure.

Suddenly he pushed me flat. "Come on let me see you do it," pulling at my trousers as I raised my arse from the ground. "Can I touch you?" as I lay back.

"Same as I did for you. But don't pull too hard," as he grabbed for my balls. I lay for a few seconds savouring the sensation of my balls being fondled and that of cock coming to full rigidity before wrapping just index finger and thumb round the shaft behind the head and pushing down, releasing the head into the air. My hand contacting his at the bottom of the stroke. I teased myself as usual with half a dozen fast tight strokes

followed either by two or three slow loose ones or stopping at the bottom of the stroke and holding the skin taut for a few seconds. The slow strokes and the stops were soon discarded, The thumb and forefinger replaced by a full tight fist.

"Keep going for fuck's sake." His hand had become motionless as he watched.

"Sorry," squeezing hard. That one I didn't mind as it seemed to impel the spunk up the shaft with extra speed. I raised my head, opened my eyes in time to see the head pulse and shoot forth a continuous thick stream of white, which landed on my belly button.

"Oooh," dropping my head back.

"Good one." I got the impression that he was of more than half a mind to try for a repeat, as he released my balls with marked reluctance when I sat up.

"Come on, Pat." My hanky was one sticky ball but would have to do. "Don't know about you but I'm starved."

We parted at the bottom or Newry Street where he lived. "See you tomorrow," and I headed along Newcastle Street towards home.

* * *

That set the pattern of our school life (more or less) for the next two years. There were interruptions of course, sickness on the part of one of us, school holidays, weekends. It became an unwritten rule that we confined our sexploits to school or on the way home. A number of incidents (quite apart from the beginning) remain vivid in my memory. Some weeks after we started I noticed one morning that he looked miserable, uncomfortable, yet excited at the same time. As was not unusual we couldn't find the time before lunch. Yet walking up the playing field he kept lagging behind.

"What's the matter?" as I reached the wall and realised that he'd come to a halt some five or six yards back.

"I can't," face reddening.

"What was that?" not quite catching what he'd said.

"I said, I can't," sounding near to tears.

"What's the matter?" I repeated. "Come on, tell me."

Keeping his head down he came over and carefully climbed

down into the field; normally we both jumped. "It's split and it hurts something awful."

"Well, show me then." He was remarkably reluctant.

"For Christ's sake, Pat, I won't touch it."

Grimacing he undid his pants and dropped them. Gingerly he pulled the briefs away from his stomach and lowered them to his knees. Hooked a finger under his limp dick and lifted it up. Hunkering down I looked closely at the swollen blood-streaked flesh. "How did you do that?"

Tears were dripping off his nose. "I've been trying to get it back for weeks," rubbing his sleeve across his face. "Like yours. I had a wank in the bath before I went to bed last night," sniffing furiously. "After, it was really soft so I had another shot at it when I got into bed" – raising his head – "and it just peeled right back" – looking at me. "You didn't say what it would feel like. It got so hard so quick. I couldn't get it back over the head" – really miserable now. "It just split. Jesus I thought it was going to burst," tears again. "Now look at it. I'll have to go to the doctor," he shivered. ''My Da will kill me. What am I going to do?"

"Don't be so fucking stupid, Pat," standing up. "I told you, the same thing happened to me, and my Dad told me it happens to lots of boys. You just have to keep it clean and leave it alone for a couple of weeks."

"Two weeks," his voice cracking. "Two fucking weeks!"

I had to laugh at the alarm on his face. "You'll find other ways, Pat," undoing my trousers. "If you can't use yours you can always borrow mine."

Sometime after that when he wasn't experiencing so much trouble I brought him off during a class in the Science Lab. We were right at the back perched on those high stools behind the workbench and I could see that he had a hard on. Whilst he was working with the microscope I slid my right hand into his left-hand pants pocket, knowing that he had ripped the bottom out so that he had more freedom to play without attracting too much attention. "Piss off, Shaun," he mutttered.

"Did you say something, Mr Cunningham?"

"No, Miss." I'd a firm hold on his cock by then and he daren't move "Well, pay attention then."

She droned on about cell structure or something as I

squeezed, and he had to remain expressionless as I milked him to explosion. I watched him try and keep his cool as his cock surged in my hand and I felt the stickiness on my palm. He was pretty good – red, but pretty good. As we were leaving at the end of the class: "I'll fucking get you for that, McKenna. I swear it."

The same week he did indeed 'get me'. On the bus. With forty other kids present. There were always mock fights on the way home and he trapped me in the corner of the back seat, ducking under my arms and clawing my zip down. No one took the slightest notice. Once he'd succeeded, despite my struggles, in getting my cock out, the only option left to me was to prevent him sitting up and leaving me open to anyone who chanced to look. He obliged me with a very quick (painfully quick) wank, catching most of it on his hand and rubbing it off on the seat cushion between my legs. He even went so far as to partially tuck me away again before I let go the seat back in front and he could sit up.

"Told you," holding his school bag in front of distended trousers as he rose to get off. Leaving me to scramble myself back to decency before anyone looked.

Apart from a few episodes like that luck must have been with us. No one ever appeared to twig what was going on. Two years later when we left school the whole thing just died. Oh we saw each other. Kilkeel is a small town. Somehow completing school seemed to draw a line under the whole thing. I saw him at the pictures occasionally; usually he was in the company of some girl or other. We would raise a hand or say "Hi" and that was that.

Did he have any regrets? At the time I couldn't see any reason why he should. I know the only regret I had was once again being thrown back on my own resources.

Robin Yeo

Misunderstandings

from *The Long Way Home*, an unfinished novel

The first few weeks of the new year, for Nicholas, revolved arosund his visits to the hospital. These soon fell into a regular routine – Monday and Wednesday after school, and either Saturday or Sunday afternoon. Adrian's mother, of course, visited every day, but she had always left by the time Nicholas arrived. Pete went regularly to see Adrian too, but they generally arranged alternate days, as one visitor at a time was easier for Adrian, and it was nice for him to see one or the other of them most days.

The doctors' confidence in Adrian's recovery turned out to be justified. Almost every time Nicholas saw him he was a little better than the time before, even if his progress seemed at first painfully slow. On New Year's Day, when Nicholas went to the hospital for the second time, he sensed already that Adrian was a little more alive inside all the bandages. It was still a great effort for him to try and communicate, and a couple of attempted words was all he could manage, but his hand was a little less limp when Nicholas held it, and the one unbandaged eye focused that much more steadily.

School started a few days into January, and the same day Adrian's dad flew back to Aden as planned. Nicholas had given little thought to the new term, and was quite surprised to find that Adrian's accident was not only a major topic of conversation, but also got special mention from the head in school assembly, along with a prayer for Adrian's recovery. Road safety classes, which had fallen into abeyance, were eagerly resumed.

His friendship with the younger boy, which had threatened to be a source of embarrassment for Nicholas in the weeks before Christmas, now acquired an unchallenged legitimacy. It was

almost a kind of prestige for Nicholas to be associated with the famous accident victim. If Kevin or one of the other boys in his class asked him now how Treadgold was, it was not with a suggestive wink but with an apparently genuine concern.

Adrian was soon able to indicate that he liked to hear about everything that was going on, even though he still found it difficult to say more than the odd word. Pete, being in the same class as Adrian, could fill him in better than Nicholas could about things of interest to him at school, so Nicholas found himself telling Adrian all kinds of things from books he was reading, the latest news on the excavation, what he'd seen on television, and what was going on at home. Adrian was always pleased to hear what Nicholas's mum had to say, and she often had some message or other to relay through her son. Once a week she would drop into the hospital herself to say hello, after coming into town for her teaching, and Nicholas could tell that she had a cheering effect on his friend, which was by no means always the case with his own mother's visits.

Towards the end of January, Adrian's speech started returning by leaps and bounds. The bandages were off his head now, and his face was beginning to regain its proper features. Both legs were still in plaster, but he was encouraged to hobble out of bed and around the ward with a pair of crutches. One Wednesday afternoon, Nicholas suddenly found that he no longer had to talk *to* Adrian, he could talk *with* +him again at last.

"You know what the... doctor said to me... this morning," Adrian asked?

"No, tell me!"

"He said... I got off lightly... I was... very lucky."

Nicholas nodded. "I know," he said. They told your mum it could have been much worse."

"Sometimes... if you've hurt... your head... you can't talk properly again... for years... perhaps never," Adrian explained.

"You're talking so much better already. It's fabulous to see you getting on so well." Nicholas smiled.

"I always knew... right from the start... when everything was black... that I was going to be alright... ," Adrian continued. "I remember everything you said to me... when I couldn't speak properly... and everything the others said to me... Pete, and mother, and the nurses...You were the best, though... it was a

bit like climbing a rope... I just had to cling on... and pull myself up..."

"It was terrible the first time I saw you," Nicholas admitted. "You were a pretty ghastly sight. I had to keep saying to myself that the real Adrian was in there alright, somewhere inside, and I just had to keep trying to connect with you."

"I could... feel that," Adrian said. "Even when... you weren't here... I could hear your voice... in my head... It's funny though... I can't remember anything... about the accident... or... having a bicycle. I can't remember... Christmas... at all."

* * *

This visit was a kind of watershed for Nicholas. Up to then he'd felt he had to keep on willing Adrian to get better, and this effort had been the constant focus of his energies. Now there could be no more doubt about Adrian's recovery, it was only a matter of time. Even if it did take a year or more to get quite over his physical injuries, as the doctors seemed to think, the main thing was that Adrian's mind was unimpaired, that he was out of bed and getting back into the routines of life — above all, for Nicholas, that he and Adrian could pick up the threads of their friendship and go forward together.

But Adrian's accident, and all that had happened around it, had brought a subtle change in their relationship. Up till now this change had been only a dim awareness, which the worry over his friend had pushed to the back of Nicholas's mind. There had been no time to think about himself. Now that Adrian was so clearly recovering, however, Nicholas began to recover his own composure, too, and he could not deny it – his own world was strangely different.

He cast his mind back to that first anguished visit to the hospital a month ago. At the time, the events of that day had seemed to centre entirely around Adrian, and the grief that Nicholas felt for his injured friend. But looking back on it now, that day had been marked for Nicholas by more than just grief. Two images stuck in his mind, or rather, two particular memories kept returning to him, so vivid and powerful that if he shut his eyes he could almost relive them. The first, of course, was sitting beside Adrian's bed, holding his limp hand and looking into his

hazy unbandaged eye. For all his terror of what might happen to his friend, and no matter how strongly he might have wished this situation had never arisen, that day had opened up a new and more intimate contact with Adrian. He had only held his friend's hand – more or less the only part of another boy's body you were permitted to touch, it seemed, and generally in a still more perfunctory way. But in the special circumstances of Adrian's injury, they had held hands – even been allowed to hold hands – with the tenderness that Nicholas knew was generally forbidden outside of your own family. Visiting Adrian in hospital had come to mean holding hands with him, and Nicholas now realised that he wanted this physical contact with his friend, needed it to continue, even intensify, as a vital part of their relationship.

How strange, then, that later the same day he had found himself in just as unusually intimate a situation with Pete. Not strange, perhaps, at one level – Nicholas had sought to comfort Adrian, and Pete had sought to comfort Nicholas, in a way that was only natural. But if he was honest with himself Nicholas had to admit that this sudden physical intimacy with Pete had been as joyful an experience as his new physical contact with Adrian. He remembered the touch of Pete's arm round his body as they cuddled together, fully dressed, on Pete's bed, every bit as vividly as he recalled the touch of Adrian's hand in his own.

Over this last month Nicholas had seen little of Pete outside of school. Though Adrian's accident had brought them together, they had made a point of visiting him on different days, and could relay any news to one another in the school playground. What with visiting the hospital three times a week, homework to do, and his mind always on Adrian's progress, Nicholas had not got round to visiting Pete again. But in a more relaxed frame of mind at last over Adrian, this idea suddenly seemed an attractive one. He should get together with Pete to celebrate Adrian's recovery.

The next morning Nicholas kept his informal rendezvous with Pete in the playground.

"How's the young man, then?" Pete inquired in his typical breezy manner.

"Oh, he really seemed so much better yesterday. Didn't you think so when you saw him on Tuesday?"

"Sure," Pete agreed. "More like his old self."

The boys smiled warmly at each other, each happy for their friend's recovery.

"I was thinking," Nicholas continued, "if I go and see Adrian on Saturday, maybe I could come round to your place afterwards."

Pete thought for a moment. "Saturday's not so good," he explained. "I usually go to the pictures with my cousin, and then I'll probably go round to his place. We could meet up Sunday, though. I'm not doing anything then."

* * *

Pete was well used to helping smaller boys with their problems, usually nothing more serious than seeing off a playground bully. But he had rarely seen bigger boys in emotional distress, and certainly not been expected to deal with this himself. When Nicholas had broken down at his house after seeing Adrian in hospital, he'd reacted by instinct. His treatment seemed to work well enough, but the result was as surprising to him as it had been to Nicholas. They had only cuddled and stroked each other through their winter clothes. But a physical bond had been established, a connection between one body and another, such as Pete had not known since the closeness with his brother in the distant past. He could sense it whenever he saw Nicholas at school. He wasn't sure at first whether Nicholas sensed it too, his mind was always so fixed on Adrian in hospital. But as Nicholas began to relax a bit, Pete could tell Nicholas also recognised the new intimacy between them.

When Nicholas finally suggested getting together that Sunday, however, Pete felt a little uneasy. There was something about the situation that made him wary, though he couldn't quite put his finger on it. He couldn't claim that Nicholas might take advantage of him — anything that happened between them would undoubtedly be by common consent. It was more to do with Adrian; weren't his interests somehow involved in the matter, and shouldn't his feelings be taken in account? But then sex, if that was what it was about, was something that Adrian definitely didn't take an interest in. It couldn't be any kind of betrayal of Adrian if he and Nicholas were to explore that side

of things together. Once again, something that should be simple seemed to get complicated, and Pete rather wished he could postpone any irrevocable decision.

The next morning, Friday, when Nicholas came over to Pete in the playground to confirm about Sunday, Pete was still apprehensive at inviting Nicholas round without any particular activity in mind. Casting round for something they might do together on a Sunday in February, he suggested they go swimming, leaving it unclear whether Nicholas would come back to his house afterwards.

"Outside the baths at three o'clock, then."

"See you there!"

Nicholas seemed content enough with the arrangement.

* * *

Nicholas's sex life, in so far as it was more than just pleasuring his body, had taken place essentially in his own head. At first, his relationship with Adrian didn't affect the fantasies that accompanied his private pleasure. What struck him, however, while he still denied to himself that his new friendship had anything to do with sex, was how the urgency of sexual release, which had almost frightened him with its force in recent months, seemed to abate to a more comfortable level. In the run-up to Christmas, as Adrian showed he felt the same joy in his company as he felt with Adrian, he had often gone for several days without needing to masturbate.

It was quite different after Adrian's accident. When the initial shock wore off, and sexual feeling returned, he first of all violently repressed his desires. How could he indulge any kind of pleasure when Adrian was there bandaged up in hospital? Then there was a week when the repressed sprang upon him with a vengeance, and he had to masturbate three or four times a day, hardly thinking of anything but the need for orgasm. And finally, just when he felt on a more even keel, there was the dream. He was on a tropical island, with palm trees, blue sky, white sandy beach, just like you sometimes see on a poster. There was a beautiful warm lagoon, crystal clear water with colourful fish swimming all around. And he was under the water, in the warm water, naked, with Adrian and Pete. There was a gentle kind of

pressure in the water that pushed them together, as if they were squeezed vertically up against each other in a deep warm bath. Everything was quite relaxed, peaceful, calm, loving. They all smiled happily at each other, sharing the delicate sensations of skin against skin. Without any mechanical action, the feelings flowed from limbs and fingers, face and breast, down into the centre of each of them, welling up in the most pleasurable zones until a warm gush of release engulfed them all.

It was the wet dream to end all wet dreams! Nicholas could hardly bring himself to accept that he was awake, uncomfortably sticky and urgently needing a hanky to wipe himself. The gulf between imagination and reality made him groan aloud, and he groaned once more as he realised its implications. But if the first time the dream came to him unwilled, the next few nights Nicholas willed it to return. It did return a couple of times, though not nearly so overwhelming as that first time. Nicholas felt terribly deprived, and tried to recapture it as a conscious fantasy. The dream seemed not to like this, and refused to return again.

Nicholas was not so foolish as to imagine in broad daylight that reality could be like his dream. But it did bring home to him, in no uncertain terms, the physical side of his feelings for Adrian. He didn't have to seek with Adrian, he reminded himself, the engulfing orgasm of his dream. Far, far less than that in reality would be worth everything he felt in the dream. But he would have to express his love for Adrian in a physical way, and he was sure Adrian would reciprocate if he found the right way of doing it. Holding hands as they'd done at the hospital was a good start.

As regards Pete, the matter seemed a lot more complicated. Much as he liked Pete, he couldn't pretend that Pete had suddenly acquired an importance in his life at all comparable with Adrian. Yet he had already been more physical with Pete than he had with Adrian, and it was in reality, not just in a dream, that he sensed the connection that had established itself between their bodies. The dream had suggested that there was no contradiction between his feelings for Adrian and his feelings for Pete, not to mention their feelings for one another. This was surely true; they could all be a loving family together, each expressing this love in the appropriate way. Between him and Adrian, he felt sure, the physical side would always be more muted, less directly

sexual. But between him and Pete? Would it be wrong to cultivate with Pete precisely that side of love that was inappropriate with Adrian?

When Nicholas suggested visiting Pete's house the next Sunday, he didn't expect even to repeat the intimacy of his last visit. Pete still underestimated Nicholas's delicacy and his inexperience, and had no real cause for concern. If the visit had gone ahead as Nicholas had proposed, they would have got to know each other rather better, but most likely would both have been very cautious of any phyical expression at this stage. Pete's hasty offer of going swimming, however, made to head off what he feared might be a frontal assault from Nicholas, was almost bound to accelerate the inevitable.

As usual on Sunday afternoons, the pool was crowded with families, and swimming conditions were far from ideal. Neither boy expected to stay very long, or to hang around once they came out of the water. There was no choice but to share a cubicle. Nicholas remembered the first time he'd gone swimming with Adrian, and how their chaste intimacy in the cubicle had subtly confirmed their relationship.

Undressing in the cubicle with Pete, though, was a different matter. Despite their modest observance of the prescribed changing ritual, Nicholas felt the closeness of Pete's body like an electric charge. Changed into their swimming trunks and packing their clothes up to put into a locker, he almost had to resist a force like that in his dream pressing him towards Pete. It wasn't at all like it was with Adrian. Much as Nicholas admired Adrian's physical appearance, it was always the spirit within Adrian's flesh that attracted him. Pete did not embody this quality of beauty, he was not beautiful by any standard, and not at all the kind of boy that the older boys talked of fancying. Just about Nicholas's height, he had large bones, a stocky musculature, and an adequate cover of fat under his skin – as against Nicholas's own rather skeletal self-image. Yet it was this very fleshiness of Pete's that Nicholas was drawn towards, and had to stop himself from reaching out and feeling.

The two friends had as much fun in the water as was possible on a crowded Sunday, but after less than half an hour they were ready to call it a day. When they padded back into the changing-room Nicholas felt a sinking feeling in his stomach.

166

He knew something was about to happen, and his tense anticipation was mixed with a certain dread.

As they towelled themselves dry, and Nicholas shivered a little, Pete fell unusually quiet. Without his flow of cheery banter Nicholas felt even more self-conscious; there was simply nothing to take his mind off Pete's body, almost naked and only inches away. A vicious circle of embarrassment developed, and Nicholas felt the blood flowing simultaneously to his face and his groin. Pete noticed the first, and seemed to deduce the second while Nicholas still sought to conceal it. His serious look made a rare breakthrough, and he spoke with the same gentleness Nicholas remembered from the day they'd first seen Adrian in hospital.

"Don't worry," he smiled, more diffidently than usual. "We're all the same, aren't we?"

They were indeed the same in the sense that was bothering Nicholas, even if it showed more conspicuously inside his swimming trunks than against Pete's bulky frame. As before, Nicholas felt a calming power in Pete's quiet tone, which immediately healed his tormenting embarrassment. He raised his eyes to Pete's and let his look reply without words. Pete reached out his hand and touched Nicholas gently on the side.

"You can come back to our place if you like," he said.

Still overcome by his emotions, Nicholas nodded assent.

As they walked through the town, Pete kept up a rather one-sided conversation, while Nicholas tried to sort out an unusual degree of confusion. The anecdote Pete was relaying went in one ear and straight out of the other, while Nicholas heard over and over in his mind the echo of Pete's other, serious voice, and those words he'd said to comfort Nicholas in the changing-room: "We're all the same, aren't we?" It sounded so simple, nothing at all profound. And yet Nicholas felt, without fully understanding why, that with these words Pete had given him a great gift.

Once again on Pete's bed, they let their bodies do the talking. This time the language was rather more intimate, and even newer for Nicholas than for Pete. The dialogue proceeded cautiously, one small step at a time. Fingers explored new areas, asked careful questions, answered by the reflex of a muscle or an inflection of breath. Usually so clumsy at expressing himself – at least, he always felt this – Nicholas found himself more relaxed

in this tremendous new adventure than he would have thought possible. With Pete, there was just nothing to be afraid of. At last they had nothing more to conceal from each other and began to pursue a heightened pleasure. There had to be one small embarrassment, of course, and Nicholas was unable to hold back a very premature orgasm. But for each boy the experience was passionately exciting and enjoyable. Afterwards they lay quietly together without speaking, and when at last they dressed again and Nicholas had to go, they parted with only few words. A spell had been cast that neither wanted to break, and each felt the need to reflect quite deeply on what had happened between them.

Will Aitken

Skinny-Dipping

from *Terre Haute* (Gay Men's Press, 1998)

I'm standing in line trying to decide whether I want Sloppy Joes or Tuna Delight when Randy Sparks bounces up next to me, T-shirt ultrawhite under the fluorescent light. He's not even pushing a tray. Come to think of it, I've never seen him in the caf during B-block.

"Hey, you don't want to eat that shit."

One of the caf Negro ladies, hair in a pincushion bun under a gold net, gives him a real dirty look as she scoops up a Sloppy Joe for the girl in front of me. He doesn't notice. He's practically dancing right here in line, bouncing from one ratty Ked to the other and pushing down hard on the chrome tray runners like he's about to do a handstand.

"You got any better ideas?"

"I got a car."

"Where'd you get a car?"

"What'll it be?" The Negro lady's spatula hovers over the Tuna Delight.

"Come on." He tugs at my arm.

I leave my tray right there on the rail and follow him to the center of the caf where the tables are close together and crowded with yelling kids. We sit down at a two-seater behind a pillar.

"Here's what we do." He leans so close I can see the pale down on his cheek. "You go ask Mr Strunk if you can go to the bathroom. While he's talking to you I'll duck out the window."

"But where are we going? Where'd you get a car?"

"I've got my permit. I'm fifteen."

"But you have to have an adult with you."

"Who's going to know unless we crash and burn? Then it's

too late anyhow."

"I don't know." I've never skipped school, unless staying home when I wasn't really sick counts. I've never just walked out in the middle of the day.

"Come on, man. It's summer." The lawn stretches beyond the half-opened windows, green and perfect as grass in a movie.

"But where will we go?"

"I don't know. We'll just go. Out to our lake. It's warm enough to go swimming."

He jumps up from the table. "You coming or not? I've got a six-pack."

"But how do I get out once I'm out of the caf?"

"Don't you know anything? Through the auditorium and out the fire door. I'll be in the alley behind the power plant."

"But the alarm will go off when I open the door."

"So? You'll be long gone."

I want to ask, But what will happen when I miss homeroom? And Latin and biology afterward? Will they call mother right away? But he's already sidling toward the windows.

Mr Strunk's standing over by a big table of giggling girls. He's grabbed an orange from one of them and is tossing it high in the air. The girl keeps reaching for it but he keeps stepping back. He has a hungry smile on his face.

"Mr Strunk?"

He glances over his shoulder at me and forgets to catch the orange. The girl scoops it up just before it hits the floor.

"What is it, McCaverty?" The smile's completely gone.

"May I be excused?"

"What for?"

"I have to go to the bathroom."

"Make it quick."

"Yes, sir."

* * *

With its windows all rolled down the little white Corvair rides like a bathtub on wheels, jolting along Route 46, shimmying with every strong breeze. Randy has kicked off his Keds and is driving barefoot, dark lines of grit under his thick toenails.

"Open me up a Malt, will you?"

I reach into the backseat for two cans. "They're cold."

"Only the best. Went home and got them."

"Your mom lets you keep your beer in the fridge now?"

"Stuck them in after she went to school." He holds the beer in one hand and steers with the other. "See if you can find some music."

I fiddle with the radio knob. Country music, *twang, twang.* Static. "Hogs are up ..." Static. "Wipe Out!" The Surfaris. Surfer music. Fine for California but kind of silly here in the Midwest. I start to look for something better but Randy yells, "Turn it up! Up!" So I do, just in time for the last throbbing run down the scale and the maniac at the end screaming "Wipe-out!"

Randy screams it too, presses the gas pedal to the floor and pulls out to pass two cars. On a hill.

Just before we reach the Plainville Bridge he jerks the steering wheel hard to the left and suddenly we're careering along a deep-rutted dirt road cut between two low hills covered with knee-high pines and yellow scrub. The road dips and we split a crater of muddy water like a speedboat, brown water splatting across the windshield. He punches on the wipers and we're looking through twin muddy rainbows.

The ruts angle upward. He downshifts, the car bucks and rattles. At the top of the ridge we skid out of the ruts and barrel straight into the woods. I can't make out any track at all. Randy spins us past stands of taller pines. Rabbits dart for safety. Red-winged blackbirds burst out of the brush, chevrons flashing. We come over a low rise flying, pine branches screeching against the side of the car. When we thud back to earth my head hits the roof.

"Slow down!"

I feel silly the minute I scream. He's already cut the engine and is leaping out of the car. A dozen yards ahead of us an old yellow school bus, axles up on cinder blocks, pokes its snub nose out of a tangle of lilac bushes.

"Grab the beer," he calls and plunges into the woods.

Sloppily stenciled black letters spell out NEW HARMONY SCHOOL DIST. on the side of the bus. Little green café curtains hang in the windows. This must be where he and his mom stay until they're ready to build.

I get the beer from the backseat and head into the woods.

The pine trees are so evenly spaced it doesn't seem like a real woods at all. I try to keep an eye out for poison ivy but after a while it's hard enough keeping track of my feet in the thick undergrowth. I stumble over a branch hidden by vines and grab for the nearest tree trunk. My hand comes away sticky with resin, smelling like Christmas.

A little farther along the ground tilts down at a scary angle. The pines march steeply down, hairy roots threading the loose sandy soil. I crouch like a skier and half slide, half fall down the hill, trying to steady myself with one hand, holding the beer aloft with the other. Halfway down I'm bumping along on my ass. I grab onto a sapling to slow down. It bends right down to the ground but doesn't break off or uproot. I dangle against the hillside, feet treading dirt. I find a foothold on a narrow ridge. The pines are taller here and more closely planted. Sunlight angles down between them in thin golden shafts. Twenty or thirty feet below I can see water green and smooth as Coke-bottle glass. A narrow dock juts out into the water. Randy stands on the end of the dock, waving his T-shirt.

"Next time take the path."

"Where is it?"

"You're on it."

He slides his jeans down over his knees. They're so tightly pegged he has to hop from one foot to the other to pull them down over his bare feet.

I follow the narrow ledge as it zigzags down to the dock.

Randy silently watches my descent, fists on hips. His white boxer shorts are dotted with diagonal rows of red and blue stars.

"At least you didn't drop the beer."

The lake's long and narrow, like a tiny fjord, pines climbing the steep hills.

"Like it?"

"It's great." I set the beer down on the dock.

"Used to be a strip mine. It's all divided up into lots now. But we're the only ones who have bought so far." It's so isolated and quiet. Can't hear anything – people, cars – except birds tweeting and the occasional plop of a frog dropping into the water.

"Skinny-dip?" He hooks his thumbs under the elastic band of his shorts.

I nod. They drop to the dock.

"What are you waiting for?"

I kick off my penny loafers and strip off my socks. That's the easy part. Pants or shirt first? Unbuckling my belt I pull down my khakis, wishing he'd go ahead and dive in but he stands there waiting. I'm thinner now than I've ever been since I was a kid, when Father used to say my rib cage looked like a xylophone, but the lumps are still there on either side of my waist. I line up the creases and fold my khakis on the dock.

"Come on already."

I unbutton my shirt but leave it on, tails hanging down. I can't look at him. If I did I wouldn't be able to take off my underpants. I slide them down around my ankles and step out of them. He's still watching like I'm the only show in town. I shrug off my shirt. I feel white and fat. The breeze is cold on my ass. My teeth start chattering.

"You cold?"

"A little."

"The water's worse."

"Really?"

"Like fucking ice water, man, but you get used to it pretty fast. Or you die."

I dangle one foot off the dock.

He pulls me back. "No fair. All or nothing."

"I don't know, Randy. If it's too cold and you jump in, it can give you a heart attack."

"Fuck that. Race you to the raft." The raft floats on oil drums close to the opposite shore, maybe a hundred yards away.

"Okay."

He leans forward and falls more than dives into the water.

I leap straight out into the air, arching my body so I barely break the smooth green surface when I land. The water's so cold it gives me an ice-cream headache all over my body. I cut across the lake so fast I'm belly down and panting on the rocking raft when Randy comes paddling up. He hoists himself onto the raft, muscles knotting in his forearms.

He sprawls next to me and lays his cheek against the rough planking. "Told you it was freezing."

"The air feels warm now."

"Ummm." He rolls a little from side to side like he wants

to sink right into the wood. The raft tilts gently and beads of water run across the planks, hitting my skin like electric shocks.

We lie there a long time not moving at all, his wet thigh just grazing mine.

Then he rolls lazily over on one side, propping his head up on one arm.

"Wish I could swim like you."

I take a deep breath and turn over on my side too. "Just a question of practice. Like anything else."

He looks down. "You're really hairy."

I look down. Compared to him I am. A copper-colored halo of curls surrounds the base of his cock but his belly and thighs are smooth and hairless.

I feel the warmth rising up inside me and roll back over onto my stomach.

"You want to teach me?"

"Teach you what?"

"Life-saving."

"Sure, why not? Not much to it. A couple of basic carries. What to do if the victim panics. That kind of thing."

"Carries?"

"How you hold the victim to tow him back to shore. Easiest one's the cross-chest carry."

"How's it work?"

"I can't show you here." Not in the state I'm in.

"Why not?"

"I mean I can't show you on the raft."

"Oh."

"Swim out a little and start drowning."

He rolls off the raft and paddles out to the center of the lake.

"This okay?"

"You don't look like you're drowning."

He bobs up and down, thrashing his arms about in the water.

"Help. Help."

I crawl off the raft, cock scraping against the rough planks. Ten strokes and I'm swimming past him.

"Where you going?"

I tread water a yard or so behind him.

174

"That's the first rule. Never approach the victim head-on. He could grab onto you and drag you down with him."

"I got it."

I dog-paddle up close behind him. He starts to turn around.

"Keep looking straight ahead." I slide my left arm across his chest and crook it around his neck. "Now lie back against me and I'll float you back to safety." I stroke the water with my right arm and lazily churn my legs. No need to hurry.

We glide along, spoon-fashion, his body now bobbing above, now resting against mine. He feels so warm, even in the freezing water. I'm sure he can feel me pressing against him.

I grab onto the raft. He doesn't try to break free, just lies there in my arms.

"Not bad."

"I told you there was nothing to it." My voice sounds like it isn't coming from me at all. He's breathing fast, like he did all the work.

"My turn," he says.

I swim out to the center and wave my arms.

"Help. Help."

He takes forever but eventually he swims up behind me and grabs me around the neck so hard my head goes under water.

"Hey!"

"Sorry, man." I lie back against him, praying he won't sink under my weight. He doesn't. He drags me along, flailing the water so hard with his free arm that we travel in wayward arcs back to the raft. My cock bobs up and down in the water like a long white fish pulled along on a line.

He clings to the raft, panting a little, one arm keeping my head above the water, his belly pressed against my back. A woodpecker starts up somewhere across the lake. It echoes over the water like someone hammering. Randy jerks away from me.

"It's only a woodpecker."

He grins sheepishly. "One more time?"

I nod.

I wait until he gets into position and then slowly dog-paddle out to him. My teeth start chattering again. Not cold. Nervous.

I swim up behind him and start to tuck my arm under his chin. He starts struggling like he's really drowning, swinging his arms and kicking at me. I've never really fought with anyone on

175

land – I don't like getting hurt. Water-fights are just my style though because water acts as kind of a cushion. It's hard to hit really hard under water and impossible to fall down. I jump on top of him, pushing him under. We roll over and over in the clear green water, twisting about, intertwining arms and legs like slow-motion wrestlers. He has to come up for air first. I pull him back down, lever my arm under his chin and drag him back to the surface.

He's gasping for breath. "Okay, okay. I give."

Instead of heading back to the raft I tow him along the length of the lake.

"Where we going?" He tries to turn around to look at me but I tighten my lock on his neck. "Scenic tour."

"You're choking me, man."

"If I ease up you'll just start fighting again."

"No, I won't."

"Promise?"

"Hope to die."

I loosen my grip and in one quick movement he flips over so we're lying face-to-face. It surprises me so much I forget to scull and go right under. He comes with me, arms around me, body against mine. We float back up to the surface, still clinging together.

I run my hands over his shoulders and down his back. I pull him to me tight. I try to press my cheek against his but he jerks his head away.

He opens his eyes wide. "What are you trying to do?"

"I don't know."

"Well, cut it out."

I don't get it at all. He's the one who started. I push away from him.

He pulls me back so our cocks rub together. "This is cool, man. I'm so fucking horny."

"Me too."

"But I'm only doing this because there are no girls around."

"Me too."

"So none of that lovey-dovey shit."

"I didn't mean – "

"Forget it. The important thing's getting your rocks off, right?"

176

"Right."

Somehow we're back at the dock, water up to our thighs, cocks bobbing in the cool air.

I reach out and touch him. It leaps up. I run my fingers along the shaft, tracing the bulge of the vein. I cup his balls. They play loose and low in the silky sac.

He slowly reaches out and touches me. I don't know who moved first but suddenly we're together again, pushing into each other. My tongue darts out to lick the beads of moisture from his shoulder.

"I'm warning you, man."

"Sorry." I kneel down before him.

"What are you doing?"

"What do you think?"

I run my tongue over the pink head and take him into my mouth. For a moment it feels like he's going to pull away but he buries his fingers in my hair and arches his back. I can feel him against the back of my throat.

"Stop!"

I look up. His eyes are shut, teeth clenched like I've hurt him.

"What's wrong?"

"I'm about to shoot."

We stand there just looking at each other, not touching, swaying a little like the light breeze is moving us.

He leans back against the dock. I crouch between his legs. His hands are tangled in my hair. Almost right away the rushing along the shaft, thickness in the back of my throat, his hips bucking like mad. He slips out of my mouth trailing a silvery strand that hangs between us an instant, snaps.

I look down in time to see my cock pouring out onto his thigh. He swirls a finger in the shiny liquid, brings the finger slowly to his mouth and licks it.

* * *

On the way back to town he's real quiet. He even drives quiet. Doesn't go over seventy even on the straightaway.

I reach over and touch his arm.

He downshifts to third for no good reason. "Might as well

finish the beer."

I reach into the backseat, unpop a can and hand it to him. He drinks it down fast.

"You don't want the last one?"

I shake my head.

"Then give it to me."

* * *

He drops me off at Meadowlark Shopping Center. Says he has to pick up his mom at the university. My lesson's at four. Says he doesn't want her to know we've been out at the lake. Says she doesn't mind him driving by himself as long as he doesn't give anyone else a ride. Says he doesn't want her to know he skipped school. I get the point.

I close the car door. "Thanks."

"Okay, man." He peels away from the curb.

Peter Szabo

Flash Gordon in Sheffield

It was not that he was even attractive. Not in a conventional sense that is, though I suppose the chestnut-red sheen of his hair which fell across his brow did have a certain beauty. Kevin was slightly taller than me and sturdier of build. His flesh was always white, even in the height of summer, and covered in freckles. The fact that he wore glasses, often held together with Sellotape, didn't help and yet when he took his glasses off he had the most amazing blue eyes.

We were both fourteen, still at school. The long hot summer of that year was almost exhausted. The fields around the village in which we lived were scorched white and across the valley the haze of the steel works shimmered beneath a deep blue sky. We had walked five miles, up to the ridge of the hill strewn with boulders which fell towards the valley. Out here in the silence it was almost possible to believe you had stepped back in time. Not that Kevin noticed, for he went on and on about Flash Gordon escaping the terrors of Ming the Merciless. We were both avid filmgoers and in those days there was often a serial accompanying the main feature. "It's only a film taken from a comic strip!" I said, exasperated at Kevin's adulation of Larry Buster Crabbe who played the bleached blond hero. "What about Dale?" I asked, referring to the heroine.

"What about her?" Kevin replied, his glasses reflecting the sunlight. I suppose what I meant was did he fancy her, or even want to be her so that he could be rescued by Flash Gordon. We never discussed sex, or if we did it was in an oblique and generally disparaging way. As far as my own emergent desires went, I had just discovered the erotic magazines full of semi-nude men which appeared under the guise of 'physical culture'. A sizable collection was building up in the bottom drawer in my bedroom, hidden beneath copies of science-fiction paperbacks. My sexual yearnings

had as yet not been expressed with anyone else. Once I'd come across two older lads at school masturbating each other behind the toilets and later I would jerk off at the memory.

It wasn't as if I even fancied Kevin or thought about him sexually so it came as a shock when on this particular afternoon, out on the edge of the moors, he suggested we lay down in the shade of the huge boulders and strip off to our underpants.

"If I'm taking my clothes off I want to sit in the sun," I said as he started pulling off his shirt. I was surprised at how muscular he was. The glasses and white skin belied his strength. Carefully he folded up his clothes then stretched out in the shade. "You going to take them off or what?" he asked, putting his glasses on top of the pile.

I laughed and untied my plimsolls. Somewhere I could hear a curlew which sounded eery in the emptiness of the moors. Placing my clothes on the ground I manoeuvred into a position in the sun. Kevin watched me silently as I lay down.

"Does anyone else come up here?" I asked. He didn't reply. Squinting in the sunlight I rolled onto my side. There seemed to be an eternity before we both responded. Looking back it was obvious we both had wanted the experience, almost telepathically arranging the situation. Slowly he pulled my hand onto his stomach then down to his underpants. He had an erection. I remembered the lads behind the toilets and leaning over started to massage his cock. Without speaking he pulled me on top of him then slowly slid down his pants. "Try this," he said as he rubbed my cock against his. I remember laughing at its size and redness. I could feel his body shudder as grabbing my head he pushed me down until my face was buried in his curly pubic hair. "Put it in your mouth!" he demanded. Hesitantly I placed my lips around his moist penis and let him slowly sink it into my mouth. I was surprised at its salty taste and at first almost gagged. Slowly Kevin began fondling my hair and breathing heavily as he sank deeper into my mouth. When he came he yelled, his fists pummelling my shoulders. Then he silently pushed me over, took hold of my hard dick and began to suck me off.

Afterwards there was an ominous silence as we made our way down the white dusty track towards the road and the bus stop. My head was racing. I wanted to ask him if he'd done this

before and who with. It was only later that I realised his skill in sucking me must have come from experience. When I haltingly asked him his face flushed and he scowled before angrily telling me to "Piss off!" So much for a burgeoning romance.

For weeks after Kevin never mentioned the incident until one evening he came to visit me when both my parents were out; he suddenly grabbed me and began feverishly unbuttoning my fly.

* * *

The summer holidays was coming to an end. I went with my parents for a week's holiday to Southport, our usual haunt as my mother's sister lived there. The entire week I spent randily scouring the beach, the back streets, the pleasure beach and amusement arcades for sex, but nothing was available. This was the mid fifties. Homosexuality was illegal. Any 'gay scene' was hidden or clandestine. As soon as I retuned home I made an excuse and went to see Kevin. His house was on a council estate in what was known as the 'rough end' of the village. A lopsided car with the front wheels missing lay across a cinder path outside his house. Beneath the vehicle I could see a sturdy, bronzed figure in baggy overalls. It was Kevin's older brother Frank. I had seen him in the past, fleetingly, on his way to work at the steel mill, a burly bruiser of a guy with cropped gold-red hair. Frank was twenty-three. Unlike Kevin he was tanned a deep brown. All the girls in the village fancied him and there were rumours that he had 'taken up with an older woman in Sheffield'.

He stopped whatever he was doing, pushed himself from beneath the car and grinned at me. He was amazingly good looking. "Wotcher!" he slowly eased himself up and rubbed his black, greasy hand against his overalls. "Kevin's not in. He's..." Frank's eyes twinkled as if anticipation at his remark, "over at his girlfriend's."

"Girlfriend?" I heard my voice waver. It sounded a million miles away.

"Patty Clough. Lass over in Barnsley." Frank straightened up and flexed his muscles. Apart from his overalls and torn sneakers he wasn't wearing anything else. "Met her at some bebop club in Sheffield."

I was astounded. Abruptly my whole world had fallen apart. I never had even conceived of Kevin having a girlfriend.

"How was your holiday?" Frank stared at me, obviously noticing my state of shock.

"Oh... good. It was OK." I sank back, turned and faced the littered garden. Washing flapped on a clothes line, a mangy dog stared indolently at me.

"He'll be back tomorrow, shall I say you called?" I could smell the sweat on Frank's body, the faint scent of the hair oil he used.

"No..." I began to walk away. "No, don't bother. I'll be in touch."

*   *   *

This was the first time I'd had to face my sexual desires and their implications. It wasn't as if I lusted after Kevin. We'd only had the two experiences which were fine but didn't fire me. It was something else. An unspoken tryst. An intimate bond broken.

I didn't return to Kevin's after that. The feeling appeared to be mutual, he never came around to see me. At school he avoided me, a guilty look in his eyes. Once in Sheffield in a coffee bar I encountered him with his girlfriend, flaunting their relationship with great relish. During that last summer term I had set my eyes on going to art school so I threw myself into drawing. I went out sketching on the moors at weekends or, if it rained, in the museum in the city. It was one such gloomy, stormy day after I'd been sketching fossils and chunks of crystal in the musty rooms of the museum that I made my way through the city, my mind preoccupied with sexual longing. I eventually decided to go to the small cinema in one of the city squares which showed mainly cartoons. Long gone now, this smoky haven of darkness and flickering screen was in fact a haunt for men seeking sex. My only experience had been a few furtive gropes, mostly from much older men whom I had managed to shun.

I bought my ticket and entered the cinema, which was practically empty. I sat down and quickly scanned the clientele. A couple of old guys in raincoats were sitting up front. A large, matronly woman with dyed black hair sat with an anaemic

looking youth. Tom and Jerry were on the screen, Jerry getting his customary beating with a frying pan resulting in him being reduced to a millimetre thick and running around frantically. I relaxed and sat back.

The next couple of cartoons I'd seen before and was half thinking of leaving when I noticed someone come in and pull off his raincoat. Obviously it was pouring outside. My heart missed a beat as I recognised Kevin's brother Frank. He stood at the back for a moment. I didn't know if I should wave or not, but as the lights went up for the intermission he saw me. Grinning he made his way over, stood next to my seat and broke out laughing.

"Want some ice cream?" he asked just as the usherette appeared with her tray.

I nodded. "Yes please... chocolate." Frank turned and brought two wrapped, oblong ice creams. I pulled the wrapper of the one he handed me, the thin coating of chocolate was frosted like mist.

Squeezing past me Frank sat down. "Just in time for Flash Gordon!" he said with a wink as the lights dimmed, the screen was floodlit green and episode twenty of Flash Gordon versus Ming the Merciless came onto the screen. Frank sat back, folding his raincoat over the seat in front. Flash Gordon had been tied to a huge silver disc. Opposite him evil Ming, his gaunt face heavily shadowed, manoeuvred an ominous-looking machine in front of Flash. Any minute he would zap the hero with atomic rays which would reduce him to pulp. A loud rumbling made Ming look up. An earthquake had arrived, right on cue. Large chunks of rock crashed down onto the machine and Ming, who vanished in a cloud of dust. A jagged piece of rock cut through Flash's ropes, and with visible relief he quickly untied himself.

Frank put his sturdy hand on my knee and whispered into my ear, his breath hot against my neck, "Kevin's told me what you two get up to." He squeezed my knee. I looked sideways, just as Flash escaped the atomiser, and Frank clutched my groin. The crumpled ice-cream paper fell out of my hand as he felt my burgeoning erection through my jeans. Silently, the film reflecting across his face, Frank unbuttoned the fly and eased my dick out, before grabbing his damp raincoat and dropping it across our knees. I was too excited, too dumbstruck to move. I

desperately wanted to feel Frank's dick, take it between my lips, but some stupid part of my brain refused to acknowledge what was happening. After all, this was Kevin's butch older brother who had 'a fancy woman in Sheffield'. Quietly, without fuss, Frank grasped my hand and pulled it beneath the raincoat. His dick was erect, moist. I squeezed it, amazed at its size. "Do it gently," he muttered. I quickly glanced around but the cinema was still practically empty. Flash Gordon was in his space ship shooting through space. Slowly I started jerking Frank off. He moaned softly, fell back against the battered, red plush seat and opened his thighs wider, squeezing his fingers more firmly round my dick.

As a shower of meteorites zoomed past Flash Gordon's space ship and Ming the Merciless appeared in a bubble screaming for Flash's downfall, Frank came in one hot gush. He sighed, pulled himself up and released his grip on my cock. "You haven't come," he said softly as he pulled out a handkerchief and discreetly cleaned himself up. I was still too awestruck to move. "C'mon," he said as the serial ended and Flash's spaceship wobbled across a mountainous terrain on some weird planet. "We can finish this off somewhere else."

Not knowing what he had in mind I managed to button my fly and pull on my coat. I felt like a fugitive as we made our way up the aisle through the smoke-filled cinema.

Outside, the rain had stopped. It was early evening, the lights of the shops were reflected in the wet flagstones of the pavement. "Where are we going?" I asked.

Frank grinned. "Just ten minutes away. I've got this room."

"Oh?" I looked at him quizzically. "Is that this older woman you see when you come to Sheffield?"

Frank broke out laughing. "Older woman? Naw..." he glanced at me and winked. "That's just a line. It belongs to this guy I know called Vince."

I stared at him. 'Vince?"

Frank nodded, took a packet of Capstan Full Strength out of his raincoat pocket and offered me one which I refused. "Yeah. Vince. He's great... we have a good time." He looked at me knowingly and lit his cigarette.

"Is he there now?" I asked as a whole, hidden world began to unfold in my mind.

"He's up at Catterick. In the army." Frank took my hand and squeezed it. "I've got a key to his flat."

To my surprise the flat was above a shop I had often visited with my father. The shop was stacked with old seventy-eight records of dance bands from the twenties and thirties – which were my father's passion – as well as model theatres which were mine. The idea of being there with my father while Frank and his friend Vince were having sex in the flat above thrilled me.

Frank ran up the two flights of stairs and unlocked the solid wooden door to the flat. Once inside I relaxed, a part of me still aware that what we were doing was illegal. Frank of course couldn't care less. He pushed open the door into the living room and switched on the light. Small red-shaded lamps flickered on. The place was a mess. Unwashed clothes lay strewn across a low-backed settee. On a round plastic table an overfilled ashtray sat next to empty beer bottles. "Gotta clear up before Vince comes back," Frank said with a chuckle.

I looked around the room. The kitchen lay behind a half-folded screen; Frank disappeared behind it and began noisily washing a couple of mugs. "You want a coffee?" he yelled. I made my way towards the kitchen and stood in the doorway. Seeing the sunlight fall on Frank's muscular body turned me on. I wanted to ask about Kevin and if he'd ever done it with him, suddenly aware that Kevin's expert cock-sucking had probably been learned from his older brother.

"So what did Kevin say about me?" I asked as Frank handed me a mug of coffee.

"Oh." Frank laughed, "that you liked sucking him off." He grinned at me and playfully thumped me on my arm. "Wanna do that with me?"

I practically choked on the coffee. Frank laughed and made his way past me towards the radiogram. "Don't get upset!" he said as he took a record out of its sleeve, "it's only if you want to!"

Want to? I'd practically come in my jeans at the thought of it. Judy Garland started singing 'The Man That Got Away' on the radiogram as Frank stood in front of me and began to unbutton his jeans. I sat forward as he fondled my hair. His uncut dick was limp, but grew firm as I started to massage it. "Suck it and I'll let you put your dick up my arse," he said, his

voice trembling. I eagerly plunged ahead, but he came too quickly for me. Laughing, he withdrew and gave me his handkerchief.

"Is this what you do with Kevin?" I asked tentatively.

Frank paused and stared at me. "Kevin? That's just playing around."

I didn't reply, though I wondered what the difference was between 'playing around' with his younger brother and what we had just done.

"You want to stay over?" he asked, rubbing his hand against my back.

"Here?" I glanced around.

Frank winked and pulled my hand against his crotch. "You could phone your parents... say you're staying with a school friend." He grinned at me. "Then we could carry out the rest of the bargain!"

It was already dark when I went out to telephone my parents. There was a sizable queue outside the cinema at the end of the street, mainly couples on their Friday night date. I felt secretly proud of my liaison with Frank. My mother sounded concerned but I invented a story about someone who was at the art college and was going to show me his work. "Well at least it's not a girl!" my mother said with a sigh of relief. I almost broke out laughing.

* * *

Frank was my first truly homosexual encounter. After that night, when he kept to his promise, I saw him regularly. Our meetings were intense and evolved into an almost silent ritual of drinking beer, undressing and caressing each other on the bed before we had sex. I often wondered if Vince ever came back, or even if he existed at all. There were no photographs of him in the place and his absence took on an almost ghostly presence. Everything was smooth sailing, we kept our meetings secret, until one evening he revealed another side of himself. It followed a bout of sex which had bordered on the violent. Frank went into the bathroom and after what seemed like an eternity appeared naked but wearing make-up. The touch of mascara and bright red lips seemed strange with his very masculine features. Slowly he leaned forward and kissed me passionately, his lipstick

smearing my face. As I wiped my mouth I innocently said, "Are you queer then?" Frank hit me hard on the mouth at that remark, resulting in a cut lip. "Never say that again!" he said darkly. "I'm not queer." In a state of confusion I left later that evening and caught the last train home.

I didn't see Frank for nearly a week after his sudden outburst. I found the mixture of violence and Frank wearing make-up unsettling. I had hoped to confront him about it, ask why he'd been so angry when I asked if he was queer. As far as I was concerned we both were and I was quite happy about it. On the day I'd made up my mind to discuss the issue I bumped into a couple of his workmates who told me that he'd left the village, gone down South and got a job in London. I was stunned, chiefly because he'd never mentioned anything about leaving.

It was the following year, when I was at art college, that I bumped into Kevin who told me Frank had got married and was living in London. He relayed the news with a particular twinkle in his eye and I wondered how much Frank had told him. I had never fancied Kevin after our first encounters and my experiences with his older brother. Years later he would become alcoholic, overweight and homophobic.

Many years later, I had come to London in search of work and ended up in an advertising studio in Soho. I was drinking in a pub in the East End which was known for its gay clientele when I suddenly heard a voice say against my ear, "Ever see Flash Gordon these days?" Turning I stared into the amused eyes of Frank. He'd lost his looks, had begun to go bald but was still sexily attractive. He pressed his hand on top of mine. "I always wanted to apologise," he said softly. I stared at him. "Yeah, for punching you on the mouth." He smiled ruefully. "You were right! About me being queer. I couldn't take it at the time."

"Oh?" I finished my beer and caught the eye of the barman who I noticed was watching us with rapt attention. "What are you drinking?" Frank asked for a bottle of Budweiser. "So what happened to your marriage?"

Frank laughed. "Shit! That was a fiasco. It lasted three months." He straightened up against the partition behind him and for a moment I saw him in his old glory. Muscular, tough. He was wearing a worn leather jacket, an open-neck black shirt and Levis.

"And Vince? What happened to Vince?" I took out my wallet as the drinks arrived.

Frank laughed and winked. He took hold of the barman's hand and said to him, "Let me introduce you!" Turning to me he grinned. "This is Vince!"

Vince was stunning. Six feet tall, lean, shaven-headed. Frank caught the look of approval on my face. "We've gotta flat in town now," he said, rubbing his hand against mine. "Come around any time."

* * * * *

Peter Szabo's novel *Does Joe Durva Still Exist?* was published by Gay Men's Press in 1999.

P. Parivaraj

A Visit to Aunty's

from *Shiva and Arun* (Gay Men's Press, 1998)

It was two years ago that very month that he made his first visit to his aunt's. He called it his first visit because he had come by himself. As a child he had often come with the others. Two years ago he had come by himself and it had been his first big train trip alone. He had enjoyed it immensely. There was a kind of freedom being alone on the train without his family. Without his father. Without his older brother. Before he took the train two years ago his father had made him sit for two hours writing and repeating instructions. Shiva supposed some people might have thought it caring that his father spent such time giving travelling instructions. Shiva knew that it was just his way of enforcing his will on their lives, but he had always been fascinated by the urchins who seemed even younger than him. They travelled without tickets, without anyone, and made money out of it.

At Chintana he had been put on the train by his father and elder brother. His father had checked the bogey number, the seat number and the passenger list three times to make sure he was in the correct place. He then asked people sitting near Shiva to "Look after him". This made Shiva embarrassed. The train pulled out on time, everyone waved. Two minutes later two of the men were asleep and the others were playing cards. He walked up and down the carriage and no one took any notice of him.

When the train stopped at his station he did as his father instructed, knowing full well that Aunt would report on him after his stay with her.

He alighted and stood on the platform for a minute, looked around and saw the Station Master's Office and headed for it. He hadn't got halfway when he felt a tap on the shoulder. It was

Aunt smiling down at him.

"So you have arrived. I watched you get down. Very good. You are careful with your bags I see. Three in all. Let me guess what's in them." She didn't though, just turned and spoke to the young man next to her, "Chinni, take young Shiva's bags and arrange the rickshaw please. Let's not stay here longer than needed. It's not clean air."

Chinni left quickly and Aunt started to follow. "Have your journey ticket ready Shivaji for the ticket collector."

They passed through the gate, Aunt first handing over her platform ticket with a nod. He walked beside her. "In one of the bags I have my study books. I got some old ones that are for next year's subjects. I want to read them in advance."

She nodded and kept walking.

Chinni was waiting with a rickshaw. He had his bicycle and on the back were tied Shiva's bags.

On the way home Aunt hardly spoke. She sat with a handkerchief over her mouth and nose. She took up most of the rickshaw seat, wedging Shiva, thin as he was, into the corner, against the side bar that dug into his ribs. She kept pulling her saree tighter and tighter over her head. As they got to the corner where she lived she said, "Ohh dear, I do hate going to that smelly railway station. And what's more these roads are so dusty nowadays. Those lorries make so much sound with their horns." She paused. "The dust gives me nose problems you know?"

He didn't think it was a question. He nodded though and half smiled. Shiva had been fascinated watching Chinni. He weaved in and out of the traffic keeping abreast with the rickshaw like a circus performer. He made it look artful. He could brake quickly and start again without putting his feet down for balance. Shiva watched him most of the way. He turned and smiled to Shiva a few times. He was a hairy young guy but his moustache was thin. When he pushed down on the pedals Shiva saw his muscles bulge.

The whole day Aunt made a fuss of him. He slept most of the afternoon, having eaten far too much at lunchtime. He had no option with Aunt. She had said a hundred times that he was far to thin. She was determined to fatten him, send him home like a prize peacock. He had to admit though that her coconut sweet was rather good.

In the evening she went off to the temple telling him to watch the house and tell Chinni the servant boy if he needed anything. He had been sent to stay with her because over the next ten days she was going to special pujas at the temple, followed by discourses. A well-known swami had come from Calcutta.

He didn't know what he was supposed to guard. She wore all her gold to the temple. The radio was an old model. The furniture didn't look special, and then there were only pots and things in the kitchen. Besides what was Chinni going to do? What she did the rest of the year for a guard he didn't know. He didn't really care because it was a holiday from home. He had books to study too. His father wasn't there either – that was great. Two weeks without his father constantly questioning him. Two weeks without his brother treating him like a peon. He walked around the house. He grinned when he saw the locks on the doors. They were the same big type that was on the temple at his place. The keys were as thick as his little fingers. The windows not only had bolts but also wooden bars. He shrugged and sat next to the radio and tried to find some music. There was music but it was the kind he hated.

It was to be two weeks in which he could study quietly. He had slipped from fifth place to eighth. His father had blamed his spending so much time at cricket practice. His marks weren't bad but his father said they were. Shiva thought that eighth out of sixty-five in the class wasn't too bad really. But he would aim at getting back in the top five. He didn't want to have his cricket stopped.

He heard Aunt coming up the steps. She smiled, went into the kitchen, and served supper for both of them. She sat facing him, adding extra curry as soon as he finished one spoonful. She told him about the visiting swami and how very wise and interesting he was. He was actually surprised she hadn't dragged him to the temple.

He thought that all the swamis he had ever heard all went on about the same impossible thing. They all extolled being so good that there would be no reincarnation after death. How it was possible for humans to be so perfect Shiva couldn't imagine. He did not express his views to his aunt. The swamis all looked alike and they all seemed to sing out of tune. They all expected

everyone to abstain from almost everything that Shiva thought was pleasant! Still they were always fat and well cared for. He didn't think that they really worked. Going from one place to the other, sitting comfortably on cushions telling the same jargon to people. He didn't think that his father really worked either. Being a pujari, a priest who simply performed rituals, wasn't what Shiva called a 'real job'.

After supper he went upstairs and sat on the balcony for a while, then went to bed and quickly fell asleep.

He was woken up by Chinni standing next to his bed. "Hot water in the bathroom. Aunt says to have bath quickly and come down for breakfast it's ready."

Shiva waited for Chinni to leave before getting out of bed. He wondered if Chinni had seen his erection under the bed sheet. He'd been lying on his back when Chinni woke him. It was still stiff when he took his shorts off and pissed, after closing the bathroom door. There was no lock on the door, but it stuck at the bottom against the frame.

When he went downstairs he had to eat three of the largest iddlis he had ever seen, covered with ghee and served with a plate of coconut chutney. He heard Aunt talking to Chinni about going to the market.

"May I go to the market with Chinni too?"

She turned and looked at him with some surprise. "What do you want there? He can get it for you. The sun is already hot. It's very dusty and smelly there too. I can't imagine anyone wanting to go when it can be fetched for you."

She handed money to Chinni. "Better you get on with your studies. Bring your books down to the front room. It's very good reading light there, and a breeze will come in that window first. It's a quiet room too."

At five in the evening aunt announced that she was leaving early. "To tell the truth I've been invited to have tiffin with a friend of mine, then we will go to bhajans together. You brush your hair. The walk with me to her place will be good for you."

He presumed that it wasn't near to the smelly market. The sky was still bright and cloudless – a soft clear blue. The sun was well angled but the pink had not started to creep across the horizon. They stopped at one corner and Aunt bartered with the woman for a string of jasmine and a handful of marigold

flowers that the woman wrapped in a leaf. They turned down the wide side street. It was lined on both sides with huge overhanging old banyan trees. It was very cool. The houses all had high compound walls. They were the big old types set back from the road.

On some of the gates were marble plaques with the house name engraved. Many had signs: BEWARE OF THE DOG. He smiled and thought they could have a sign on their front door at home: BEWARE OF THE FATHER.

"What are you smiling at, Shivaji?" Aunt had caught his smile.

"Ohhh, a big dog sign and a small dog."

She stopped at a gate. It was wrought iron and had a brass handle. In the driveway was a white Ambassador car. A young man was in the driveway playing with a small dog. There was no dog sign on the gate. The dog ran up to the gate and wagged its tail. It looked very well cared for. A red collar was around its neck. Aunt spoke to the dog. The young man came up the drive. He was tall and thin, Shiva thought he was really beautiful. His skin was a soft bronze brown colour. He had shorts on, and Shiva noticed the fine hair on his legs. He had a thin moustache that might have been trimmed at the ends, it was so neat.

The young man smiled. "Hello, Aunty, mother is expecting you, she is waiting inside. Let me hold the dog and open the gate for you."

He seemed very friendly and called her Aunt. They must be good friends, Shiva thought. Aunt didn't allow too many non-family people to be that friendly. The boy looked too bronzed to be a Brahmin though.

Aunt turned to Shiva. He thought she was about to introduce hm. He was wrong. "Thank you, Shiva, you can go back now, don't dawdle either. There is no one in the house you know."

Somehow it sounded as though Chinni wasn't a proper person or something. He stood for a second and smiled at her. He turned slightly to smile at the young man, but he was bending over patting the dog. Shiva turned quickly and briskly walked down the road towards Aunt's house. If she was watching, and he knew she would be, he might get marks for that! Maybe...

He rang the door bell and heard Chinni come and lift the

wooden bar. He smiled and Chinni smiled back. He crossed the room and heard the wood drop back on the catch. He walked up to his room and lay on the bed, thinking about the young man he had seen, and the dog.

* * *

He wasn't sure how long he had been there dreaming. A soft knock startled him. Shiva knew that it must be Chinni. He looked at the small bedside clock Aunt had put on the bedside table. It couldn't be tiffin time. The door opened slowly. Chinni put his head in.

"You went out walking, would you like some hot water to bathe before having tiffin? There is a pot ready in the kitchen if you want me to bring it up for you."

Chinni spoke without expression on his face. Shiva realised he was almost staring at him though. He thought that Chinni looked a bit like the young man he had been thinking about. Only older, more mature. And, yes, somehow less innocent looking. More physically mature.

Of course he was much less innocent, Shiva thought. He most likely had a dozen experiences with girls around the town. Shiva sat up. "Yes, alright, bring the hot water. I think I will have a bath before tiffin and starting to study again."

Shiva heard Chinni go down the stairs two at a time, a light thud thud thud. He took off his shirt and pants, put on a cotton towel and picked up his soap and walked to the bathroom. He still had his shorts on under the towel. There were already two buckets in the bathroom, one empty and the other filled with cold water. He put his towel on the wooden peg. He stretched up and looked through the high small window. He could only see sky, and it was almost dark.

The pink he had seen walking home was now turning to grey. He liked the greys of the evening that slipped across the sky just as the stars started to shine. He stood staring out of the window and wondered where the moon would be. He then realised it would be on the other side of the house. He hardly heard the door open. He turned to see Chinni put the pot of hot water on the floor. He poured some of the cold water into the empty bucket and started to mix hot water. He dipped his little

finger into it.

"You can make it hotter if you want. There is plenty of hot water in the pot."

Shiva bent over and tested the water. It was alright, he didn't want it too hot. He noticed that while Chinni was downstairs he had taken his shirt off. He didn't like to stare too much. He could easily see the long line of hair that ran from his throat down to his navel and disappeared somewhere into the lungee. Two small fans of hair spread across his chest. He was muscular and very wiry, the kind of person Shiva thought who could work hard and not feel the strain. He didn't know for sure, that was just his idea.

Chinni went to the bathroom door. "There is no one in the house, you can take your shorts off to bathe if you wish. Put them in the bucket and I'll rinse them later and put them on the line to dry for you."

He smiled and closed the door, but not hard against the frame. What a strange thing to say Shiva thought. He often bathed without his shorts in his bathroom at home. He knew that many of his friends never took them off to bathe. They would bathe, dry and then wrapping the towel around themselves, stand wriggling and pulling the shorts off. He had seen many boys do it and the wriggling always made him laugh to himself. They looked like they were doing some crazy dance. It had been the topic of a lunchtime discussion between Sam, Sreenu, Ramana, Laxman and Abdullah. Like many of their conversations at school it started and ended nowhere.

Shiva knelt beside the bucket and poured one mug of warm water over himself slowly, then another. He was thinking of the young guy with the dog and it was making his penis hard. He squeezed it for a few seconds, felt that unique sensation, and tucked it between his legs. Then all he could see was the little bunch of thick black hair. He picked up the soap, ran it over his head and worked his fingers around to make a thick lather. He closed his eyes tight and put the soap down so that even with his eyes closed he could find it. He poured water over his head and started to make soap lather again. He thought he heard the door, but he couldn't open his eyes. Then a little light swept across his face and he knew that the door must have opened.

Chinni spoke. "You want me to pour water over you?"

Shiva wasn't sure if he wanted Chinni to pour water or not. He didn't have much option as he heard the mug being lifted from the bucket and felt the warm water running nicely over his back. Chinni then massaged his scalp with soap, poured a little more water and made it lather again. He paused. Then Shiva, with his eyes still closed tightly against the soapy water, felt Chinni rubbing soap across his shoulders, across and down his back. Shiva was glad he had tucked his hard penis between his legs. He would be embarrassed if Chinni saw it.

Chinni rubbed his back gently, then moved down to his thighs. A exciting feeling crept through Shiva. He felt his tucked-away penis go even harder. With a strange shock he realised that Chinni was now rubbing soap over his buttocks. Suddenly a new exciting feeling gripped Shiva. Chinni was rubbing his soaped hand all over his testicles and up and down his hard penis. He stayed kneeling, not really knowing what to do. Chinni took his hand away and poured water all over Shiva. Shiva wiped his face and looked up. Chinni didn't have his lungee on, just his shorts, where there was something poking hard against the material. Shiva looked up at Chinni and saw that he was smiling. Not grinning, just smiling. It was a soft kind smile, a knowing smile. Shiva felt that his whole body was alive in a new way.

"With all this extra hot water I could also take a bath." Chinni paused. "If you don't mind?"

For a few seconds Shiva was confused. It always happened when someone was friendly and then used that 'master-servant' tone. The tone of 'upper and lower caste' used just as often by those who were so disgustingly called lower caste. Shiva always had to control himself when this happened. Chinni had just washed his hair and rubbed his back and run his hand over his balls and hard cock. Now he was asking if he could bathe next to him! Shiva knew it was his caste that perpetuated this injustice. Why in a so-called free India did people still accept it?

He smiled and shrugged his shoulders. It was the same shrug that many of the guys made at school when caste things came up. In their group it didn't happen much. Sometimes though a new guy would be with them. The shrug was meant to show a non-recognition of anything that smacked of some taboo that was outdated, unwanted and demeaning. But Shiva knew that deep inside very many of them this rubbish still permeated their

lives. Usually it was somehow imposed by elders and parents.

Shiva played cricket with a friend, a so called 'harijan' lower-caste boy. His name was Ram. A brilliant guy to know if you needed a quick answer in physics. Ram always seemed embarrassed to offer or take anything from other students who he thought were 'upper'. Sometimes even a glass of water seemed a problem. And of course there were still 'backward' Brahmin students who thought it was right or smart to pull their caste rank. All of Shiva's close friends made stinging remarks when others showed this leftover shit.

The worst was 'Brahmin' Murty Ramana. One day when he made a show over water, not once but twice, the three of them held him down. Each pissed on his legs. They put spit on their fingers and ran it across his forehead. He couldn't believe what was happening. He said nothing. Next day he came to school smiling and told them just before the bell rang, "I didn't bathe last night or this morning, so if I smell of piss it's your bad luck."

What Shiva was really wondering was if Chinni would take his shorts off too. With a smile and a quick movement Chinni did just that. He flung the shorts over to the wooden hook on the wall. Shiva turned just slightly to see if they caught on the hook. In turning his own hard cock flipped up from being tucked tight between his legs. It thumped on his stomach. They were both looking at each other – more precisely, at each other's cocks. Chinni came and knelt in the same position in front of Shiva. He took hold of his cock and was slowly drawing the foreskin back and forth.

"Is this what you do?" he asked with a smile.

Shiva shook his head. "No. All I do is hold it like this," he took his own now very hard cock and held it near the head, "and I just squeeze it like this. It makes so much feeling that I have to stop after a few minutes."

Chinni leaned across and taking Shiva's hand away put his own there and started to work the foreskin up and down. "Does thick white stuff come out when you just squeeze it?"

Shiva sat still thinking. "No."

He realised then that he knew what Chinni was talking about. It was the semen stuff that came out inside a woman when you had sex and mixed with the woman's stuff and made babies.

He knew that much from Pradeep's biology book. He was not into botany and biology – pulling flowers apart and cutting up frogs and rats and stuff. His interest was chemistry and physics and maths. He had read it in Pradeep's book when they were asking each other revision questions for some term exam.

Chinni took Shiva's hand and placed it around his own cock.

Shiva was filled with so many different new feelings he didn't speak. He mouth felt dry. He was holding Chinni's cock and doing the same to him, running the foreskin up and down. Something was happening to Shiva. His body was filled with strange and exciting sensations. He enjoyed holding Chinni's penis like this. He had often thought about doing this and other things with his friends, but there had never been a chance. He had often wondered what it would be like. Now he was experiencing it, he was holding someone else's. It was hard and much bigger than his, and it felt good. He was fascinated to feel something so thick and long. He imagined that one day his would also grow big.

Then his mind went blank. He felt this... sensation grip him. He thought at first it was pain. Then he thought he was going to piss. But it wasn't pain and no piss came – it was so different and it somehow numbed him. He was going to tell Chinni to stop, but he couldn't.

Then he felt something happening, something deep inside his crotch, somewhere inside his balls. A strangely new exciting searing sensation ran up his cock. His legs went stiff. A fluid shot out, not once but three times. He instantly knew what it was. This was Pradeep's book in reality. He felt his body unwind as though he had been wound up like a clock spring. He knew this must be semen. He felt excited and relaxed and exhilarated. He looked at the semen. The first two shots had landed on Chinni's arm and the last one on his hairy leg.

He was still holding Chinni's cock and pulling the skin up and down. All of a sudden Chinni groaned and started to bend towards Shiva. He stopped, he thought Chinni must be in pain. As soon as Shiva let go, Chinni grabbed it and moved the skin up and down fast. Shiva watched fascinated now. Then the semen shot out thick and milky. It landed on Shiva's stomach and leg.

Chinni smiled and relaxed and leaned back on his legs. Shiva

was still squatting too, just holding his still hard penis and moving the skin up and down very slowly. Fascinated with himself, almost.

They just sat looking at each other peacefully.

Shiva was thinking. He had learnt the word for this in English. The word for doing this, with your hand, not inside a woman. It was called masturbation. Pradeep had showed him the word, Shiva had read it and not commented because it had confused him. The explanation had said 'self abuse'. Shiva had thought that this meant to hurt oneself sexually. What they had just done together was to masturbate. He couldn't see how it was an abuse.

It wasn't painful. It was, he thought, the opposite. He didn't really know what word to use in his mind for the feelings that had engulfed him. He smiled. 'Fantastic' would do for now.

His first question to Chinni was, "How many times can you do this, I mean, every day, or what?"

Chinni thought, or looked thoughtful. He was pouring water over Shiva's stomach and legs. "Some men say that if you do it too many times you will get weak. Lose your energy. I've been doing it every day since I was fifteen and now I'm twenty. So that's a full five years. I work just as hard as any man. I don't think I'm weak."

He paused and smiled. "I watched a rooster once. He would chase hens around every morning and afternoon when I let him out. He screws every hen he can catch, struts around like a peacock afterwards. He forgets he is just a rooster. I reckon I'm as good as any of those cocks." Chinni laughed and Shiva laughed with him. "I do it almost everyday. I'd sooner get a tired arm from doing this than pulling water from your aunt's well in the summer." He stood up and taking Shiva's arm pulled him up too. They stood drying each other.

Chinni collected their shorts, the empty pot and bucket and went downstairs. Shiva smiled when he heard him going down the steps two at a time. He walked to his room. He didn't want to study! He did wish though that he had Pradeep's textbook with him. He just lay on the bed thinking about how great it had felt.

He felt somehow that he was free of something. It wasn't definable, but it was there. He felt almost released from

something. He felt that some secret that had been locked up in him was now out and free, open.

He heard the front-door bolts being opened. It must be near nine o'clock and Aunt was returning. He got up quickly and put his shirt on, buttoning it up as he went down the stairs. He was hungry. That would make Aunt happy.

After supper Aunt went quickly around locking doors and sent him to his room. A silence fell over the inner house. He lay on his bed. His penis was hard again. He wondered if Chinni would masturbate tomorrow, and if he would do it with him. He had liked the feeling of holding Chinni's hard cock. He wanted to hold it again. He wanted to run his hands over his hairy chest. He wanted to feel his muscular arms.

He fell asleep with a new sense of contentment.

*　*　*

However on the next afternoon he saw his fantasy for the planned evening dissolve.

"This evening you will have to be in the house by yourself, Shiva, Chinni babu is coming with me. I have all of these rice cakes to take to the temple and distribute to the poor at the gate. He won't return until I come home. You will have to be careful."

She stood up and rubbed her back. "If you are going to bathe this evening, do it early if you want hot water. I want to lock the kitchen outer door."

Chinni was sitting and packing the rice cakes into a basket. "If it's too early for you to bathe before we leave, I'll heat up some water for you when we return."

Aunty clicked her tongue. "What nonsense, fellow. Talking about bathing at nine o'clock in the night. Really you are senseless at times. Anyway," she paused, "it's a waste of firewood."

Chinni kept his head down and went on packing the cakes. Shiva caught his eye a few seconds later and they communicated that their dream had been shattered.

Shiva knew that Chinni slept in the outer verandah room and Aunt would lock that side when she went to bed. He waited for them to leave. He knew that he had plenty of studying to do. He knew too that his mind wouldn't be on his work. It was

like trying to study three hours before going to see a new movie, or the next night after seeing a super movie. He sat in the front room and listened to the radio for a while. He got bored. It was the type of classical music his father liked. He turned it off. He thought that it sounded like people in pain.

All day he had been feeling the urge to do it again. He would wait until everyone had gone to bed that evening. He went upstairs and decided to bathe while the water was warm. He had an erection the whole time he was bathing. In the end he couldn't wait. He knelt in the same place and position as he and Chinni Babu had been the day before. He masturbated himself slowly remembering yesterday.

The only part missing was Chinni, Chinni holding his cock, and him holding Chinni's. That was the bit he desired!

The time passed slowly. At 9.15 he took a study book down and sat in the front room.

He heard Aunt and Chinni coming up the steps. He jumped up and unlocked and opened the door. "Now look, Shiva, I have a terrible headache. I sat too near to that loud P.A. system. My head is unbearable. Chinni babu will get your supper. You will have to manage yourself. I'm going to bed." She handed Shiva the keys, "Lock up carefully and double-check the locks." She turned to Chinni: "And you, don't make a mess serving the food. The kitchen's clean you know." Aunt held her head and walked towards her bedroom. They heard the door close and then the bolt lock.

They looked at each other with a knowing sly smile. Chinni winked at Shiva, and Shiva felt himself blush. A wink was what a hero gave a heroine in a Hindu movie. A wink was something secret, somehow connected with love and sex. They went into the kitchen and ate together – something that would have horrified Aunt if she knew. Chinni took the plates outside to the cleaning square, came in, smiled and closed the door quietly putting the keys on the right hook.

They went upstairs together silently, holding hands. Chinni turned and closed the door at the top of the stairs and dropped the wooden bar. He turned and put his arms around Shiva and smiled and hugged him.

Shiva smiled back and said, "I couldn't wait." He paused. "I mean, I've already..." He paused again, he didn't really know

how to say what he had done, this new discovery! "I thought that it wouldn't be possible together tonight."

Chinni just grinned. "I thought you might have done; neither of us could have thought that poor Aunt would have a headache." He smiled and added, "Want to try again?"

Shiva didn't know if it would come out again so soon, the semen, but he knew something. His penis was starting to get hard again just thinking and talking about it. He also knew that if it didn't happen for him, he could do it for Chinni, to Chinni. The thought of that, holding Chinni's cock and watching Chinni, made him really hard.

They were standing on the open roof verandah. Chinni leaned across the distance between them and drew his hand up between Shiva's legs. The sensation made Shiva shudder with excitement. He drew the hand slowly across his crotch and pressed slightly on the already hard cock, and Shiva felt it twitch.

Shiva couldn't resist the urge, the temptation to do the same to Chinni and with daring pulled his lungee up quickly. He slid his other hand under the lungee and rubbed Chinni's hard cock still imprisoned inside the shorts. He stepped even closer and slid one hand up the leg of the shorts and rubbed the end of the cock. There was already some fluid there.

Chinni hugged him close. They moved into the bedroom. Standing together they took each other's clothing off slowly. Shiva couldn't manage the pin that held Chinni's shorts up. Chinni flicked it open with a smile. The shorts fell down and stopped when they hung on his cock. Shiva slipped his hand inside the shorts and flicked the cock out. It was like a spring. They stood there for a long time, Chinni just letting Shiva explore him. Shiva ran his hands all over Chinni's body, up and down his chest and stomach. From the balls, which he caressed, around the pubic 'nest' and up through the hair that ran in a fine line to Chinni's throat. Shiva felt exhilarated being able to feel the hair on Chinni's stomach and chest. Looking into Chinni's eyes and watching the expression on his face, Shiva knew that he was enjoying it too!

Chinni moved to the bed and they sat facing each other, legs intertwined. Then Chinni did something that blanked Shiva's mind out. He leaned over and took Shiva's penis in his mouth. It was just so contrary to everything a Brahmin learnt. With all

of the taboos about this hand for that and this hand for other things, saliva not meant to be swallowed, fingers not touching the mouth when eating. Now Chinni had his cock in his mouth. Shiva's mind stopped. For the first few seconds, the first few movements, he was shocked. He felt himself go tense with a shock of disgust. He was going to pull Chinni's head away. But between thinking of the protest and the words to express it the realization struck, the realization of having a hard erect cock being sucked for the first time.

In an instant, the sensation of what was happening overran all the old taboos! The feeling was indescribable, he had never imagined such a sensation could exist!

Chinni withdrew his mouth and raised his head to look at Shiva. Shiva just sat motionless with excitement. He blinked his eyes a few times and sighed a little. This was an unbelievable sensation. He, Shiva, knew now exactly what he wanted to do.

The day before he was due to go home Shiva felt a sudden fit of depression. He knew what he was going home to. How could he live without this, this everything? How would he ever find a friend like Chinni again? A new and exciting page had opened. A short chapter, and Shiva saw it closing.

"You must be homesick, Shiva, you don't look happy." Aunt put her hand on his shoulder. "Still it's only until tomorrow and you will be home. Cheer up."

He smiled pleasantly at Aunt.

* * *

On the train home he slept the whole way. He was so tired. He and Chinni had hardly slept two hours that last night together. The elderly man on the berth below him woke him just as the train crossed the river, about fifteen minutes from Chintana. He got up and taking his small toilet bag walked slowly to the bathroom at the end of the bogey. He waited his turn, bending down and looking out at the rice fields as the train slowed at the junction lines. He began to feel depressed. Somehow he wished the train would just keep on going, and not stop. That he and it could just travel on.

The thought of being home and his father's demanding ways, his brother's jibes, his brother-in-law's snide comments

made him feel listless.

A few minutes after he had returned from the bathroom and sat down the train began to slow again. He picked up his luggage and walked to the door. The train had slowed down at the crossing signal. When it eventually chugged and stopped at the platform he almost let the crowd just push him along the platform. He looked around uninterestedly to see if anyone was there to meet him. He was glad he saw no one. Shiva thought about walking home, but then he knew his father would want to know why he took so long to reach home after the train had arrived. Whatever excuse he used for walking home instead of taking a rickshaw would be criticised or commented on. He managed to get through the day smiling and not showing his real feelings, telling everyone about his stay with Aunt. Well not quite all – just the edited and censored version. In the evening he stood in front of the mirror. He looked at himself. There weren't any signs of change, but changed he had.

Andrew Clements

Playtime

from *Air From Other Planets* (Gay Men's Press, 2000)

When Mark was twelve the school summer holiday was an endless round of sunny days and carefree play. Together with his friend Robert he would spend most of his time whizzing round country lanes on his bike or huddled in Robert's partly converted loft making plastic model aeroplanes or pouring over the latest issue of *Flight Magazine*. But once a week, on a Thursday, Robert's mother had to go to work in the afternoon and his brother Steve, who was sixteen, was charged with looking after him. Steve, however, had other ideas and would instead disappear out with his mates, leaving Robert with the house to himself for a couple of hours.

The two boys were quick to appreciate the potential of this situation – once a week, from two to four in the afternoon they had an opportunity to get up to absolutely anything they wanted, with no possibility of anyone ever finding out. Although they were both just about on the fringes of puberty and knew nothing, as yet, of masturbation, orgasms or any such thing, they were both nevertheless frantically horny.

It began as a game where they took it in turns – one was the Nazi interrogator while the other was the prisoner. The prisoner was required to strip naked and lie on the bed whereupon he was ruthlessly tickled and his genitals roughly handled in an 'interrogation' that could last anything from five minutes to half an hour depending on how cruel the interrogator was feeling or how long the prisoner could stand it. They quickly established however that Robert was much happier being the torturer while Mark was far more interested in being the victim. Both boys were excruciatingly ticklish, but while Robert could stand it for only a short while, Mark could happily have lain

there all day while his friend's fingers played over his body.

It was never certain until the last minute that Steve would go out and leave his brother. Mrs Jarvis didn't leave the house until one-thirty and was home again three hours later. She waited across the road for her bus and Steve had to wait until he had seen her actually get on before he knew it was safe for him to leave. The minute he did so Robert would be on the phone to Mark.

"All clear, come on over."

"I'm just finishing my lunch. Give me fifteen minutes."

"Okay, but not a minute more. Don't you dare be late."

Mark was always in the middle of lunch when the call came. As soon as he had put the receiver down he would have hot cheeks and a raging hard-on. On the very threshold of puberty it was already large enough to show in his trousers and his problem now was how to return to the dining room, where his mother sat at the table, and finish his dinner without doing anything to make her suspicious. He developed a strategy of pretending to carry on the conversation after Robert had hung up. This gave him time to concentrate on something other than the afternoon's anticipated pleasures so that his willy would behave itself and he could at least avoid the unthinkable horror of his mother noticing it.

"Was that Robert?" she would ask as he came back to the table.

"Yes. " Mark had to work very hard to appear nonchalant. He couldn't allow his voice to show any hint of excitement or his manner to give any clue that the activities they planned that afternoon were so far from innocent. "Yes", he would say. "Mrs Jarvis has gone to work but Steve's there. We're going to play football in the garden."

"Well make sure you're back by five o'clock for tea and do be careful cycling up that road."

"I will," he would chirp. But now he had the problem of getting up from the table, beneath which his willy was again seriously misbehaving itself. But necessity was always the mother of invention and he quickly mastered a technique of turning away from her as he bent and pushed his chair back, while giving no hint of the discomfort he caused himself.

As he pedalled furiously round to Robert's house, half a

mile away, his swollen crotch would rock about on the saddle; he always loved the sensation and would grind himself in as hard as he could as he toiled up the hill. Once there the routine was always the same. He would let himself in the back door and go to the foot of the stairs. Robert would be waiting at the top. "Ah!" he would shout, "the prisoner is here at last. Get up here now."

Whilst everything they did together was physically harmless, Robert, once established in his role as the torturer, had shown himself to be wonderfully creative. When it came to exposing and exploiting Mark's vulnerabilities he was on a steep learning curve, such that with each session their games grew increasingly intense. One of his early discoveries was that Mark's feeling of nakedness was greatly enhanced if he had no access to his clothes. Thus he would make Mark strip on the landing and climb the loft ladder stark naked. Following him up he would draw the ladder up and secure the trap door, leaving the clothes behind. Sometimes he would send Mark downstairs with no clothes on and with a task to complete, such as to make them a drink or to locate various items hidden about the house. There would always be a strict time limit and a forfeit to pay if he didn't make it back in time.

In another game Robert would sit and watch while he made Mark do jobs such as vacuuming the carpet or washing the dishes, always stark naked, and would make endless comments about how silly he looked or how his willy boinged around. Then he would take the vacuum cleaner and press the nozzle against Mark's balls or put it over the end of his willy and make the skin vibrate. Back in the attic Mark would find himself with his wrists tied to a beam above his head and Robert would spend ages tickling him. He quickly discovered Mark's most sensitive places and accordingly gave these particular attention. He also refined his techniques, using a range of methods from digging vigorously into his ribs to brushing up and down with feather-light strokes.

Mark's genitals naturally received the greatest attention. His foreskin would be stretched cruelly, both forwards and backwards. Once held firmly back, the end of his willy would be rubbed with a dry flannel or stroked with fingernails. Sometimes Robert would even put tiny strips of Sellotape on it

and peel them off at varying peeds. 'Quiztime' meant that one end of a pyjama cord was tied around his genitals and the other end tied to a sandcastle bucket which was then allowed to hang between his legs. Robert would sit on a stool in front of him with *The Golden Treasury of Knowledge* open on his lap and would ask him questions. Every time he got an answer wrong, or didn't know it, Robert placed a marble in the bucket. Mark's general knowledge was pretty good, but even so it was never long before he was unable to stand it and he would beg his friend to untie the bucket. But Robert would only free him from this torment once he had agreed to be his total and absolute slave and to obey any commands he was given for the rest of the afternoon.

One such trial was often to lick Robert's willy. Robert always found this a hilarious idea and went under the cheerful misapprehension that Mark disliked it. In fact he loved to get on his knees and have Robert take his willy out and place it in his mouth, to have to lick it thoroughly, paying close attention to his friend's instructions. His enjoyment was only slightly marred by having to pretend not to like it – if he let on he actually enjoyed it there was a danger that Robert would find something else to make him do instead.

On one occasion, when Mark was happily trussed up in the loft and Robert was rolling his balls with one hand and tickling his ribs with the other, they heard the back door close. They both froze. Steve was home, unexpectedly early. Fortunately for them Robert had let the loft ladder down and in one brilliant, panic-stricken movement he shot down it, grabbed Mark's clothes, shot back up, hauled up the ladder and shut the door. Steve called out to them and Robert answered, trying to keep control of his voice while his breathing was desperately short. He untied his friend, who got hurriedly dressed. Scarcely thinking what they were doing they flew around the table, trying to make it look as much as possible as if they had been quietly working on a model aeroplane. Their secret world had come perilously close to being discovered and the shock was enormous. Part of the attraction of all these games was the acute sense they both shared of just how naughty it all was. The consequences of being found out were unthinkable and their greatest fear was of the embarrassment, which would be overwhelming, unbearable and utterly unavoidable. They had escaped this but the shock

had greatly unsettled them both.

For Mark it also did something else. It sparked off the pleasant and enduring little fantasy that Steve had indeed caught them and far from blowing the whistle, had actually joined in. Mark had this vague idea that Steve, being sixteen, would know all sorts of things that they didn't yet and he would be able to teach them. He wasn't sure just what things these might be exactly, but he was certain there were things, to do with willies and stuff, that an older boy would be able to explain, or better still to demonstrate. He was also very taken with the idea of being tormented and played with by Robert and Steve together. He didn't make very much sense of this, he just knew that it was a bloody exciting idea and it didn't half make his willy go stiff.

One day when he was round at Robert's he caught a glimpse, by pure chance, of Steve getting out of the bath. He had never even seen his own father – not that he could remember anyway, his wasn't really that sort of family – and this was the first time he had had proper sight of a naked man. It was only the briefest of glimpses as he happened to run past the door, but it was a defining moment in his twelve-year-old life. For Steve had what appeared in that instant to be a medium-sized squirrel bouncing around between his legs. In that short but intense moment Mark was electrified and his brain managed to register a huge amount of information. He saw the sinewy, athletic thighs with their coating of fluffy hair. He saw the flat, strong stomach and the little band of hair running down from the navel to spread and become a thick bush. He saw the vein standing out along the shaft of Steve's willy, the roundness and particular shape of the head, the fullness of the balls. He sensed the springy texture of the genital flesh. In the blink of an eye he took all this in and the shock went through him like a bolt of lightning. He was infinitely curious and consumed with a desire for... what? He wasn't really sure. Some sort of closeness, as yet undefined; a need to be in some way connected to this fascinating body.

He wanted to have an exclusive and secret link with Steve. He wanted Steve to teach him things – extremely private things about willies and balls and men's bodies. In his favourite fantasy the two of them would go away camping together. They would pitch their tent in some remote wood and there spend all day climbing trees and wrestling. Then at night they would snuggle

down together in the tent and Steve would tell him show him all kinds of wonderful things – things that only boys knew about. The next day Steve would tie him to a tree, naked of course, and spend the whole day subjecting him to playful and exquisite torments. And they would pass a whole week like that, or maybe even two, hidden away in their own secret and intimate little world of maleness.

Mike Seabrook

First Love

from *Full Circle* (Gay Men's Press, 1997)

It had begun when he was thirteen and a half and Peter Butter-worth was sixteen. He had been punting a ball about with a few cronies in break one morning and the ball had flown far into the next pound of the quadrangle – by unwritten but rigid convention reserved for members of the upper school, and strictly *verboten* to juniors. The etiquette regarding the division of the quad was unwritten. School rules, on the other hand, on the subject of running in densely populated areas, were very clearly written indeed. Hales had hared after the ball without a thought in his head for either, at the precise moment when Butterworth chose to walk round a corner of the School House building. Butterworth was two and a half years older and three inches taller; but he was lightly built and graceful, whereas Hales, even at thirteen, was square-rigged and powerful for his age. He was also carried along by the momentum of his headlong rush after the ball. Butterworth was bowled over, Hales rebounded several feet from the force of the impact, and the two of them finished in a sprawl of arms, legs and school uniform.

"I... I'm sorry," muttered Hales, sitting up and feeling slightly sick. He sat up, trying to rub several places at once, principally a badly gashed knee that was protruding through a gaping rent in his trousers. Knowing how jealously the upper school guarded their privileges, he fully expected to be booted without ceremony back to his own territory. The older boy too sat up and made a gingerly exploration of the various points at which he felt damaged. Then he looked, a little dizzily, at his assailant. Hales saw a black cloud of indignation pass over his face, confirming his apprehensions. Then, to his great surprise, the other boy looked at his gashed knee, by now bleeding

profusely, and his frown cleared. "Better get something done about that," he said mildly. "Come on, I'll take you to the first-aid box. There's one in the Prefects' Room."

"Nunno, I'll be all right," he had replied, embarrassed. "It's only a graze." But he was still feeling sick and a little dizzy from the collision and his crashing fall to the unyielding hardcore of the quadrangle, and had not felt inclined to hurry to his feet, now that the prospect of a booting appeared to have faded. Butterworth pulled him up and led him off anyway, ignoring his protests. They went through the corridors of the senior end of the school, where Hales had rarely gone, and eventually stood before the Prefects' den. Butterworth knocked, at first lightly, then with a firm, confident rap. When there was no answer he boldly pushed open the door and led Hales into the sanctum. In that moment he became a hero to the young Brian Hales.

He stood looking about him, his damaged knee forgotten in his keen interest in these glamorous and forbidden precincts. It was a small, cosy room, dominated by a broken-down ping-pong table, which stood in the middle, barely a square inch of its drunkenly canted surface visible beneath a litter of essay paper, cricket boxes, rugby balls, scarves, half-eaten sandwiches and other debris. Hockey sticks and sports bags hung from a row of pegs that ran along one wall, while blazers, jock straps and every other kind of garment were strewn about the floor and the half a dozen battered and threadbare armchairs. It was, Hales felt immediately, the most comfortable room he had ever been in, wholly masculine and reassuring.

Butterworth crossed the room and reached a green metal first-aid box down from a shelf, and set about making businesslike repairs to Hales's knee. He worked quickly and efficiently, without fuss. Hales was surprised, and vaguely impressed, by the gentleness with which he cleaned and dressed the wound. By the time he had finished they were already friends.

It had been an unusual friendship in the rigidly hierarchical society of a boys' school, where differences in age were treated like sacred charms far up into the senior echelons. Lofty members of the Upper Sixth might legitimately talk to their immediate juniors in the Lower Sixth, but beyond that the convention was absolute: you moved among your peers; lower boys you passed by as the idle wind which you respected not.

Butterworth was a lone wolf and a law unto himself. He was utterly immune to the blandishments of fashion. In a school where prowess at games was the universal currency in which everyone's relative worth was reckoned, he was, at his own casual, dismissive estimate, a duffer at rugby and a total dead loss at cricket; and for the cult of games he expressed excoriating contempt, openly jeering at 'hearties', whom he dismissed, in their hearing, as 'brainless assemblages of superfluous muscle'. Sustaining such heresy on the wave of his own kind of excellence, he went his own way – which was to be quite overtly and outspokenly intellectual, in his diligent application to the classical languages and their literatures and his unconcealed love of them. By the time he reached the Sixth Form he had made a beginning on textual emendation, and acquitted himself without discredit in a couple of donnish exchanges in the pages of the *Classical Review*, he also produced, for his own amusement, an uninhibited translation of *The Frogs* of Aristophanes that left the classical staff of the school simultaneously scandalised and bursting with pride. And over the next two and a half years he contributed as much as anyone and more than most to Hales's education, gently ridiculing his adolescent certainties, unobtrusively introducing books and ideas into his path, and talking, endlessly talking and laughing with him, sometimes instructing him in his surreptitious way, but most of all, always there, and never too busy to spare time for his young friend.

When Butterworth was in his scholarship year, by this time himself a Prefect and contributing his twopennorth to the squalor in the chaotic room where he had ministered gently to Hales's wounds, Hales was in the Lower Remove. He had filled out and was already a good way towards being the good-looking young man who would take Ronnie by storm a few brief years later. He was neither a 'blood' nor a scholar, performing adequately but without distinction at both games and work while Butterworth was gliding effortlessly to an open scholarship to Trinity; but Butterworth exerted to the last a quiet, civilising influence over him, stiffening Hales's diffident, uncertain disposition and bringing out such talents as he had in work and even in the despised games. Hales, for his part, had come, within a month of making Butterworth's acquaintance, to regard him as an oracle, the fount of all wisdom.

The compliment was not undeserved. Peter Butterworth was unspoiled by celebrity, and remained a wise and sensible boy, gentle and affectionate; and Hales was aware, in a vague way which he never sought to put into words, of how good his friend was for him. He never knew, because Butterworth never said so, that Butterworth was in love with him. It didn't matter unduly, because they were both conscious that there was love between them, of a kind; but both felt instinctively that it was not something that ought to be put into words, for fear of spoiling the bloom. Butterworth yearned in secret, but he was too scared of losing what he already had to articulate the more that he desired. So he kept his yearning to himself and waited, hoping. Why he directed such devotion to such an apparently mediocre object he could not have said, except that there was something distinctly appealing about Hales's diffidence, something almost coquettish, though anything of the kind would have been the last thing to enter Hales's honest, straightforward head.

In the end it was not a great surprise to Hales when Butterworth decided that his moment had come. One summer afternoon, when they had known each other for about six months, they were walking after school across the vast, shaggy golf course through which the school cross-country teams ran, talking as always about anything and everything that came into their heads, Butterworth imparting knowledge and Hales absorbing it. After several miles they were in need of a rest. Butterworth turned abruptly off the grassy walk between two stretches of fairway and pushed through a light screen of bushes. Hales followed him into a small, light clearing. They stripped off their blazers and ties and sprawled on the light, springy grass.

A discussion of cricket turned into a light-hearted argument, spiced with laughter and mutual schoolboy abuse, and then into horseplay, ending with them rolling breathlessly together on the turf. Though Hales was already rather the stronger of the two, Butterworth was still quite a lot bigger, and used his long, wiry limbs to wrestle his friend into submission. He sat triumphantly on his chest, propping himself on his hands over Hales, so close that he could feel his pants of breath on his own face. Impulsively, without stopping to realise what he was doing, he bent forward and kissed Hales. At first it was a timid, hasty peck; but when the younger boy made no protest or attempt to wriggle free he

slid down, took him in a long, hard embrace and kissed him again, full on his lips, spending all the bottled-up passion of six months and an expressive, affectionate nature in that first, rapturous contact.

They stripped quickly, urgently, without words, with a sense of inevitability about it that they were both clearly aware of. After that they found time almost every day to go somewhere private to masturbate together, giving and taking mutual pleasure which in Butterworth was raised to the higher powers of ecstasy. Again, he kept the deeper, darker currents of his feelings to himself, sensing that it would be dangerous to let them too far out of their captivity deep within him.

Then, one day a few months after their first sexual contact, they had gone wandering one evening through the woodland that ran for miles from the far side of the golf course, carrying on, as always, an animated discussion. They talked about fungi, which were sprouting in profusion in the moist autumn woods, birds, and the occasional small animals that they heard scuttering about in the underbrush. They were both conscious of the usual undertone of sexual arousal, and the pleasurable anticipation of its imminent gratification; but they were good enough friends, and easy enough with each other that it didn't obtrude itself or cast too oppressive a foreshadow as they strolled. From time to time one of them would say something that demanded a physical response, and there would be a brief scuffle, or they would chase each other among the trees. Then they would saunter on, laughing, getting their breath back, savouring the poignancy of friendship.

They turned off by tacit agreement at a well-known clump of birch trees and headed into a circle of rhododendrons, escaped decades ago from a nearby baronial estate. In the middle of the clump was an irregularly shaped grassy clearing, just big enough for two boys to stretch out in the dappled light. They undressed without haste, looking at each other's bodies and taking pleasure from seeing each other's arousal. But this time, instead of going into his usual clinch with his young partner, Butterworth had held him in his arms only briefly, looking down from his superior height into Hales's face with a great tenderness in his mild brown eyes, and then he had slid slowly down his body, flicking out his tongue to lick Hales's smooth white chest. He paused to lick

and tease his small brown nipples with his tongue, then sank to his knees in the damp grass. Then, gently but with a firm, determined certainty about him, he ran his tongue up the length of Hales's small, very hard penis, and slipped the tip into his mouth.

For a few moments Hales was so surprised that he was transfixed. By the time he had registered the amazing, shocking thing his friend was doing to him his blood was already running cold from the pleasure of it. His entire body was tingling and trembling from the hitherto unplumbed depth of sensation. He lifted his chin and gazed glassily up at the gently waving birch and beech leaves high above the dark ring of rhododendrons. Then he closed his eyes, letting the late sunlight make a warm, red curtain of their lids, and gave himself up to the incredible, blissful new sensations flowing in a powerful beat, like the tide, from his genitals.

Butterworth teased and fondled every fold of him with his tongue, sending wave after wave of electric shocks through him. Then he released him, to run the tip of his tongue and then his lips up and down the length of his erection, round his small, tight scrotum and back to the tip again. At last, feeling the rhythmical throbs in his friend's body coming closer and closer together, he took him back deep into his mouth again, feeling the tip of his penis thrusting urgently against his palate, and sucked him hard until Hales, with a long, gasping moan of relief, spirted a stream of semen that seemed to go on and on, flowing round every corner of his mouth and trickling down his throat. Butterworth relaxed, suddenly becoming aware that his entire body had been tensed like a coiled spring, and made small, gentle licking motions with the tip of his tongue against Hales's softening penis, wishing only that the moment could go on and never end. He wished with all his soul that they could be captured and frozen in that moment for the rest of time, like two flies in amber. In fact, being the wise and practical boy he was, he swallowed, savouring the unfamiliar taste, and let Hales go.

Hales stood for a few moments, observing closely as the feelings of bliss ebbed and ceased. Then he looked down at the top of his friend's head, resting in the faint dark fuzz of his incipient pubic hair, the fair hair tousled against his white lower belly. Moved by a simple instinct of gratitude, he ran the fingers

of both hands through the fair, straight hair. "Stand up, Peter," he said after doing this for a while. Butterworth, sensing what was to come, rose shakily to his feet, trembling all over. Hales dropped briskly to his knees before his friend.

* * *

After that, though, it was never quite the same between them. Something fragile had been broken, and could never be reforged. They were still friends, and they still pleasured each other frequently, sometimes in the same way as they had among the rhododendrons. The pleasure was so great that they were both keen to renew it, though for different reasons. But where Butterworth was a solitary youth, with few acquaintances and hardly any friends, more than content with the one passionate relationship, Hales was a much less complicated spirit, with many pals in his own year. While Butterworth was bookish and reflective, Hales was an enthusiastic joiner of any cliques and coteries going, a ready participant in whatever rags, mischief and antics anyone might happen to suggest to improve the shining hour. As time went by he began to hear what his cronies had to say about 'people like that Butterworth', as he overheard on more than one occasion. When he considered the sort of things they would say if they knew what he got up to with his friend, his blood ran cold. So, gradually, never fatally but damagingly enough, a chill crept between them. They saw less of each other by degrees, and when they were together there was a guardedness between them in place of the old careless openness.

Butterworth saw, quite clearly and early, what was happening, and was sensible enough to realise that he could do little or nothing about it. He got on with his work, moving methodically towards his scholarship, continued to devote a necessary minimum energy to the avoidance of cricket and rugby, and spent many of the hours between grieving quietly and alone, grasping whatever his young beloved still saw fit to offer him, and being grateful. He had enough sense of his own dignity to know that he was never, whatever he felt, going to grovel or beg for favours from Hales.

He made an exception to this once only. A few days before he was due to leave the school he sought out Hales, now a hefty

and, ostensibly at least, a considerably more self-confident sixteen-year-old, in morning break. "Come for a walk with me tonight, Brian," he murmured in his ear, while Hales, having the grace to feel no little of a heel for doing it, could nonetheless not help shooting a swift, covert glance round his pals. But they carried on booting their ball about, drifting away with the tide of their game, to Hales's somewhat guilty relief. Butterworth had seen the nervous sidelong glance and diagnosed it correctly. "Just one last walk across the golf course, Brian," he said softly, without a trace of pleading. "For old times' sake. I shall be leaving next week, and I'd like to have a last time with you. We've been good friends..."

Hales felt a sharp stab of guilt and shame scorch through him. He was aware that he had treated Butterworth shabbily, even brutally, when all he owed him was gratitude for giving him friendship, loyalty and pleasure without limit or reservation, and for teaching him a great deal. He realised – dimly, but the realisation was there – that his friend had been a profoundly civilising and shaping influence, and had made a contribution to his growing up that he might never expect to fathom, let alone repay. All this came to him in a series of frissons of feeling, wild, formless, inchoate and inarticulate. It left him feeling nothing he could have expressed but a vague but extremely uncomfortable feeling of mingled guilt and sadness coupled with an overwhelming sense of impending loss. It was all over in a few instants of time, but it had been strong while it was passing through him, and it left its mark. He looked levelly at Butterworth, with a sadness in his face that Butterworth had never seen before. It made him look older, turned his ordinary, boyish face, for a few seconds, into one of transcendent beauty. Then it was gone, and it was the face of Hales the schoolboy, whom he still loved, looking at him with much of the old affection.

"Of course I'll come with you, Peter," he said, and for one last time all the old affection and easy friendship was back in his face and tone.

The walk was not a great success. Though they were both trying – perhaps too hard – they could not re-establish the old rapport. And when Butterworth tried to take Hales in his arms and kiss him, Hales wriggled awkwardly in his embrace, and

blushed hotly. Butterworth saw how things stood, and sighed as he released his friend, feeling his erection collapse precipitately into his pants. They turned back then, by unspoken agreement, both sadly aware that something had just come to an end. In that moment a great deal about Brian Hales was revealed to Butterworth, in his difficult and uncompromising self-vision; and something in him writhed briefly, whimpered, and died. When they reached the point where Hales had to turn one way for his house and Butterworth went the other way for his, they stood facing one another, not knowing what to say or how to go about saying it.

Eventually Butterworth stuck out a hand, and Hales, feeling a conflicting cocktail of relief, shame, sadness and a vague, indefinable regret, took it, shook it awkwardly and then held on to it for a moment, as if not knowing how to let it go. They were both rather glad when they turned their respective corners and passed out of each other's sight.

With his friend departed for home and then Cambridge, Hales quickly and assiduously diverted his energies elsewhere, feeling relief that potentially dangerous emotions could now be left safely dormant in their cage, where they could not betray him, bringing risks of losing him face among his widening circle of friends.

It would be some years more before Hales would understand that there was a simple, not specially important but fundamental difference between himself and other men. When it came he was able to draw on unsuspected reserves of resilience and inner strength to deal with the knowledge, and the immense additional pressures from outside, without collapsing under them. It was then that he finally knew and acknowledged his full debt to his friend; and then, too, that he savoured fully the grief that comes from first acquaintance with the bitterest, most poignant of betrayals: betrayal by oneself. But all that was to come. For the time being he took away from his relationship with Peter Butterworth one legacy that would echo and resonate through his life: he was never afterwards proof against a certain kind of looks. The lethal cocktail required a combination of masculinity with prettiness: a gracefully built boy, all blue eyes and clean blond hair, would ever afterwards set off images in Hales's mind of golden days when youth seemed impregnable

and school and the companionship of boys seemed as if it might never end, when the sun was always bright and the breeze always cooling; and Hales would be lost.

Ken Shakin

The Dusty Trail

from *Real Men Ride Horses* (Gay Men's Press, 1999)

We all played the game when we were boys. Except the sissies. They played house with the girls. But boys will be boys, and in a man's world the name of the game is war. And for some reason no war has as much fascination for American boys as the war between the Cowboys and the Indians. At that age you don't know what genocide means. You only know what you see on TV and nothing fires the imagination of a young couch potato growing up in Suburbia quite like the mythology of the western. The wild West might have been created in Hollywood for all he knows but sitting in mom's den it's true history real as the wood paneling. Hedged in on all sides by cloned houses, green lawns and blacktop, a boy dreams of dusty trails leading to unpredictable adventure.

We played Cops and Robbers too. Brave men in blue defending private property from the desperate poor. We played Americans and Nazis. It was fun to goosestep and shout "Heil Hitler". Which had an exotic ring back in the days when the only skinheads were in the marines. Occasionally we even joined in with the current strife. The cold war was the war of our fathers. For us it was just another TV movie. We knew it simply as Kill the Commies. As with our fathers, it didn't really matter who we killed so long as they were the bad guys. Nowadays I imagine these kids all wanna be the bad guys. Hitler, Charles Manson, or the Unabomber. But back then we played with GI Joe and we bowed our heads in prayer at school and we believed in the powers-that-be. We were the good guys. That was clear. The problem was finding someone to play the bad guy. In all war, real or make-believe, someone has to be the bad guy. Someone has to lose. Someone has to get killed.

Tex tells me that growing up on a ranch was like growing up in Bonanza. Horses, unpaved dusty trails. Ranch hands, raw hide, stirrups, cowboy hats, cowboy boots, Cowboys and even Indians. The Indians were still there even if no longer a danger to white men. I suppose growing up in Suburbia was a bit like growing up in *Leave It to Beaver*. For both of us the grass was greener somewhere else. Just as I dreamed of living on a ranch he dreamed of moving to a house in the burbs. Ten years later we each ended up in a one-room apartment in the big city. And ten years later I run into him in a crowded bar and inspired by something an aging hippy Indian told me I ask this aging yuppy cowboy if he ever played the game. Something I never thought of asking back when we were young men thinking only of the future. I must say it came as a surprise to find out that although he grew up on a ranch, as a boy he too played more than any other game the game of the wild West. They caught robbers and killed commies but their favorite was ours, good ole Cowboys and Indians. At least they didn't have to pretend the mall was a prairie. Authenticity counts for something. Even in a game. I imagine they had real Indians to play the Indians.

He chuckles at my fantasy. It's triggered a memory. He smiles sadly and looks up at the video screen above the crowd around the bar and sees another place, another time, remembering a story never told. A story he will never forget.

There were Indians around. That's for sure. Not many. And not integrated into the social circle of a rich boy. There was one reservation far away. Other than that among the poor people living in town were always some Indians or half-breeds. You could see it in their faces. The oriental features, the red-brown complexion mixed with white, black, and whatever else. Tex as the son of a wealthy rancher certainly wasn't going to play with some drunken half-breed's boy. His friends were the sons of the other ranchers. They weren't forbidden to play with poor boys, but why would they. Indians, Blacks, Mexicans, Chinese, and poor white trash were seen as not quite human. Something else. Poor and dirty. And stupid. In other words deserving of being poor and dirty. So when it came to playing Cowboys and Indians Tex and his buddies had this same problem convincing one of their own to play the part of the Indian. To be the bad guy. To get killed. To lie down and play dead, like a dog.

There were plenty of non-whites working on the ranch. All sorts of breeds. Tex grew up thinking of them as all rather the same. Dark people. Niggers. The word was used in passing without much meaning. A crude way of referring to the help. As a little boy he even played with one of the Mexican's sons, a boy named Pedro. He can't remember exactly what they did. Mostly just exploring or hanging out doing nothing. They were friends, as on par as the rancher's kid and the ranchhand's kid could be. At that age it almost works. When the two were alone they could be two boys, classless except for their boots. But when in a group with the other rich boys it was different. Then Pedro became the token poor kid, teased and isolated. A few times they did in fact get him to play Indian. Goading him with a crown of feathers and a bow and arrow. Laughing at him. Even at that age they sensed what was going on. Pedro would reluctantly take the disguise. And run. No one likes to be chased by a gang of boys with guns even if they're only toy rifles. He played along, willing to do almost anything to play with them.

Tex remembers one real Indian boy. A friend of Pedro's. He barely noticed him and probably would not remember him now if not for the fact that they ran into each other later as young teens and had a strange, sexual encounter. By that age he had no friends who weren't rich white boys like himself. The dark boys gradually came to be less visible. Seen but not heard. Recognized but kept in the background. In their place. The classes keep to their divides, trained to keep the glass walls in place. Their children follow suit, as soon as they start making the transition into adulthood. As soon as they start puberty. So for all the images of Indians in the Wild West (it wouldn't be quite so wild without them) growing up on a ranch left Tex with few wild memories. Which might explain why the one exception, short as it was, left such a vivid impression.

He was riding his bike on a long trek through the dry landscape to a stream he liked to swim in. I find it ironic that with all those horses around he rode a bike. He reminds me that this is the 20th Century and when you're around animals all day the last thing you want to do is ride a horse. For boys bikes were the thing. Later the motorcycle and then the car. As a teenager Tex often went for long bike rides always seeking some new trail. He describes the landscape as endless trails of dust

leading through dusty plains with some grassy hill in the distance to aim for. He remembers that day enjoying the free and open landscape flying along the dirt road on his Schwinn racer thinking about nothing much except getting away, being alone with himself, searching out a lonely spot to take off his clothes, swim, and maybe jerk off in the sun. He'd heard that Pedro and the local boys sometimes went to a spot far away. Four hours by bike. A long hot ride through some of the driest terrain to get to a swimming hole. More like a tiny creek, but cold and fresh. Though he and Pedro no longer hung out together they still talked sometimes. Pedro was an expert pathfinder. He knew all the remote spots, the undiscovered nooks. Places to prove your manhood with a bottle of tequila. Pedro had talked about this one trickling stream where he liked to go. Just a crack in the dusty earth where water comes. Pedro made it sound enticing. A map loosely scraped in the dust to point it out and the next day Tex is off in search of a mirage.

The ride there is draining and invigorating at the same time. The more he pedals the more he sweats the more he drinks from his water bottle the more he sweats and pedals on through the hot wind to dry off. The cycle energizing the cyclist. As the blood gets pumping the mind gets free. It's as close as you can get to flying without leaving the ground. Four hours he rides until he thinks he'll never get there. It isn't hard to find. Just further than he thought. By the time he reaches the pass from where the creek can be seen it's high noon. He's thoroughly exhausted, hot and dehydrated. He can barely push down on the pedals anymore and all he wants to do is dunk his head in the stream and drink.

When he gets there he drops the bike and lunges for it. Nothing to dive into. Or even swim. More like bathing in a sink. He dunks his teeshirt and wraps it around his head. He throws it in his mouth and in his face. This tiny stream of cold water dribbling out of the parched earth is a miracle, a lifesaver. Imagine all the cowboys who stopped here on their long journeys, who thought they were dreaming when they saw it and slid down off their half-dead horses, kneeled down and sunk their burnt heads into it.

He looks around. He's alone. Not another soul. Nobody. No animals even. Maybe some insects. A stray bird flying over.

The prairie has a silence dry as the parched ground. Loud in its lack of sound. It rings in the air interrupted only by the wind. Hearing this silence he feels alone, finally, as alone as alone can be. So he takes off the rest of his clothes. His sneakers and socks first. Then, looking around again as though anyone else might actually be there, he shyly pulls down his shorts and undershorts. Free at last. Naked under the endless nothingness of sky and prairie. A small creature in a great big universe. The freedom makes him horny. He relaxes finally into his long-sought solitude. He puts his feet in the water. Holding on to the rocks he squats into the trickling stream in an effort to submerge himself in the shallow depth. He manages to get wet, enough to cool off. The burnt skin dunked in icy water. Enough to feel ecstasy drying off in the warm breeze. He lies back on the hot dust with his feet still in the water feeling his skin tingle in the sun. His dick gets hard and he feels it spring up. He puts his hands behind his head and enjoys the feeling. He closes his eyes. Nothing to see but a fiery red canvas. The sun blasting through his eyelids.

He's enjoying a serenity of freedom that evokes images of flying off canyons into bottomless clouds of dust when at one moment his blind vision is shaded and the realization that something is casting a shadow on him jolts him out of his reverie so that he opens his eyes and flinches his body, looks up and sees a dark face.

"Hey."

"Hey." What else is there to say. He's naked in the middle of nowhere and suddenly exposed to this strange intruder. One is never as alone as one thinks. Where did he come from? Was he watching me the whole time? He recognizes the face. It's that Indian boy, Pedro's friend. He should have figured he wouldn't be alone in a place known to the local boys, solitary as it seems. Maybe that's why he came here. Not just to be alone. Yet his embarrassment at being caught with his pants down is complete. He would cover himself but that would be even more embarrassing. So he pretends it's nothing. And his shamed hardon sinks.

He's aware that the Indian boy is studying his body. Silently. He has to say something to break the silence. "What's your name again?"

"Sonny."

Doesn't sound Indian. "I'm Tex."

"I know. Pedro talk about you. He say you got a big room, the whole attic of the big house."

Shy: "Yeah. It's not so big." A lie. It's an enormous space for a kid. Filled with expensive toys including an electric train set landscaped with mountains. "You come here a lot?"

"Sometimes." The Indian boy's words are short and expressionless. It reminds Tex of the Indians in the old movies. Poker-faced with searching eyes. The boy is still studying his body. They are the same age, that precarious age when boys turn into young men. Their bodies are developing with each night's sleep. The Indian is so obviously staring at Tex's body that he has to mention it.

"Whatta ya starin' at?"

"You got red hair around your dick." Fascinated.

"So?" Defensive.

Then the silence. Tex is at the age where being seen naked is a turnon. In spite of himself his dick starts to react. His sex life has been only with himself. Another body is yearned for. Something to rub against like he rubs against his pillow at night. But something that responds. Just being seen is an incredible elation.

Without blinking an eye the Indian turns to the side and pulls out his dick to pee. He lets a stream of piss stain the white clay ground. Tex is even more embarrassed now. The fact that he often jerks off thinking about the other boys peeing or jerking off overtakes his thoughts and guilt sets in. He turns away, anxious not to look at the Indian boy peeing. But it's too late. He sees him in his mind's eye. The reddish brown skin against jet black hair. The well-formed physique, not as skinny as his own. The fact that he's wearing only a pair of shorts. No shirt, no shoes. Penis in hand, peeing. He did in fact look at the boy's penis. The image lingers in his thoughts as he hears him zip up and turn back around and then actually lie down next to him with his feet plunked in the water.

Out of the blue: "You jerk off a lot?"

The question abrupt, but natural and uncomplicated in a way that makes it disarming. Tex has no choice but to answer. "Sometimes."

"I like to come here to jerk off sometimes. In the sun. No

one around."

Tex feels his hardon return stronger. It won't go away this time.

"You got a hardon."

Thanks.

"I got one too." And the boy pulls it out. Simple as that. And then he's tugging on it, whackin' off, unashamed, carefree.

Tex touches himself. He jerks it. The two of them jerking off together, separately. Right next to each other without touching. It doesn't take long before the Indian boy is groaning. "Um gonna shoot it," he says and puffs out his chest. He shoots his jism in the air towards the sky letting it fly where it will. Big creamy drops falling on his chest, stomach and arm, on the dust around him. And on the arm and chest of the boy next to him. Tex opens his mouth. The smell of the other boy's jism brings it out of him. He stops stroking himself and painfully lets it go, following the lead, shooting more cum than he ever shot. Hot liquid splatting all over his thin body leaving him sticky and exhausted and thoroughly embarrassed.

But the Indian boy is still carefree. "That was good, man. Always feels good to shoot the juice."

Before he can answer the Indian boy rolls over on top of him and pins him down. "Let's wrestle."

"No, you're hurting me." He's taken by surprise and says the wrong thing. The words sound whiny and wimpy. The intimacy is too much for him. He can feel their chests sticking together with jism. The embarrassment is overwhelming.

The Indian boy laughs, enjoying the game, the mess and the roughness. "Whatsa matter. You sissy. Fight." He commands him to resist. But he can't. "Whatsa matter, rich boy, you can't fight?"

It's all happening too quick. He tries to push the Indian off of him but the boy grits his teeth and holds him down. "C'mon, fight, sissy boy. You think you better than me cause your father rich, huh?"

Tex can smell the jism. The intimacy is sensual and undeniable. He looks into the other boy's oriental eyes. The brown face angry but laughing. He wants to push him off. Or maybe he wants to kiss him. Maybe both. Confusion overtakes him and all he can do is surrender. He stops resisting and lets

himself be pinned down, going limp under the strength of the stronger boy.

"Sissy." The Indian gets up, stands over him, and looks down. "You can't fight. Get outa here."

The mood changes. He was friendly a minute ago. Rough but playful. Now he's aggressive.

"Go on, get."

The rich boy may not be able to fight but he knows his place and he can defend himself with words. "I can stay here if I want. It ain't your land."

"It's my land. I say you gotta go." He's serious now.

Tex props himself up on his elbows, but he's not going to get up. He looks up into the angry eyes, his own eyes squinting in the sharp rays of the sun, unable to see clearly, to understand the change of mood. Stubborn and ready to defend his turf.

"You go, or I gonna beat you up."

The threat makes him move over slightly, but he refuses to be pushed around. After all his father is one of the richest men in the area. His father owns cattle. And the hands who work with the cattle. His father owns the Indian boy's father in a way. "I don't have to do anything you tell me."

"Go!" he screams kicking dust on him. Tex starts to get up and the boy kicks him down. "Go. Get outa here!" Each time he tries to get up the boy pushes him down kicking him further along the path. "Get, you sissy." He grabs his clothes and starts putting them on even as the boy kicks sand in his face. Finally the Indian pretends to lunge for him, forcing him to flinch and scramble for his bike.

That day Tex rode away from the scene of his first sexual contact, his entrance into manhood, like a scared chicken flapping its wings. That day he came to understand finally what he'd known all along. Admitting to himself that he liked to dream about other boys and their bodies and their roughness. That it turned him on. He knew then that he was a coward in their eyes, that he wanted them to love him like he loved them. Now he knew what the poor boys thought of him. What had happened would never have happened with his own friends, the sons of the other ranchers. The jerking off. The lack of embarrassment that allowed for it. The intimacy. The fighting. The brutal honesty. Even if his friends sensed that he was different from

them they never said anything. Now that it was said – implied in coarse and blunt terms by a poor Indian boy but said nonetheless – there was no turning back.

He tells me that he has never quite achieved that intensity since. He's had plenty of hot sex. Fucking deep, crying out in ecstasy. But nothing will ever compare to that intimacy, the sheer frankness of this boyhood exchange of jism and emotion. Sometimes he thinks he's been running away from that scene ever since. His legacy remains intact. His innocence lost for good. Like a coward riding away from the battle to become something he wasn't meant to be. A deserter. Free from the war but not free.

He did once see the boy again, years later. He was passing through his home town on his way to the family ranch for a visit with the daunting task of buying a last-minute present for his parents, something to get for people who already have everything. Driving through noticing how a small city has grown out of what was once just a little town he thinks about how he too has changed a lot since then. Then, driving through the parking lot of the new mall he sees Sonny, the Indian boy who taught him what's what, and the image of time gone by hits him square in the face. It's an unsettling picture. How people become something they never could have imagined they'd ever be. The skinny boy now a big man with a wife and a baby clinging to the wife. Unmistakable. That's him alright. With a beer belly and a woman to match. They look poor, dumpy, shabby. A depressing sight as they walk together hand in hand towards the mall entrance. Tex from inside his red Mercedes convertible lets his eyes follow them thinking how unfair life is. The inequities seem randomly appointed. In youth we are all at least young. It's not so important. But the older we get the more the lines are drawn, the distinctions made obvious. A part of him wants to go up to the Indian and give him a check for ten thousand bucks. Another part of him wants to drive by and yell: "Go, get outa here, you low-life." Now who has the power. The Indian may have won the battle but the cowboy won the war. He should drive by and say something. See if the guy even recognizes him. Let him be jealous of him and his fancy car. He should do something to make up for lost time. Blow him a kiss?

All he does is drive on. Out of the parking lot. Away from

the mall to avoid meeting them and out of town along the dusty dirt trail that leads to his ranch, a trail that has since been paved.

POSTSCRIPT

A Letter from Ivan

Dome 23
Irkutsk 47609-244
Siberia

20 March 2085

Dear Robin,

Hello from Siberia! I got your name from this old book
I discovered – not the original kind on woodpaper of course.
The thing is, I'm really interested in history, and I was
browsing through the system on the subject of 'gay people',
who seem to have been kind of forerunners of the New Way,
though they sure had a lot of problems in those days.

I don't suppose this letter will ever reach you, as I've just
worked out that if you were the same age as me when you
wrote your book (I'm fifteen and three months), you'd be at
least a hundred by now, and most likely you didn't survive
the Big Disasters anyway. But maybe I'll continue, and in
another ninety years someone might find this an interesting
document – some hope!

Ours was the country where the New Way was first
invented, and for quite a time now this is how most people in
Siberia have lived. It seems we had to, after the Big Disasters in
the early part of the century. Radiation was such a problem
that they built these big domes to live in – though the earliest
ones are just museum-pieces now. We still have to be careful
how much time we spend outside, and kids don't go outside at
all until they're five years old. In Dome 23 we have eight
hundred and fifty-six people at the moment (one more
expected next week), we are very well-organised and all care
for each other. We've decontaminated the fields and woods
for at least ten kilometres around. I think it's warmer now

then it was in your time, and we grow most of our own food. We don't travel very much, but we see everything that happens all over the planet on our screens. Our newest construction is a big salt-water swimming-pool, built underground, complete with seaweed and a few crabs.

I guess the biggest surprise for people living the Old Way is that we have about three times as many females as males. My mum Katya is very lucky to have a boy, as well as my big sister Liza (she's gone to college in Moscow). There are fifty of us in the boys' dorms, a whole mixture of colours; our mums raided the sperm bank for all the variety they could get. Funnily enough, though, I look quite Russian, with a touch of the Mongol I guess.

This afternoon we went out skiing, probably for the last time before the snow melts. As it's Saturday we don't have afternoon school, and Alexei (my partner) is playing chess, which I find a real bore. So here goes.

I did enjoy your book *All Boys Together*, but some things surprised me. It seems that in your day you had very little love with other boys, so when you had sex, it was all a bit traumatic (if that's the right word). It's very different for us in the New Way, cos we're taught from quite young that love is the most important. In the little boys' dorm you each have your own bed, but most nights you have to sleep with one of the other boys (in turn), to make sure you still love them. Sometimes you don't want to, if you've had a quarrel or you'd rather sleep with your best friend, but then you cuddle up together and they don't seem so bad after all (at least that's the theory!). Of course you do kind of sexy things even when you're little, but it's not quite the same as when you get bigger, I'm sure you know what I mean.

When you're about twelve or thirteen, you move up to the big boys' dorm, which is just along the corridor. It's up to you to make the move, but the others give you a bit of encouragement. It's rather funny, cos you feel a bit awkward with the bigger boys, though at that end they're only a year or so older than you. The big boys have their own rooms, that is, two partners share a room, or sometimes three if they're not sure who they want their partner to be.

I was very keen on Josef, whose 'father' (we still use that

word) was African, from Senegal his mum told him. He's got soft chocolatey skin and a big beautiful smile. Josef's partner then was Nikolai; I remembered them from the little boys' dorm, of course, but they'd both grown a lot in the last year or so. When you're ready to move to the big boys' dorm, any of the boys you like must let you become his partner, at least for a few months. You can try out two or three first, until you find someone you really get on with, but I moved in right away with Josef and Nikolai.

They really made me welcome, and I soon loved Nikolai as much as Josef. We'd roll around all cuddled up together, then each in turn would get 'special treats' from the other two. It was Nikolai who first made me spunk off, and we still have a laugh about that every now and then. Of course I soon learned what they liked to do; I guess most boys like much the same kind of thing.

That's the way it's supposed to be when you move up with the big boys. They're supposed to give you all the attention, make sure you get all the best sexy feelings; you don't have to do anything to them if you don't want to. One boy in our dorm, Markus, just used to lie there and let his partner do everything to him without doing anything back; he got rather a bad reputation. But of course if they're nice to you, it's only normal to want to enjoy things together.

When you're thirteen, sex is so exciting that you think that's what being partners is all about. But after a year or two, you realise that you can have nice sex with a lot of people, but you need something else in a partner as well. Even love isn't quite the right word, I think, cos there's the love you're meant to have for everyone in the Dome, especially the other boys, but then there's the kind you discover over time, when you feel on the same wavelength about things. At least that's how it is with me and Alexei.

We knew each other of course in the little boys' dorm, but Alexei was a very keen student, and used to spend hours in the computer lab even when he was ten or eleven. I was more into practical things, I loved to grow plants even when I was very young, so we were rather on different tracks. Alexei wasn't so lucky as me when he moved to the big boys' dorm. I think he was in too much of a hurry to find a longterm

partner, perhaps because his mum got ill and died. Things didn't work out well with him and Jorge, and he had to have counselling for a while. I like to joke that he was a plant that needed some special nourishment, but it really was a little like that. Everyone knew that he needed a new partner. I'd been with Nikolai and Josef for a year, but I gradually came to realise that they loved each other more than they loved me. I felt so sorry for Alexei that I'd go and give him a cuddle without thinking that we might become partners. But talking with him made me realise how childish I still was in so many ways, and I soon grew to love that seriousness of his which used to put me off.

We've been partners now for six months, and we've had some wonderful talks together about everything. He's got the brightest blue eyes, and I don't know anyone who's so completely sincere in all he says. When I wake up and realise it's Alexei in bed with me, it just seems so good to be alive. As you can imagine the outside world can be quite a scary place, and in a couple of years we have to go off to college. There are hostels for New Way people in quite a few cities now; Alexei thinks we should go to Vancouver, where he could study informatics and I could do their famous course on arboriculture. But they still have some funny ideas over there, Mum's been to America and doesn't like it very much.

Well as I said, Alexei has been playing chess this afternoon, but he should be back quite soon and it's my turn to clean our room. I'd better sign off now, so to Robin or whom it may concern,

love and best wishes from,
yours sincerely,
Ivan